JYNA
MAENG

To every person who was told
they were not good enough.

You are.

CHAPTER I

The sandstone walls flew by as Arla hurried down the southeast tower stairs of the castle. The heavy dress dragged behind her, picking up the dirt and debris through the various corridors that led past the castle keep and into the main passageway.

Almost there.

A roar of laughter tumbled down the corridor, showing the way. Savory aromas of sweetened garlic beef and fermented cabbage danced in the air as she neared. Her entire body vibrated in anticipation.

Soft light beamed through the slightly ajar wooden panel door hitting the ground in a long streak. She approached slowly, her stomach fluttering as she nervously squeezed her lower arm to stabilize herself. Through the crack of the door, the great banquet hall of her father's castle boomed with jovial life.

Rows and rows of fresh fruit and rare meats from across the five kingdoms lay across the long refectory tables as a hundred or so High-Born women and men stuffed themselves to the brim. The grease of duck fat dripped down their chins while shades of red and purple wine stained their lips. Any other day, her mouth would have watered at the sight, but she was too nervous now to focus on the food.

Decadent shades of crimson and bright sapphire dresses showed off the women in the room, a sharp contrast to Arla's pastel lilac dress, whose large shoulder frills and long sleeves were clearly no longer the style of the more open-shoulder designs of the court ladies. Arla's heart beat fast against her chest as she pulled her sleeves down even further, making sure her forearms were completely covered.

Arla knew she looked like a clown.

The pale powder was caked onto her face too thick, settling into the creases of her fair skin, making her look much older than her sixteen years. And the shade of pink hastily brushed onto her cheeks was alarmingly loud, which made her resemble a cheap porcelain doll more than a girl who was trying to look regal.

But this was honestly the best Arla could do to look like the princess she was. No one had taught her the techniques to make her appear more like the other court ladies she was watching now, whose skin glowed against the sun with no imperfections to be seen. Seeing these beautiful women made her want to crawl into a small tomb and wither away from anyone's view, but she couldn't let such thoughts deter her. Not today.

With sweaty hands, she pressed her palms down the satin skirt of her gown, failing to smooth out the deep wrinkles of the rarely worn dress she had dragged out of a dusty trunk from her armoire. The top part was too loose. The entire thing was too loose, in fact. This dress was formerly tailored to an older woman with more curves and a larger chest that showed her womanly figure, unlike Arla's smaller, shorter body that would have looked more like a boy's if someone didn't notice her long, thick black hair that curled in all directions at the ends.

Adjusting the small golden crown on her head, she took in one long, uneasy breath and pushed against the door, slipping into the room.

Joining the celebration was like entering a parade. Arla was instantly swept up in the energy of boisterous laughter and fast-paced music as noble families of Ulsana ate and sang along to the plucking strings of gayageums and the beating drums made of leather and wood. No one had noticed her enter as they danced past, too enthralled in their own inebriated celebration. Arla wanted to join them, to hold their hands and dance with them in a circle as they did, but now was not the time. She stayed close to the wall to not get trampled on and made her way forward until she finally got close enough to see...

Ah, yes. There they were.

In the front center of the Great Hall, standing side by side on an elevated tiered platform was her father, the King of Ulsana, Mathus Seojin, and her young stepmother, Queen Ametha Seojin. They were draped in gold fabrics and coats of pure black fur, stripped from the hides of ferocious menturabeasts who were infamously hard to kill.

Mathus was a mountain of a man, while Ametha stood tall and thin. Their enormous, gilded crowns caught the light of the thousands of candles set in the room, making them glitter like deities.

And in her stepmother's arms, bundled in warm wool, was the newly arrived prince of Ulsana, Jun Seojin, Arla's baby brother.

Looking at them, bathed in the warm glow of the fire torches lined along the walls and radiant jewels hanging around their necks and wrists, filled Arla with longing. To the king's left was an empty space, where Arla should have been.

"My king." An older man, dressed in aquamarine velvet, bent low to the ground. "In honor of your new son, I have brought jewels from my visit to Checeia, along with one-of-a-kind paintings from Viloxian herself."

Her father simply nodded in acceptance, showing no gratitude in his eyes. His face was axen, fortified by an unrelenting will. Known as the most powerful fire-wielder of the lands, his sharp expressions only supported the terror he usually brought on to his subjects.

The older man bowed again, lower this time. "May the Whispers bless the new prince as your ancestors did you." He waved his hand. "*Indui-ter-ani.*"

The air curled around his fingers, sending a small breeze over the young prince's nose, tickling him into a fit of burbling giggles.

Queen Ametha smiled as she adjusted her son in her arms. It was tradition to present a whiff of magic to a newborn royal on their hundredth-day debut celebration in hopes that it would bless them with stronger magic than their own. If only it actually worked like that, things would have been much easier for Arla.

Her feet shifted from side to side. She had practiced this. She was ready.

Lifting her dress, she peeled away from the wall and approached the platform.

She bowed quickly before climbing the three steps up toward her stepmother. The moment Arla laid eyes on her new brother, she thought her heart might burst.

He was so happy. So full of life.

The start of something new.

"He's so beautiful," Arla spoke softly, to show Ametha she meant no harm. The queen gaped at her, wide-eyed. Arla expected this. She was supposed to say, "I would like to pay my respects to my brother." But her heart got the better of her and instead, she sheepishly reached out her arms, wanting to hold him. "May I—?"

Ametha clutched the prince to her chest, turning away from Arla like she was saving her son from being touched by a disease.

The laughter and music evaporated into silence.

A tower of gold and fur stepped between them.

The warmth of the flames fizzled out as Arla was overcast by the shadow of her father. King Mathus Seojin looked down at her with the type of cold expression that sent shivers down her spine. His sharp eyes narrowed. "Why are you here?"

Arla swallowed hard as she tried to control the shaking of her body. No matter how many times she heard the disdain and hatred dripping from his voice, she never got used to it. She scratched at the sleeves of her forearms. "I–I wanted to say hello to my new brother."

"You are mistaken," he replied in a warning tone. "Go back to your chambers."

This was the moment she had practiced.

I belong here. I am your daughter. I am part of your family too.

Those were the words she had repeated over and over again in the mirror of her bed chambers and those were the words that should have come out of her mouth, but instead, she asked, "But can't I stay?"

She knew she said the wrong thing. Her father's eyes flared, the color of fire and loathing, but his body remained rigid, containing the fury. "If you were welcome here," he said through a tightened jaw, "you would have been invited."

His words gnashed against her skin, exposing a part of her she wished was made of stone instead of the fleshy bulb it was.

"I'm sorry, I—"

"Out." Her father pointed at the grand front double doors on the other end of the Great Hall. Arla looked out at the crowd, who stared at her wrinkled dress and her jester makeup. She could almost hear their muted laughter and contained disgust. She didn't know it was possible to feel even smaller than she already did.

Without argument, she bowed her head to Mathus and walked slowly down the center aisle towards the doors. The crowd parted for her while muttering to each other, but she did not look them in the eye, for fear that she would burst into tears.

"Let us hope our new prince is not like her," a man murmured to another.

"He must," someone else replied worriedly. "A tragedy like that can't happen twice, can it?"

Arla reddened as she quickened her pace, down the parted channel of guests until she crossed to the other side of the grand mahogany doors. The moment she knew they couldn't see her anymore, she took off at a full sprint.

T he warm glow bathed the guests in joy and merriment as they continued to pay their respects to the boy. Arla could see the tops of their heads through the window from where she sat on a cold, marble bench. The outdoor garden was empty this time of night; it always was.

Her father's grand castle had many gardens dedicated to flora and statues that paid respects to their myths and legends. And each was planted with flowers and other decorative plants from different regions of their kingdom to represent all the beauty Ulsana had to offer. This one in particular was the smallest of the gardens, dedicated to spring flowers that grew on the Endezee Mountains, but the fall season had turned it desolate, leaving it very unpopular during this season.

She sniffled up rogue tears that threatened to escape from her traitorous eyes. What did she expect was going to happen?

A stone statue crouched beside her against the marble bench she sat on. The gray rock was carved into the shape of a grotesque creature with the head of three snakes and the body of a lion with four legs, each ending with the claws of an eagle. It had one outstretched claw, its five talons faced up, exposing its palm up to the sky.

The moon was only a sliver in the sky, unable to combat the darkness surrounding Arla's vision of the dinner plate balancing on her lap. She had managed to grab a few quick things from the kitchen that were left out before she came here.

She scooped a small amount of salty crab rice into her mouth as she watched the glowing window, trying to distract herself from the ache that bruised her heart. Her stomach immediately knotted from the new gluttonous arrival.

She grabbed one of two leaf-wrapped gelatins from her plate and placed it in the stone creature's outreached claw. She patted its front leg. "One for you, one for me."

The evening wind pierced through her dress, through all the gaps between the satin material and her skin, chilling her core, but she refused to let it push her indoors. At least, not yet. Even if her fingers were stiffening from the cold, there was no other spot with this great view of the banquet. Through the window glass, she saw her father gently smooth a finger over her brother's soft cheek.

The look her father gave his son...

She tried not to pay attention to the tightening in her chest, nor the hollowness that crept up from the dark. Her eyes stung violently as the wind picked up.

Be grateful, Arla. This is fine. This is good.

She stuffed another spoonful of rice into her mouth. Salty goodness burst onto her tongue and kept the sorrow at bay, for now.

The crowd inside cheered again as they raised a glass. "To the new heir of Ulsana, Prince Jun Seojin! May he live a long and prosperous life!"

Arla raised her own cup of water, trying to heave up a smile from the pit in her core. And when they clinked their cups together,

Arla clinked hers to the lifeless monster next to her, the sound of it echoing loudly in the empty garden.

CHAPTER 2

Arla didn't know what time it was. She never knew. The heavy velvet curtains in her bedroom blocked any light from the outside world, so when she woke up each morning—or oftentimes afternoon—it always felt like night to her. She lay in her bed, staring at the peeling paint on her ceiling. She had woken an hour ago, but hadn't moved because... what was the point? No one was waiting for her to wake up.

Yesterday was her baby brother's hundredth-day celebration, a debut to the world of his existence and health. Up until then, no one outside of caretakers and immediate family was allowed to see him. Immediate family should have included her, but her father made sure she was not allowed to see Jun.

She had hoped that maybe the birth of her new baby brother would have changed things. Now that her father had an heir he could be proud of, maybe he could be persuaded to let her take part in their lives. But she was wrong.

So now, Arla merely lay in her bed, wondering how long it would take for the day to end.

There was a time when servants rushed into her chambers and flew open her curtains, forcing her from her slumber. They would wrestle down her long coal-black hair and put her into the newest styles of dress all the while telling her the busy schedule she would have that day, which usually consisted of meeting visiting nobles, learning to read and write, or practicing magic with Norendra.

She remembered vividly the way her father used to smile at her, the way he did at Jun yesterday. He would always have her by his side, saying that whatever matters he was involved in, involved her too. She would be so proud to be given such responsibility at such a young age.

But all that stopped when Arla's tenth year came and went and she still could not hear the Whispers. It was then that her father realized that Arla was the only pure-blooded High-Born in history to not be able to wield magic.

Almost overnight, his kind gaze shifted to disgust.

You're no daughter of mine.

She had thought he was just angry when he said those words and he would quickly remember how much he doted on her before. Instead, his coldness grew until... She lightly touched her covered forearms, careful not to press too hard on them. After all these years, they were still tender.

Arla's stomach grumbled, demanding to be fed, which finally made her roll out of bed. If there was one thing that kept her moving, it was her hunger. At least, she still had that.

As she made her way to the window, she knocked her knee against the sharp corner of her nightstand. She sucked in her breath, clutching it to her like a wounded animal. No matter how many times she walked this path, she always managed to find a way to hit that corner.

She squinted her eyes, preparing herself, and slung the curtains open, letting in a wave of warm, bright sunlight into the bedroom. Through the glass, she saw court ladies and gentlemen flirting and giggling in the gardens of the more popular courtyards while servants tended to horses on the other end still carrying the High-Born nobles arriving from their morning ride.

The ache returned.

The truth was, Arla was more like a ghost than a princess, roaming the corridors of the castle, neither living nor dead, disregarded and unimportant.

How long can I keep living like this?

Her stomach growled angrily. *Alright,* she snapped at it.

After she dressed, she made her way down the plaster stairs and into a passageway that led to a crack in the stone wall. The southeast tower, where she lived, was full of these cracks, neglected and emptied in favor of upkeeping the central keep and northern towers of the castle where her father and stepmother stayed.

She wiggled herself through the gap, getting dark scuff marks on her dress. *Damn it.* She could never keep anything clean. Another thing Norendra said she was terrible at.

Add it to the list, I guess.

The crack led to an inner chamber splitting out into convoluted smaller tunnels underground. She dragged her hands along the familiar stone, knowing each and everyone from her years of exploring alone down here. With a few turns and climbs, she popped up in the passageway next to the royal kitchen.

She ducked into the bustling cookery where Low-Born servants ran around like headless chickens, preparing the lunch menu that would be served in an hour. It was humid here, with fires boiling large pots of water and the scent of citrusy herbs and nutty spices prancing in the air above.

Someone knocked against Arla's shoulder in an attempt to rush past her. They didn't even look back. Still, Arla reflexively uttered a small apology and bowed before swiftly grabbing a flaky scallion pancake from a nearby plate on the center table before disappearing back into another tunnel.

The air darkened and then with a couple more turns, the bright blue sky opened up to her as she entered the small, empty garden.

The stone monstrosity was waiting, its claw opened up to her. She tore a piece of the pancake and placed it in its palm, patting each of its three snake heads. The gelatin she had left the day before had mysteriously disappeared, as it always did. She wondered if servants were cleaning during the times she was not here.

The small Endezee garden was more cheery-looking in the daytime; the fall may have taken away its flowers, but the vines remained hardy and entangled around the statues and benches, marking its intent on returning its blooms in the spring.

She bit into the greasy pancake, savoring the sharp scallion against the sweet bread. Even if her stomach would protest later, it was worth it. Any other princess in the other four kingdoms would have been dining with her family by this hour, but Arla had stopped being invited years ago. For years, she kept trying to find ways to convince her father she was deserving of being let back in, but they almost always failed, often with scars and tears. Maybe it was time she gave up.

Arla looked up at the central tower of the keep from her bench, finding the window was left slightly open for the morning breeze to freshen the room. She could see Ametha rocking the new baby prince through the glass, passing by it, back and forth. They had moved the child into his own nursing room, a place that Arla knew well.

Very well.

And that's when another idea sprang to life.

She waited until most of them had fallen asleep when her step-mother would retire to her bedroom to visit her father for at least a couple of hours before returning. It was just enough time for her to do what she needed to do without being caught.

Arla slipped into the underground passages, weaving and climb-ing until she entered undetected behind a hidden door that was covered by a tapestry in her brother's room.

She never knew why Ulsana's castle had so many secret passage-ways. The nobles knew of them, but they had never bothered to fully explore them all. Hundreds of tunnels coiled and bobbed all over the castle, and the only ones they cared about were the ones that led them to the safety of the outside in case there was a siege. But the others were left unexplored without curiosity, which meant no one really knew where most of the cavernous tunnels led. Arla would have never known either if she hadn't accidentally tripped into one when the wall of the southeastern tower cracked. The only time she was grateful for her clumsiness.

She listened for footsteps behind the hidden door of her brother's room, and when she heard none, she slowly opened it, hoping the tapestry muffled most of its sound. She pushed back the hanging cloth and surveyed the nursery. A woven basket held firm by wooden legs stood near the other end of the wall.

At first, she thought maybe he wasn't there until she saw tiny arms and legs kick up from inside. Arla peered over the crib and saw a fully awake, wriggling baby, his face so round and milky-smooth, it almost startled her how pillowy it looked. No wonder people loved to touch baby's cheeks.

"Hello, Jun," she said in a hushed voice. "I'm Arla, your sister." Jun stared at her with big hazel eyes, like he was studying her trustworthiness. "I wasn't allowed to meet you earlier," she said. "But I'm here now. So... hello." She gave him a small wave.

As if he understood, Jun cooed and wriggled happily at her presence, which warmed her deep into her bones. It had been a long time since someone had smiled at her like this. A truly happy one that told her they were glad she was there.

She often wondered, in the first hundred days of Jun's life that she wasn't able to see him, whether she would resent this new light in her father's life, but when she saw Jun, she knew she could never blame him or anyone except herself. She had lost her father's love on her own, by disappointing him over and over again.

She checked the light underneath the door, watching for shadows, but there was nothing, which gave her the courage to pull up a chair next to his crib, careful not to make a sound. "I heard children like to hear stories. Should I tell you one?"

Jun gave her a toothless smile, releasing a dribble of drool onto his cotton shirt. She knew he couldn't really understand her, but she still took this as a sign. She was told once that speaking to children was beneficial for their development, so she hoped she was being helpful to him now. She pointed through his window to the outside, across the plains far past the castle to a shadowland that blended with the night.

"Do you want to hear the one about The Forest? I know a lot about that."

She was telling the truth. When one had a lot of time on her hands like she did, with nowhere to go but back and forth inside the same castle for years, it gave way to an insatiable reading habit. And the subject that captured Arla's attention since she was a child was the deadly and mysterious forest that lay at the edge of Ulsana. Granted, she was no expert, but she believed she knew enough to tell stories to an infant.

"Before humankind appeared on this land, there was a forest that held all the magic in the world. It was beautiful and extraordinary." Arla gestured with her hands, tall trees, and floating magic, wriggling her fingers. "It had a language, spoken only by the trees, but The Forest was kind and decided to grant High-Borns the power to hear its Whispers and use its magic. They said you could just walk in, and it would grant you magic." Arla feigned a menacing frown, hoping to increase the entertainment factor. "But one day, The Forest darkened into a place of death and disease. It shut itself off and no longer gave its Whispers to the people, killing anyone who stepped into it."

For a moment, she wondered whether she had gone too far. Should she talk about death to a child?

Jun squealed, not bothered at all.

"So, to survive," she continued, "the five most powerful noble families split into five kingdoms, protecting the Whispers they had left, only allowing High-Borns to birth children with other High-Borns to protect the magic in their bloodlines."

Arla leaned closer to Jun. "That's where you come in. Father is the only one left that can hear the Whispers of fire. And your mother... she comes from a long line of strong magic, too." Jun kicked the blanket off of him like he was excited about this part. "And that's why father is so happy with you. He thinks you'll have strong magic, just like him."

She reached in and pulled the blanket back over him. "I hope you can hear the Whispers Jun."

For your own sake.

What time was it? Longer than she intended for sure.

Just as Arla was about to pull her hand away, Jun grabbed her index finger tightly. His small, pudgy fingers barely wrapped around her own, but his grip was surprisingly strong. Her entire heart filled at that moment as she sat there, Jun's hand holding her as if to say he wanted her to stay.

"I'll come back and tell you more stories, I promise."

He smiled at her, a bright, innocent grin. She knew he didn't understand anything she was saying, but a silly part of her still hoped maybe he did, in some way, deep down, the way souls could speak without language.

She was excluded by her father, but with Jun, there was still hope. Maybe in time, they would become close and, in that way, she would still have a family.

She thought about what it would be like to have a sibling to finally share life with. She imagined herself sneaking cupcakes to Jun when he got older. Passing looks of knowing while Ametha wasn't looking. How they would complain about their father and understand what no one else could about being a Seojin offspring. Jun would cry, clinging to her arm at night, begging for one more story before he was forced to sleep, and she would smile and stay a little longer for at least one more tale every time.

"When you grow up," Arla said softly, "don't hate me, okay?"

Jun gurgled and waved his tiny hands in the air, taking her finger along with it. She giggled, waving her finger with his hand still gripped tight around it, making it look like he was dancing with his arms.

"Get away from him!"

Arla hadn't noticed the door open behind her. *Oh no.*

Ametha pushed her aside and grabbed Jun, hauling him into her arms. The sudden movement drove Jun to cry out. Ametha tried to hush him as his cries swelled, filling the entire room. "It's okay, it's okay," she assured him, bobbing him up and down. "I'm here now."

Arla shot straight from her chair, backing away. "I'm sorry. I will leave."

Her stepmother threw her a glare, but then her eyes quickly flicked up to something behind Arla. She didn't need to turn around to know who the queen was looking at, but she did anyway.

Mathus's large frame blocked most of the light coming from the hallway. "How many times do I have to tell you to stay away from him?" he seethed.

With trembling hands, Arla bowed; her rapidly beating heart didn't warm the ice that froze her to the ground. "I'm sorry."

There was no use in explaining, in arguing. It always fell on deaf ears.

Mathus remained standing in the door frame. His obsidian eyes, empty of emotion, stared down at her. She knew that look.

He held out his hand.

Her heart raced inside her chest.

No. Please.

She looked past him towards the sanctuary of the hallway. Maybe she could squeeze by him. No, there was no room.

Her eyes darted to the hidden door. If she ran, the punishment would be worse.

"Please, I won't do it again." She was close to tears now. She didn't want to do this.

There was no mercy in him. Just a command. "Give it to me."

Obediently, Arla placed her shaking arm in her father's palm. He pulled up her sleeves, revealing patches of thick, raised tissue, the crisscrossing of sizzled skin that had healed years ago. He slid his hand up to a fresh, untouched spot, pressing his thumb deep into her arm until the skin around it turned white.

Arla took in short, deep breaths, bracing herself.

It will pass. It will pass.

Mathus was an entity of calm malice as he said, "*Hal'en.*"

His thumb glowed red, sending roots of lava into Arla's forearm, pushing white-hot pain up her arm, across her shoulder, and down her spine. She screamed through her tears as her knees buckled underneath her, but she did not fall because she was still held up by her father's vice-like grip.

Don't faint. Don't faint.

"You have failed me in every way," he growled. "Even when I ask you to disappear, to stay away, you fail me."

The hatred in his voice so expertly drowned her.

The disappointment of having a daughter with no magic shamed him in front of his court and all five kingdoms. The rumors made him look weak. That his bloodline was not as pure High-Born as he wanted everyone to believe.

"Will you continue to disappoint me until my dying breath?" he spat.

The pain was so excruciating that she couldn't think straight. It was almost over. Her vision was getting blurry. Her head was getting faint. The sharp tang of burning flesh filled the room as Jun wailed louder.

Almost over.

And then, mercifully, Mathus tossed her arm away from him, stopping the blaze of pain in her body.

Arla collapsed to the floor, sweating and shaking uncontrollably. She pulled her arm to her chest, cradling it. Tears streamed down her face as she choked back sobs.

Her father turned to Jun in Ametha's arms, who was red from screaming. She watched her father's face soften, putting a gentle thumb across his chubby cheeks, the same thumb that had permanently set another mark on Arla's arm. He smiled at his son with the love of any doting father, and it was like the air had been sucked out of the room.

"Do not come here again," he commanded without turning to her, his voice devoid of guilt or regret.

Arla dropped her head in obedience. As she pushed herself up, she struggled at first but managed to muster enough strength to do so quickly enough that he wouldn't get angry again and fled the room.

CHAPTER 3

Arla curled next to the stone monster in the courtyard, trying to fit herself into the curved crevices of its lion-bodied side to protect her from the natural elements and everything else in the world. Even when the high afternoon sun beamed heat across the castle grounds, it provided no warmth for her. A few days had passed since her punishment, and her tears had long since dried.

This was how it always went. As it always would.

All her life she had wished she had magic. She willed it. Dreamed of it. Prayed for it. But it never came and that's why her father hated her so much.

Why did the Whispers decide it would only be her to be deaf to them when they had blessed her family line for decades?

Her forearm throbbed underneath her sleeves. They would take weeks to crust over and heal again. Another scar on the speckled field of her arm. *Is this going to be my life forever?* She leaned against the statue, which remained in its permanent crouched position, overlooking the courtyard.

"Stupid girl."

From the shadow of a marble column adjacent to the garden entrance, Norendra stepped out, materializing from nothing.

It wasn't surprising anymore when Norendra appeared from the darkness. The First Advisor to the king heard the Whispers of shadows, allowing her to control and move freely within them. Arla had seen Norendra appear randomly enough times to assume that all shadows were doorways for her former magic teacher and to always be ready for her.

Norendra was wearing her usual plain black dress that always fell an inch above the ground. Her long brown hair was tightly braided and wrapped around the crown of her head. It looked almost painful to have such a hairstyle, but Norendra, in her mid-forties with her perfect posture and stern face, felt no pain. She was a pillar of discipline and rules, and she stood now, looking right at Arla.

"Let me see." Norendra held out her hand, but Arla didn't budge.

"It's nothing," Arla replied, hoping she would drop the subject.

The older woman snatched her arm up, pressing deeply into the fresh wound, which made Arla yelp in pain. Norendra didn't seem to care as she pulled back the sleeve to see the burn was already bandaged. She inspected it for a minute. "This is terrible work. You wrapped it too tightly. The wound needs space to breathe."

Arla reclaimed her arm, trying not to sound sarcastic. "I'm sorry, next time I will do better."

"You apologize as much as you eat, Arla," Norendra reprimanded. "Next time just do it right instead."

"Loosen that gauze tonight, or I will do it for you." It sounded almost like a threat. Norendra moved to leave before swinging her head back around. "And don't go to see the prince again, understand?"

Arla nodded, which sufficed enough for Norendra to leave, oblivious to the fact that Arla just lied to her. She had promised her brother she was going to read him stories. It felt more important than a promise to a teacher who, when she had first discovered Mathus was burning her, said in a shocked state, "But you're not even worth hurting."

The statue was providing no comfort today, and the fall wind was starting to pick up. Arla uncurled herself and headed inside.

She was going to find new material for her brother and read to him again tonight. She would be quieter and more vigilant, she convinced herself. She would not get caught again. Because the risk of being burned again by her father was not as bad as the stark loneliness she felt in all the waking hours of her day. If there was a chance to fill the hollowness of her life with Jun, then the scars would be worth it.

There were two libraries within the castle walls. One was exquisitely grand. A beautiful place with the most precious and rare works in all the land. It was the one Arla had loved to peruse as a child, but it was not the one she went to now.

Down near the catacombs where the past rulers lay was another library, significantly smaller than the grand one that her father showed off to guests. This one smelled of rotting wood and was only frequented by the royal scholars and herself. And it was also the only one that held the history books of The Forest.

When she arrived at the small underground library, one large candle flickered in the front, providing light to the servant who was dusting the front shelves of the library. The entire cave-like room was awash with amber and browns that made it look ancient, which was probably true. Arla gave the servant a quick acknowledgment and grabbed a spare candle from a table, using the servant's flame to ignite her own. After that, she scurried to the back of the stuffy shelves where the darkness gladly accepted her.

Here, she was free to roam and pull out any book she wanted, and she knew which would provide her with the stories she would need to refresh her memories. She squatted low to tug out a thick textbook: *The Forgotten Forest: A History.*

There was a squeal.

A ball of brown fur scurried past her hand. Arla let out a yelp and fell on her bottom. She almost gagged, realizing that a rat had grazed her hand. She held her palm like it was severed and bleeding. She hated rats. They defecated everywhere and ate a lot of food in the kitchens. Food she could have eaten herself.

She couldn't believe rats were in the library, openly running around like this. Wasn't the servant hunting them? To her left, she saw the dark hole the rat disappeared into. She shuddered, imagining how many more lived in that disgusting orifice. Arla was about to get up to find a washing basin when she noticed a crack above the hole.

Something was on the other side.

With some hesitation, she eventually dared to lean forward to see through the crack.

Paper. It was some sort of paper.

She placed her rat-infested hand on the stone beside the opening and to her surprise, she realized it was loose. She pulled at it, wiggling it back and forth until finally, it popped out of the wall. She reached into the dark, praying no nasty rodent touched her again, and felt crinkled paper leaning against the side. She gently dragged it out and saw it was a book.

Tattered and burnt, the leatherbound book was thin, barely the size of Arla's palm. And it had no title. It looked like the remains of what used to be a beautiful thing that had turned hideous from an attack. *So strange...*

Arla got up and moved to a nearby table that held a candle to get a better view. The spine of the thin book crackled as she opened it, and she flipped through its inconsistent pages, as there were clearly chunks and pieces missing, until she landed on one that read:

The Forest plays tricks.

Arla looked up at the top right of the page. It was barely readable from whatever had damaged it, a combination of sunlight and fire, but it was clear what it was.

A date. A month and day, but no year. This wasn't a book. It was a *journal.*

Someone's journal.

Arla flipped to the front of the journal. Its first entry.

I went into the abyss of The Forest and have survived its death, but it lingers still.

Her heart drummed in her ears. The person who wrote this journal—they had gone into The Forest, *after* the Darkening, and survived?! This was life-changing! This was the first-ever survivor of The Forest! Arla couldn't believe it. Of all her years reading, never had anyone ever mentioned a survivor after the Darkening and now here it was in front of her. Proof!

And *she* had found it! She had to tell her father; he would be so elated! She had to—

"What are you reading?"

Arla startled, twisting around to see a familiar lanky dark man with sunken eye sockets.

"Good morning, Simion," Arla replied, wishing he wasn't there.

Simion Yubal's hands were folded behind his back, holding a thick book. There was something chilling about him. Maybe it was the way he looked down on everyone or the slow way he spoke, like a snake about to strike. He was only a few years older than Arla, but his demeanor resembled that of an elderly man, closer to death than to his best years.

"Another fictional tale?" His eyes glided over the beat-up journal. She slowly closed it and placed both hands over the peeling cover as nonchalantly as possible so as not to raise suspicion. Simion used knowledge as a weapon, so the less he knew about her or the journal, the better.

"Mathematics. Astronomy. Medicine. These are the subjects worth reading, not imaginary tales," he lectured, the flame of the candle darkening his sunken eyes even more, making him look almost monstrous.

"They are all worth reading," Arla responded. "Besides, I don't just read fiction. I read history."

He scoffed. "The past belongs to the dead. We need to look to the future."

"I disagree," she quickly retorted, her feet firmly pressing against the ground.

"No one cares that you disagree," Simion replied. "No one cares about your opinion at all, Princess."

Arla flinched at the insult. Of all the High-Borns that had hurled hurtful words at her, it was Simion who always hit the mark. Because what he said was most often always true. He used his knowledge to strip you down and twist you in ways that hurt. A dark trait for a Royal Scholar.

Royal Scholars acted as a living knowledge trunk for nobles to use for strategizing future plans, making judgments between feuds, and enacting future laws. A position two notches down from an advisor and one that Simion filled with glee.

"So how does it feel to no longer be heir to the throne?" he asked in a detached manner that made one believe he wasn't interested, even though he surely was, or else why would he have asked? "It must be difficult to see a baby have more promise than you," he stated.

"As long as the king and queen are happy, I'm happy." She was telling the truth. Arla didn't care about the throne.

Simion smiled. It was a devious smile. The kind that made Arla cringe. "I saw you at the banquet yesterday. Did you really think you were going to hold your father's attention by crashing the prince's party? It still won't solve all your problems, Arla. You're still *you*, after all."

Arla's face grew hot. He was always trying to get a rise out of her for sport. Sometimes Simion would jab at her in front of his peers, a competition to see who could get her to cry first. She was ashamed of how long it had worked. And how it continued to work even now as she fought the feelings rising within her.

"I j-just wanted to see my brother," she stammered, her hands tightening around the tattered journal.

"Half-brother," he corrected.

That was enough for today.

"I have to go." The wooden bench scraped against the floor as Arla backed away.

"Oh, that reminds me," Simion continued. "I wanted to ask you something." He leaned closer to her, a move that made Arla flinch. Through glinting white teeth, he asked, "Did you poison the prince?"

"What?" Arla shouted, her voice ringing against the rocks and shelves of the library. "Why are you asking this?"

Simion laughed, a hoarse, scratchy sound that was like nails chipping against iron. "Haven't you heard? The young prince has fallen ill."

Entering the throne room was like crawling into thick molasses. She could feel the tension of worry as the tall turquoise- and gold-painted walls bounced back the flurry of chatter and debates among a huddle of men and women.

In the center front, Mathus sat on his imposing throne adorned with rubies, diamonds, and gold siphoned from the fertile Ulsanan ground while his wife sat on a significantly smaller, less appealing chair by his side.

Arla had not even made it to her designated seat before someone wailed in grief. Arla jerked back as Ametha cried into her sleeves. Her usual perfectly curled golden hair was tousled in an unkempt way and her bright cerulean eyes were duller, drowning in worry and despair.

"Silence, woman!" Her father's vein on the top of his head bulged.

Arla quietly slinked to a simple wooden chair to the left of the king and queen, far enough away that she would not disturb anyone, nor be seen by *them* clearly, but she could see them. It was a miracle that she even made it to this chair.

Whatever was happening was bad enough that her father did not bother to kick her out, or maybe he hadn't noticed her entering. Simion had told her just moments ago about this meeting, and she was determined to know what was going on.

Arla looked across the room. All twenty of her father's advisers were standing before his throne, along with a sprinkle of the eldest Royal Scholars, arguing and debating like clucking roosters, and at the top of the flock was Norendra. She stood at least five inches taller than almost everyone in the room, except the king, of course.

Did Norendra suspect her of poisoning her brother? Arla examined the room for any accusatory glares coming her way. Who else thought she had poisoned him?

Don't worry, Princess, Simion had said at the library doors an hour ago. *The physician has already concluded it wasn't poisoning.*

They did not truly suspect her, but that did not stop Arla from her real concern. How sick was her baby brother?

Half-brother.

"Your son is severely ill, Your Highness." The physician in the center of the room was sweating, clearly afraid of the repercussions of telling the truth. His round face matched his short, rotund body, and he looked like he had not slept in days as he stood in front of Mathus. "I do not know what has overcome the prince, but whatever it is, there is no human-made cure for it."

Ametha let out another cry as she clutched her chest. A gloom fell over Arla as she remembered Jun's bright brown eyes and his smile as he squeezed her finger. How could he be sick? She just saw him a few days ago, and he was healthy and happy.

The temperature rose. Waves of heat emanated from her father's body, singing the fur on his cloak. In a low, dark voice, he asked, "How long does he have?"

"I do not know for sure." The physician wrung his hands. "But I do not expect him to live past the month."

An audible gasp spread throughout the room.

Arla wanted to cry out just like her stepmother. *Only a month?* This could not be true.

Mathus gripped the end of his armrest. The physician's eyes widened, knowing what this might mean for him. "Please, my king, I speak only the truth."

"You were supposed to cure him. You have failed at your one purpose," Mathus said. "And you will be punished for it." He lifted his hand.

"No... please."

The physician's begging wouldn't do him any good. The king loved when they begged; it made it more enjoyable for him. Something that made Arla sick every time.

But it was hard to focus on what was happening when all Arla could think about was that sweet, innocent face, pale in fever, crying out to an empty, dark room. *How could this have happened?* Dread filled her. *Was it her? Was she really cursed? Was it her fault?*

Just as her father opened his mouth to speak, the round physician shrieked. "I can cure him! I can cure him!" Mathus's hand slowly lowered. The physician shuddered in slight relief. He was safe for the next few moments. "There is a legend of a healing plant that can cure any and all ailments," the physician croaked. "We can get this plant and it could save the young prince... but..." He was sweating profusely now. "The legend says it lives only in the heart of The Forest."

Arla leaned forward. She had read about this years ago. Out of the dozens or so books left of The Forest, only one spoke of the healing plant. They said it grew plentiful in the days when The Forest still granted magic, and it could heal anything that ailed the creature that ate it.

"You... You can send for someone to fetch it for you, my king," the physician suggested.

Arla forced herself not to gasp, not to make any sound. The throbbing of her healing burn reminded her to stay quiet even when she wanted to reject it. There was a reason no one went into The Forest after the Darkening; books and journals all told of hundreds of people trying and never being heard from again. Nearby villages would hear screaming through the trees every night for years until people learned to stay away.

Arla looked at her father, who leaned back in his chair, his brow furrowed in contemplation. Was he really considering this idea?

"Your Highness," a plump male advisor said, "we do not know if this plant really exists. It is a legend, after all."

"I am not a fool. I know it is a legend." Mathus retorted before turning to his first advisor. "What do you think, Norendra?"

Her face was calm and calculating. She did not speak hurriedly or with anxiety like the others. "It is worth pursuing, as one of many avenues, my king."

Mathus nodded. His eyes fell on the physician again. "We shall try this method and I will hold you personally accountable for its results." The physician retracted, paling. Mathus spoke to everyone. "Send out soldiers to retrieve this plant. If it exists, they will get it. In the meantime,"—he looked to Norendra again—"send me more physicians. All of them."

Norendra bowed her head in agreement, but the other advisors were not so on board.

"My king, you cannot be serious!" an advisor shouted. "Sending soldiers there... It would be a suicide mission. With the army numbers as they are, we cannot spare that many to go."

He was right. They were going to fail. No one went into that death trap and lived to tell the—No, that wasn't true. There was one person who survived, and their journal rested in her pocket right now.

Arla swallowed hard, building up her courage. She hoped she wouldn't be punished for speaking up.

"There is one person who—" Arla started to say.

"Soldiers are Low-Borns, Docannon" Mathus replied. "Are you saying the prince's life is worth less than a handful of Low-Borns?"

"Never." The advisor's eyes darted from Norendra to Mathus and fell back into silence.

"Your Highness," Norendra said. "Despite Docannon's unruly outburst, he does have a point. Might I suggest we don't send our best soldiers, in case it is a myth. We do not want to lose our most valuable fighters. We could send the expendable ones."

Mathus nodded in agreement. "Send them then."

But another advisor spoke up, a middle-aged man with golden hair. "The Forest is the source of all magic. What will a handful of Low-Born soldiers do against all the unknown magic it contains?"

"I found a journal that—" Arla began again.

"You are right, Gerald," the king gleamed. "It will be better odds to send High-Borns. They'll have the magic to combat whatever is needed in The Forest. Shall we send your son? What was his name? Wilkins?"

Gerald's face paled. "Your Highness, he is my only heir."

"As is my son."

Gerald's eyes darted to Arla. She knew her father was technically wrong, he had two heirs, but in Mathus's world, only one mattered.

Arla tried again. "The journal tells—"

"Then it's settled," Mathus finished. "Tell Wilkins to meet the soldiers at dawn at the main gate."

"Please, Your Majesty—" Gerald pleaded.

"You shame yourself, Gerald." The king looked down on his advisor with disgust. "You beg like a Low-Born."

Gerald's head dropped, defeated.

Arla inwardly sighed in frustration. They weren't listening to her.

No one cares about your opinion at all, Princess.

If this mission failed, her brother was going to die. She had to tell the soldiers or maybe Wilkins about what she knew. The journal and all those years of knowledge she gathered about The Forest to give them the best chance of survival. But how was she going to give all this knowledge to the soldiers before they departed? There was no way.

Unless... Arla went with them.

Arla's breathing shallowed. An idea was brewing.

Their chances were slim, but with her, they could at least have some defense against what they didn't know. She was starting to sweat now as the other advisors shuffled around, making plans on which soldiers to send.

But... she couldn't do this, right? There was no way. She was not equipped. She was not smart enough. Or strong. Or agile.

Not to mention, she would probably die, like the hundreds before her who had entered that place.

"We will find a cure for my son," Mathus boomed across the throne room. "He will be saved one way or another."

For a fleeting moment, Arla saw the worry in her father's eyes.

Something vibrated in Arla, watching her father look at everyone in the room. She had never seen that expression before.

Jun's round, smiling face bloomed in her mind. Flushed in pink and giggling. And then his skin faded to a sickly gray, the light dimming from his eyes.

She clenched her fists, unable to bear the image. She had to try to save him, if not for her, then for her father. And if she did... then maybe... maybe Mathus would smile at her the way he used to and remember that she was his daughter too.

She knew a lot about The Forest, more than the soldiers at least. She could help navigate them to the plant, *if* there was a plant.

She could do this.

She had to.

CHAPTER 4

Arla knew this was stupid. She had never left the city grounds in her entire life. She had never held the weight of a cold steel sword in her hands. She had never slept outside her fire-warmed bed chambers on any night. Which ultimately meant that she was not an adventurer, and the likelihood of her survival was slim, but if there was a chance, no matter how small, that she could succeed, then she was going to take it.

And she was going to do it fast before she changed her mind.

Arla snatched the largest bag she owned from her armoire. It was made of durable cloth with one leather strap meant to bind across your chest to carry it. The bag was big enough that she could have packed her two pillows and a small canine if she wanted to, but instead, she stuffed it full of clothes and supplies.

What did one bring on a trek into the deadliest place of all five kingdoms? Probably a weapon. Arla had stolen a paring knife, wrapped it in cloth, and placed it in the bottom of her bag. She could've taken a larger one, like the chef's knife, but she was afraid it would jostle in the bag and stab her through the cloth. So, the small paring knife would have to do. She also brought a bunch of forks—no idea why, she just did. Maybe in case, she had to eat something or dig something up with it.

Anything and everything could be useful, right?

She donned simple tan pants and a plain cotton buttoned shirt with a maroon jacket on top in case it was chilly. Was it cold in The Forest? Or hot? No one knew. Because, again, it was a death trap in which no one had survived, except the owner of her journal, who, as far as she had been able to read—which was not much yet—did not mention the temperature. Also, she wondered if she should pack a thick blanket. She didn't know. The list of things she didn't know could fill its own book.

She had not slept at all through the night when the first rooster cried into the dawn. She draped a ragged brown cloak over herself and immediately hopped into the secret tunnels deep down into the earth and then reappeared in the main courtyard of the castle.

It was a plain square, with the central tower overlooking its activities. The entire enclosure was walled with the gray stones of the castle that bordered it along with the front gates that were now half-opened. Soldiers and other servants tied supplies to a large wooden wagon, which in turn was tied to four horses, preparing for the trip out.

Arla sighed in relief. The wagon was big enough for her to fit in.

She slinked behind a barrel, trying to be invisible, a trait she was naturally gifted in. People tossed burlap sacks of something into the wagon. It was a simple four-wheeled cart, with the entire top of it covered in a beige cloth arching over the wooden bottom frame.

There were too many of them attending the wagon for Arla to simply jump into it. She needed a distraction.

And then Arla heard the last voice she wanted to hear at that moment. Across the courtyard, Norendra stood, in all black, pointing the soldiers to various supplies. "Faster," she barked. "You must leave as soon as possible."

Arla's fingers fidgeted below her cloak. She needed to hurry. She crawled to another barrel, hoping some brilliant idea would come to her, and that was when she saw an unattended shield on top of the barrel. Maybe if...

She lifted the shield slowly, so no one would notice. The weight of the steel pressed against her hand as it screeched across the wooden top. It was way too loud.

Panicking, she silently dropped the shield.

Arla crawled to another barrel. What else could she do? And then she had it, but it was going to be noisier than the first idea for sure. Staying behind her barrel, she put out her two feet and pressed her heels against the top of the barrel next to her; it tilted slowly. Yes! It was just light enough at the top.

This would have to be quick.

With one swift, unladylike grunt, Arla kicked the top of the barrel next to her, tipping it completely over. The barrel knocked into the one beside it and that one knocked into the one beside that until a series of barrels toppled over, causing a big commotion.

When everyone's eyes were on the strewn barrels of rice and grain, Arla dashed toward the abandoned wagon and threw herself into the draped back of it, banging the edge of the wooden bed with her knee. She hissed, curling into a ball in the wagon. *Every time.*

Now inside, she rolled to a corner, rubbing her knee in self-pity. She burrowed into a pile of blankets and bags of unknown objects and threw them on top of herself, hiding every inch of her presence.

She knew no one would have let her go if she had volunteered publicly. No matter how much her father wished she was out of his life, he would not risk losing a royal over something Low-Borns could do instead. She was sure no one was going to notice her absence for at least a day or two, which would be long enough for the wagon to arrive at The Forest, where she planned to reveal herself. By then, it would be too late for them to turn around.

As she lay there, suffocating under heavy bags of whatever was in them, Arla imagined herself at the end of all this, storming back into the castle, the plant in her hand. The entire throne hall would rejoice, and Jun would be healthy again. And her father would approach her with a look of gratitude. Maybe he would rest his hand on her shoulder and thank her. Maybe he would finally say the words she had waited for all her life.

She touched her finger, remembering her brother's firm grip and his tiny fingernails. She was going to save him no matter what and when she did, her father would finally see her as something better than a disappointment.

Time must have passed quickly when she was daydreaming because before she knew it, the wagon lurched forward as the horses pulled it along out of the castle gates and through the city borders.

It was a three-day trek to The Forest and the soldiers had packed well for it. The wagon was plump with food rations, weapons, clothes, and other sleeping supplies, which were all slowly crushing Arla. Each bump in the road that the wheels rolled over shifted the items in a way that made them dig into her chest and stomach. Maybe she shouldn't have layered so many things on top of herself.

At first, the soldiers were silent, not speaking much, until they were a bit away from the castle. Only then did they start to converse.

"Does anyone know where the heart of The Forest even is?"

The wagon's top cloth allowed light and air into it, which also meant it was thin enough that Arla was able to cut a small tear so she could see what was happening outside. She craned her neck to peer through the hole and followed this voice to a man riding the only white horse in the brigade. The sun shone on his entire being. His soft, alabaster skin complimented the golden hair that slicked back in the most perfect way on his head.

This blond-haired beauty wore the bright bold colors of a High-Born. This must be Gerald's son, Wilkins Dermarcu. She had never met him before, but she had overheard once, while traveling through the castle tunnels, of court ladies murmuring compliments on his considerable wealth.

Wilkins's face was stretched in worry. He must have been the one to ask the question.

"It's at the center." The deep voice vibrated through the wooden bed into Arla's entire being. She turned her neck to see more through the tear. It was a soldier, taller than the others. His steel armor boasted the emblem of Ulsana at the center of his chest plate:

an image of The Forest with twin blades crossed diagonally in the center of it.

It was quite strange, how proud Ulsana was of being the keepers of The Forest and yet so afraid of it at the same time. This tall soldier's short, wavy, dark brown hair fell over his sharp-jawed, olive-toned face. He was the most serious-looking young man she had ever seen and the most handsome. Even more than Wilkins.

...Not that it mattered...

"The scholars were able to tell us at least that before we left," the dark-haired soldier continued. He sounded bitter like the scholars did not give him as much information as he wanted.

She looked as wide as she could and realized there were at least fifteen soldiers of all various ages and genders walking alongside her side of the wagon. She could only imagine there were more on the other side.

"Soldier, you address me as 'my lord' when you speak to me," Wilkins reproached.

The serious young man simply replied with a silent, deadened look.

"Did you hear what I said?" Wilkins repeated, tightening the grip on his reins.

"It is Captain Treterra." He didn't even glance Wilkins's way this time.

Captain? This person seemed too young to be a captain. Although he had the frown of a much older man, he still looked, at most, a few years older than Arla.

"Excuse me?" Wilkins's eyes narrowed.

"If you want me to address you as a lord, then address me as captain. If titles are important to you." Captain Treterra continued to look forward, his expression level and calm, which made the insult more barbed.

Wilkins turned scarlet. He looked around, expecting the other Low-Borns to be as appalled as he was, but he found no sympathy among them. The legion followed their captain down the road, their faces suppressing any emotion they might have truly been feeling.

Was this what her father's advisor was talking about? What was his name? Docannon? He had implied the army was dwindling. Was it so dire that they were appointing young men as captains? Or was Treterra really that skilled?

Although, it wasn't entirely unheard of, was it? She had read about young captains like this one before in history books. It was rare but not impossible for a teenager to lead a small group of soldiers like this one.

"If you are the captain, then where is your horse?" Wilkins spat. "Captains usually ride."

"I march with my soldiers." The answer was curt and to the point, an end to the conversation.

Wilkins was the only High-Born amongst them, excluding Arla, so he must have known he was outnumbered. An argument here would not be won, so Wilkins lifted his chin and continued on to the front.

Arla was just as shocked as Wilkins was. She had never seen a Low-Born so openly dismiss or insult a High-Born like that, ever. That type of tone would have gotten them publicly flogged, or worse. She stayed staring through the cloth. When she was sure that she wasn't in any danger of missing out on more conflict, she laid back on her side and pulled out her journal.

The captain was right, the heart was at the center. Every book had spoken of the heart in some way, shape, or form. They all told of how The Forest had given a "gift" to humankind from its heart, saying it rose from the earth, *wailing*. When she had first read about it, it was strange to her that the books described the "gift" in such a way.

Simion had argued the "gift" was magic, but Arla thought maybe it was the plant and if it was *wailing*, then maybe the plant could make sounds. Or was it a form of speech that had changed over hundreds of years? She didn't know.

She opened the journal with a soft crack of its burnt spine. She hadn't had the time to really read through the survivor's journal but now felt like a good time to finally settle in with it. It was difficult to travel with. On one hand, it was delicate, threatening to turn into a pile of dust at any moment given its condition, so she had to be careful with it, but she also had no choice but to keep it with her and damage it further by touching its pages, because she needed the information within.

She flipped through it, trying to see if there was anything about the heart of The Forest. Had the person been there?

No. Nothing about that.

The rest of the journey was uneventful. They passed by various villages and farmlands of Ulsana that gave them no problems and villagers simply looked at them from afar without interacting much.

She watched them go by as she drank from the waterskin stored in her bag.

It wasn't until nightfall came that her bladder finally decided it could no longer store anything else. Thankfully, the wagon had stopped as the soldiers took their first break for the day. As the soldiers talked amongst themselves, eating their dinners, she was able to squeeze her way through the pile of bags and blankets and quietly but hurriedly topple out of the wagon to relieve herself.

It was surprisingly thrilling. She felt like a mysterious creature of the night, living a secret life without anyone knowing. She did this again the next night and was still never caught.

Truthfully, she was surprised they never noticed. Maybe because they had not sent their most skilled fighters. Norendra advised her father to send "expendable" soldiers. Not their most valuable. Maybe this was why the armored men and women seemed either too young or too old.

The first two days, the soldiers spoke amongst themselves casually, but the third day was when things started to shift. Tension grew amongst them as they got closer and closer to where The Forest would be. They walked stiffer, staying tightly together. Even the captain kept a hand on the hilt of his sword at all times.

The chill found them before the trees even appeared over the hill.

And then in a blink, it loomed before them.

They were finally standing at the edge of The Forest. Death's door. Even through the rip of the wagon cloth, staring at it felt like peering into the abyss to nowhere. The trees that bordered it stood tall and slender and dead. With no leaves and charred black trunks, the branches reached up into the sky, their tips as sharp as spears.

And the grass... Although the grass below them now was vibrantly green and healthy, as it reached the edge of the hollowed trees, the dirt turned to black ash and the grass died, replaced by string-thin, onyx-shaded blades of what looked like obsidian ice poking up from the ground on the forest floor.

"I don't know about this, Leo. The Forest is cursed." The strained voice came from a short, lanky soldier who, judging from his round face, couldn't have been more than twelve or thirteen years old.

Pale and brown-eyed with black hair, this soldier's monolid eyes were wide with the terror of any child who approached a place like this. He looked far too young to be in any type of armor, especially the one that hung on him like an oversized barrel which only made him look smaller.

The young boy looked to the captain, seeking direction. "Leo?"

Leo? Was that the captain's name? Were soldiers allowed to call their captains by their first names?

Captain Treterra—or Leo—kept his gaze forward. If he was worried about this thicket of skeletal branches and wood like the rest of them, he didn't show it. He patted the boy's shoulder. "It will be okay, Uro." It wasn't meant to comfort him; it was meant to tell him to be brave.

The young soldier named Uro nodded, but it did not stop him from tightening his grip on his sword. A sharp-faced, female soldier stepped beside them. Arla had to admit she was struck in awe when she saw her and was surprised she did not notice her before.

The soldier's height matched Leo's, with a diamond-shaped face and umber-toned skin, her braided hair was tied behind her to reveal her high cheekbones that glowed in the sun. She was beautiful, straight-edged, and strong, everything Arla was not, who would describe herself as more a soft, uncooked ball of dough.

"Your talking is wasting energy," this young woman said curtly. "Save it for whatever comes."

Leo lightly tapped her shield as he spoke, smirking. "See, Uro? Be more like Rose here. Stoic, logical, and focused. All her energy is going to be used very efficiently today."

"That is correct," Rose replied, in a strangely monotone voice.

Her face was serious, not understanding she was being teased, which only made Leo and Uro smile wider. A ping of jealousy struck Arla's heart. These three seemed close. What was it like to have friends like that?

The envious feeling would have lingered if another chill did not throw Arla back into the situation at hand.

They were about to enter The Forest.

The place where no one, save for one, survived for as long as Arla had been alive, or longer. Part of her was screaming to jump out of the wagon and run home, but she pressed it deep down, muffling it with sheer will. She wasn't going to turn around now.

For a moment, no one moved. They all seemed to take a combined moment to look at what was before them. And then Leo took the first step into the shadowland.

CHAPTER 5

Darkness crept above them, slowly draining the light away from everything and making every part of The Forest look sinister. The trees and plants were sharp and foreboding, grimacing towards the sky, devoid of leaves like they were burnt until only their hollow, scorched skeletons remained. What was even stranger was the silence. There was no chirping of birds or the scuttle of lizards underneath curled fallen leaves. It was a symphony of desolating stillness.

Wilkins's horse fretted in nervousness, reeling backward, not wanting to go any further. The noble cursed and kicked the horse with his heels, demanding the animal obey, but it wouldn't. The horses pulling the wagon seemed to be spooked too as they stuttered to a stop. Arla could barely see through the rip now. With the fading light, her vision was limited, turning most of the soldiers into shadowy silhouettes.

"What was that?" Panic spiked in Wilkins's voice.

She didn't like the sound of it because it made her own heartbeat jump. Feet shuffled in uncertainty, crunching against the black vegetation blades beneath them.

"Did you hear that?" Wilkins croaked.

"Something is wrong." Uro's voice shook in the dark.

Arla's eyes strained, feeling like they were going to pop out of their sockets from how hard she was trying to see through the ripped cloth, looking for any movement or shadow.

And then it happened.

A bloodcurdling scream burst through the soldiers.

The walls of the wagon thrashed violently, knocking Arla out from under the blankets and spewing items everywhere. Something splattered on the other side of the cloth, staining it a dark crimson.

Screaming.

There was so much screaming.

The sharp ring of swords leaving their sheaths. The ground quaking from something large slamming into it. The clattering of metal armor. Ice filled Arla's veins.

Death was here.

Something ripped through the top of the wagon, splashing something wet onto her leg. She screamed, clinging to the edges of the wagon bed.

Above her was a long, thick tree branch, covered in blood and black ooze.

It was *moving*.

The branch lifted, raising the wagon along with it. Arla dug her fingernails into the wood, trying to hang on.

And then it stopped. Black sludge spilled from a gash Arla couldn't see, spilling more of the muck over her legs, and the branch fell, hurtling her and the wagon back to the ground. The wagon crashed sideways, tossing all of its contents over to one side and Arla along with them.

Clamoring out of her hiding spot, Arla strapped her heavy bag behind her back. She had to get out before another *thing* smashed the wagon to pieces. She pushed herself up and swung open the doors. Immediately, she was blasted with the sounds of unnatural screeches and the crackling of stretching bark.

Arla gasped.

Chaos descended on her in a whirlwind of metal and wood, blood splattering everywhere as the trees tore through the soldiers.

The *trees*.

Their rough, raw-boned branches stretched unnaturally and struck out at the soldiers, cutting through their shields and armor. Their darksome trunks grimaced, like ancient faces with no eyes or mouths.

She had barely gotten her bearings when she saw something shoot out at her in her peripheral. She dove to the ground just as another branch crashed into the wagon, splintering it to pieces.

Wilkins uttered words that made him fast on his feet. He looked like a blur. He dodged the branches, whose sharp tips threatened to skewer him clean.

Arla rolled to her left, just in time to see a soldier get impaled by a thick, blackened branch. Fresh, hot blood splattered onto her arm. She opened her mouth to scream, but nothing came out, her voice strangling in terror.

Run. Run. Run.

Arla crawled through the mud and dirt, dodging falling soldiers and branches alike. She could barely comprehend everything that was going on.

Fast. Everything was moving way too fast. She was an animal whose instincts propelled her legs forward. There was nothing in her mind except the will to survive.

The ground shook.

By the Whispers, the trees were stampeding in unison now. Their jagged roots crawled across the forest floor like hideous spiders, and they were coming toward her. Arla scrambled to her feet and ran as fast as her legs would go.

A wall of metal slammed into her, sending her tumbling forward and entangling in someone else's arms and legs. They rolled in the dirt until she found herself straight on top of him. She looked down to see Leo, his mouth agape.

For a moment, all time stopped, and they just stared at each other. His dark umber eyes flared with surprise and the aftermath of fighting fury. Her cheeks flushed. He was even more striking up close. That square jaw. The thick brows angled downward into a deepening frown that only accentuated his sharp eyes.

Before she could stop herself, she meekly lifted her hand in a greeting gesture. "Hi."

And then the world spun again, faster than ever before. Leo's eyes darted to something behind her, and he pushed her headfirst into the ground beside him which filled her mouth with ash dirt. A sharp clash of wood on metal rang as Leo fought back an attacking limb.

Leo pointed at the rocks behind her. "Hide!"

Without hesitation, Arla scrambled behind the rocks he pointed to, holding her bag like it was a child. The stones were taller than her standing, which meant they were enough to protect her.

Leo pointed to someone, shouting something. She didn't know what they were saying. There was too much going on. And then she saw the captain bellow out the young soldier boy's name.

In a blink, Leo had gripped his shield and blocked a sharpened branch from tearing through Uro and swung his blade. The limb was too thick to cut all the way through, but the captain had sliced it deep enough to make it bleed. Without missing a beat, Leo swung again, hacking away at the bark until he eventually severed the branch from the tree. Arla had seen guards train in the castle, but it was nothing compared to how this captain held his weapon. It moved like an extension of himself. Focused and intentional.

Arla yanked the journal from her pocket, flying through the pages. The delicate paper began to catch and tear against her trembling fingers.

Focus. Did the survivor talk about the trees? How to stop them? There was no mention of them in the history books. Why didn't the journal warn me of this? Were those the missing pages?

Bark splintered between the rocks, knocking the journal out of Arla's hands. Shouting, she scrambled back away from it, barely able to snatch the journal back up from the ground and stuff it into her pocket. Her back hit another cold stone, shaking her spine.

She was trapped.

She needed to push it away or run or attack. If only she had a sword, or—*of course!* Her hands dove into her bag, rummaging as the limb thrashed around, looking for her. It bent and whipped at her legs. She screamed, kicking it back as she pulled out her paring knife.

She drove the small blade into the tree limb, releasing a spray of black ooze against the rock, but there was no scream or writhing or any reaction at all from the tree. And then Arla realized... it did not feel pain.

A small branch from the limb extended and wrapped around her ankle. The tree yanked her down, sending her flying onto her back. Arla grabbed her bag as she was dragged across the ash. Lifting it above her, she dropped the heavy bag onto the branch, snapping it in half. The rest of the limb retracted, taking her paring knife with it.

Sweat beaded her forehead. That was close.

Leo's voice roared out to his soldiers. "Into the woods!"

Soldiers rushed past her. Before she could react, Leo had sprinted to her side and grabbed her hand, not stopping as he ran deeper into The Forest.

They ran faster than Arla could take. Her legs felt like lead, and her heart threatened to burst from her chest, but every time she slacked, Leo's hand tightened and dragged her further and further until they couldn't hear the thundering trees anymore.

Her large bag jostled from side to side, its heavy contents pulling her down.

"Drop the bag!" he shouted back to her.

"No!" she shouted back.

The land thundered with the pursuit of roots stretching out to grab them. One brushed the back of her heel, but Leo just tugged her forward, racing past everything. Her lungs were on fire, and she didn't know how much longer she could keep this pace.

And that was when the landscape changed around them. Where the trees were skeletal and blackened, they shifted into tall evergreens that seemed calm and not so... evil. The ground no longer shook, and the light started to beam back through the canopy. Like waking up from a terrible nightmare and into the morning sun. The change was drastic and sudden like they were in a completely different woodland.

The thundering of pursuing roots disappeared.

That was when Leo finally stopped.

It took a couple of minutes for Arla to gather her breath. She had never run like that in her life. She couldn't wrap her mind around what had just happened.

The trees are alive?!

"You shouldn't be here," Leo snapped, tossing her hand out of his. He spoke to her so casually, like he was reprimanding a child, rather than speaking to a High-Born.

Even though Arla knew all the High- and Low-Borns did not hold her in high regard, she was still a princess, and usually, Low-Borns spoke to her with indifference, rather than the contempt he showed. And even if they did speak with contempt, it was usually done in the servants' quarters where they thought she wasn't listening. Wilkins was right, this captain did not care for titles.

Leo shouted for his soldiers, who slowly reappeared from the trees.

Twenty had come, and judging from the amount of blood on their metal armor and their sunken faces, they had lost a lot of fighters. She remembered the blood bathing the ground as bark limbs pierced through their armor into their chests. The smell of sharp iron and toxic fumes.

The world dipped sideways as she felt bile bubble up her throat.

"Princess Arla?!" Uro gasped. The young boy sped to her. He didn't appear to be hurt in any way. "What—How? Are you alright?" He pulled a handkerchief from his side, offering it to her.

She had thought to reach for it when she suddenly puked, emptying her stomach of her breakfast. There was so much blood on that forest floor. She had never seen someone die and to witness so many perish so violently in a matter of minutes...

She retched again.

Uro crouched next to her, unfazed by the stench, and offered her his handkerchief again. "It's okay, it happens to all of us."

When she was sure she wasn't going to throw up again, Arla gratefully took the cloth and wiped her mouth. The young boy helped her unfold herself and stand straight.

"Thank you," she said hoarsely, the acid having weakened her throat.

He accepted her gratitude with a smile.

"Out of the way!" Wilkins pushed past the soldiers and when his eyes fell on Arla, his mouth fell open. He paused, his eyes searching for something inside his mind, and he turned to a nearby soldier. "Was she walking with us the entire time?"

It seemed Wilkins was wondering if she had been there and he had just missed her. Like the invisible thing she usually was.

"Why did you follow us?" Leo, who had just watched her throw up without offering any help, had his arms crossed as he stood before her now. His eyes were full of judgment and anger. She didn't know why, but it made her wish she had thrown up on his feet and sullied his boots.

She cleared her acid-sore throat as best she could before she responded. "I'm here to help you find the healing plant."

There was a silence amongst them where one could only hear the slight breeze fluttering the pine needle leaves. Leo looked at her like he was disappointed in her answer.

Wilkins burst into laughter, almost keeling over. "You?" he choked back a heave of more cackling. "You're going to help us?" He howled in glee. "What are *you* going to do? You can't fight. You can't use magic. You have no weapons or horses or—" He couldn't seem to finish, he was laughing so hard he was having trouble breathing.

Arla tugged at her sleeves, wishing she could turn into a small mouse and scurry away. Saying it out loud, it *did* sound foolish. She curled slightly into herself and focused on looking at her dirtied boots.

Wilkins's booming laughter finally died down to a minor chuckle as he wiped a tear from his eye. He let out a big sigh and then pivoted to Leo. "I think we should return to the castle now, so the king doesn't have our heads when Princess Arla over here inevitably dies."

"No!" Arla shouted. "If we go back now, we'll never get the plant in time. We need to hurry before my brother—"

"I'm not going to be executed because you decided to join the ride." Wilkins grimaced.

"If we return without the plant, we will be executed regardless." Rose flicked black sap from her sword before she returned it to its scabbard. She seemed unscathed as well, except for a couple of dents in her armor. Her impassive eyes quickly surveyed Arla's ooze-stained legs and arms and the bag she carried with her. Arla had a sinking suspicion Rose had assessed that she was weak and would die soon as well.

Leo nodded in agreement, although his sour expression did not shift. "Rose is right. We have no choice. Our task was to get the healing plant and that is what we'll do." He turned his cold gaze to Arla as if he was blaming her for making their lives even more difficult than they already were.

Arla curled away from the look, wanting to be that small mouse again, but something else stirred in her. In a voice much higher and squeakier than she wished it was, she said, "Captain, I've read every book there is on The Forest, and I can help you with what I know."

"Any book that was written about The Forest was from before The Darkening," Leo retorted. "It won't be much help to us now." He turned his back on her, walking away.

"I also have a journal from a survivor!" she shouted after him.

Leo froze. The soldiers gasped and spoke amongst themselves again.

"A survivor?"

"There is no such thing."

"No one has survived this place."

When the captain turned, his eyes were narrowed. "And how do you know this person survived The Forest?"

"They said so." The minute those words left her mouth, Arla realized that the journal could have been a trick. Someone pretending to have survived and making up riddles.

Leo was probably thinking the same thing as his eyebrow arched, almost waiting for her to think about what she said. "So you trust the words of a stranger you've never met?"

"I know it sounds stupid, but I think it's real," she insisted. "I found it hidden away behind a stone in the library. And the way they talk about this wood, it feels real."

Leo rubbed his furrowed brows with his forefinger and thumb. "I know that you live cooped up in your castle, *Princess*, so you may not know this,"—he looked down at the bound pages in her hands—"but this is the real world with real consequences. You have to be careful in whom or what you trust."

In other words, he was saying she was a naive, ignorant castle brat who believed in fairytale journals with no real understanding of blood and battle. Arla's face reddened in shame. It wasn't untrue.

"We need to make camp," Leo announced to the rest of them. "Rose, tend to the wounded. Uro, build a fire to ward off any other *life* that might come for us."

And with that, Arla's time to speak was over, and she was left with just Wilkins standing beside her.

"What an insolent Low-Born bastard," Wilkins growled at Leo's back, who was now too far to hear him.

She knew no one believed her and worse yet, they thought she was a joke, and for a minute, she agreed. Of course, the journal could be false. She had no idea. She didn't even think for a second that it could be a trick or some joke. But something in her gut told her it wasn't. The way the survivor talked about their journey, the messy scribbles slanted like they were hurriedly jotted down against the back of a rock, it seemed real to her.

Regardless, it did not deter her; she was here now, and she still was the only one amongst them who knew the most about this place. She was going to get the plant as fast as possible before worse things than the trees came after them.

CHAPTER 6

They chose to settle against a colossal rock that jutted out from the surface of the forest floor, no doubt hoping to protect themselves from any butchering trees that might find them. The fire was quickly set as the soldiers huddled around it, trying to keep warm from the sudden drop in temperature when night fell.

Arla felt a bit out of place amongst all the beaten-down warriors, so she kept her distance, choosing to sit on a moldy log a few feet away.

Before they camped, the soldiers had bandaged themselves up and gave a moment of silence to those they lost. Some even broke into tears, but then the tears dried, and their faces hardened again as they removed their armor and settled by the fire.

The calmness seemed strange compared to the insanity they had just endured. Arla wondered if that was what the life of a soldier was—fighting for your life one minute, relaxing for dinner the next. They couldn't hold onto grief, because their lives demanded they continue on.

The thought of this saddened her. How difficult this life must be.

Waxed cloth rustled open around their packed food, which included dried puffs of rice and dehydrated meat. She was in awe of how, even in the fighting, some soldiers managed to grab and haul sacks of supplies from the wagon with them. She barely managed to hold onto her own bag.

For a long time, they sat in a quiet hush with only the sound of their repetitive chewing to be heard. Amongst the thicket and the trees, there was still no chirping of birds or critters that normal woods would have, merely the slight breeze of the wind brushing up against the plants and their own exhausted bodies.

Arla kept a suspicious eye on the trees that now towered around them. They were covered in green needles, as most pine trees were. So different from the ghostly sharp branches of the ones that bordered the outer edges of The Forest.

But were they safe?

The branches groaned, creaking and moving forward. Arla jerked back. *Were they—? No.* It was just the wind, making their bark-covered limbs dance. The lifeless, unmoving, non-killing branches.

She took a deep breath to calm herself. All that puking and running had tired her out.

The trees used to be trustworthy here; their leaves were described as soft as cotton and flourishing with never-ending flowers and fruits. It used to be a place of plenty. Although these trees didn't have fruit or flowers, they did look less menacing and more like the trees the books described.

If she had to guess, the ones with leaves were safe, or at least it seemed that way. Who really knew? Maybe the needles would start shooting down at them like deadly shards of glass.

She flipped through every inkling of knowledge she had of The Forest in her mind. Remembering passages describing the woods as the most stunning place in the land. So different from what it was now. Past scholars described how light beamed from within the stones and moss and the songs of the birds could draw tears from even the most hardened pessimist. How beautiful this place must have been. Arla wished she was alive back then to see it.

She looked down at her feet, where a mixture of black ash and whitish fungus-infected dirt lay. It was so uninviting, like it would give you hives if you laid on it.

To have such a lovely place turn into this, what could have happened?

She glanced up at the dark tree canopy, sending a silent plea.

Please don't start moving and try to kill us.

She tugged the journal from her pocket and noticed it had bent where her pocket had folded against her hip. A small, childish part of her drooped. Norendra's words floated in her mind. *Can't keep anything pristine.*

Flipping through its pages, the journal still didn't mention anything about trees. She had checked before, but it was under duress, and she wanted to double-check just in case. She stopped at a page that contained an illustration of The Forest. The image was sketched in a hurry, one would have thought it was a blob of black scratches if one did not look carefully. And that one person was Arla, two days ago when she had seen this black blob before.

Arla squinted her eyes, choosing to look carefully this time. In the center of the drawing was a group of dead trees.

She looked closer. The tips of their branches were sharp like lances and dripping from them... *blood*.

It was here all along. Which only meant one thing. This journal was real. The survivor had gone into these woods. How else would they have known about this? Energy surged through her.

"I knew it!" she shouted. She was so filled with glee that she forgot about the tired, mourning soldiers within earshot. A pang of guilt hit her, but luckily, they didn't seem to hear, as they were wrapped up in their own conversation.

A conversation that piqued her interest.

"Do you think the stories are true?" a soldier asked no one in particular. "That The Forest can grant magic?" A consensus of grunts and nods spread across the soldiers.

"Maybe a long time ago, but it doesn't now," another responded.

Uro excitedly turned to Leo. "Maybe it still can. To be just like the High-Borns would be amazing."

Leo shook his head. "Why would you want to be like the High-Borns?"

The bitterness in Leo's voice was so raw, Arla started to suspect his hatred towards them was more personal.

Uro mumbled, "So we could have magic."

"What a ridiculous thought," said Wilkins, who emerged from the woods, still fumbling with the drawstring along the waistband of his pants, coming from a privy break.

He looked at the soldiers like dumb brutes. "You cannot gain magic without pure High-Born blood pumping through your veins."

Uro turned red and bowed his head, shamed by Wilkins's tone. The others grew quiet. She understood their desire. When Arla couldn't hear the Whispers, there was nothing she wanted more than to have magic. She would have done anything for it.

The young boy grabbed a stick and poked the fire, probably trying to take attention away from his reddened face. It was then that he turned and noticed Arla sitting alone. As the others changed the subject and spoke about something else, Uro got up and approached her.

Does he need something?

When Uro reached her, he held out a piece of dried meat. "Would you like some, Your Highness?"

"Oh." Arla paused, not used to this kind of gesture, so she wasn't sure how to react. Was he being sincere? Looking at his face, it seemed it was... She held out her hand, accepting the gift. "Thank you."

He smiled and turned to go.

"Oh! Actually, I have something too." She pulled open her bag and shuffled through a pile of forks and string and pulled out a small bag of banana leaf-wrapped sticky rice and mung bean. She grabbed a handful and placed it in Uro's hands. "For you."

Uro's eyes beamed, looking at the wraps, which puzzled Arla. It was only a snack.

"Uro." Leo's harsh voice cut through the night. He stood a few feet behind the young soldier, blocking the light of the fire from reaching Arla. Without his armor, Leo wore black pants and a beige tunic with leather bracers around his wrists. The tunic had a simple

V-shaped neckline held together by a crisscrossing string which only revealed more of his toned chest. "What are you doing?"

Uro's face blushed as he sheepishly replied, "I was just hoping to share a meal together with the princess. It's been a... tough day."

Leo's cold expression remained unchanged. "High-Borns don't eat with us. It's their rule." He was warning Uro to stay away, just like the others. His gaze shifted to her, his dark brown eyes piercing through her thin layer of confidence. It was suddenly colder, as she felt frost riming up her skin. "Isn't that right, Your Highness?" he practically growled.

She knew that tone well. Hatred and disgust. She could feel it seeping from him like poison.

Wilkins plopped himself next to her, making her small log tip more toward his side. "It's true. Although, I would say the princess barely made the requirement." Arla's ears heated in embarrassment. "Now go away, soldiers." He waved them off like dogs.

Hurt crossed Uro's face as Leo shifted his hateful glare to Wilkins. The young boy bowed his head low to Arla and followed Leo back towards their fire.

She frowned and scooted away from Wilkins. "You shouldn't be so mean to them."

Wilkins ignored her, taking three sticky rice wraps from her bag. He took a bite out of one, chewing loudly as chunks of glutinous white rice stretched and rolled in his mouth. "Did you see his face? So happy to get *this*?" He coughed and laughed at the same time as he threw the rest of the wrap onto the ground, stepping on it. "It's not even that good. Low-Borns will eat anything. Such pigs."

He stuffed the other two into his pockets.

A flare of heat went through Arla.

She wanted to stick her hand into his throat and pull out the rice, hoping he would gag as she did it. And just as fast as the scalding rage came, it subsided. She was a little shocked at herself for having such a violent desire. She had never thought like that before.

"I'm usually served at least three to four courses, and with friends..." Wilkins looked at her, utterly disappointed. "But these are desperate times." He smiled at her, a wide, fake smile. "So, I guess this stuff will have to do." He grabbed two more wraps.

This thief looked different from the pale, terrified young man she saw when they were being hunted by the skeletal trees. Was this the face he gave to the court ladies that made them swoon? He reminded Arla of a fox, sly and cheeky, willing to do what it took to survive.

She couldn't bear to keep looking at that grin, so she looked at the soldiers ahead of them instead. They were hunched over the fire, and she couldn't help but notice Leo's intense stare boring into the flames ahead of him, his lips a thin grim line. He leered at the fire so hard she thought he was trying to make it explode.

She chewed on the dried meat, hoping Uro would see how much she was enjoying it. Her stomach churned and tightened from the salt. Still, it was very good. She bit into it again, more dramatically in case Uro didn't see it the first time.

"Is that the journal?"

Before Arla could stop him, Wilkins plucked the journal from the top of her bag. He pulled at the pages, bending the spine all the way back, and folded it, which made Arla cringe. He licked his finger and flipped until he landed on something that caught his eye.

"*The water was so beautiful,*" he read out loud. "*It spoke to me in ways no one else could understand.*" Snorting a laugh, he said, "Is this a journal or a diary? This belonged to a woman, didn't it? Was she in love with The Forest or something? What is this flowery language?"

Arla's face grew hot. She snatched the journal out of his grubby hands.

"Is this what you read all day, Princess? Romantic diaries? We all wondered what you did with all that spare time you had."

We. He meant the other nobles in the royal court. While they were busy attending parties and gossiping, or training in weaponry or artful talents, Arla was huddled away in tunnels and libraries. As much as she loved her books, she had dreamed of joining them one day, if they would have her. But they never did.

Still laughing, Wilkins chortled, "Oh, I'm sorry, Princess, I didn't mean to offend you." He didn't seem sorry at all.

"This person was probably swept away by what they saw. Water is very important here," she defended as she glided the survivor's pages back into her pocket, apologizing to it inwardly. "Ancient scholars wrote that the water was so essential it beat with the heart of The Forest itself."

Wilkins scoffed. "Those scholars have been dead for hundreds of years. What do they know?"

Without another word, Arla got up and settled closer to the crevice of the rock, away from his amused chuckle, trying not to let him see her irritation that she was sure was painted all over her face.

Wilkins, fortunately, did not follow.

CHAPTER 7

They were lost. Arla knew it, and she knew that Leo knew it. Wilkins cursed as he tripped over a fallen twig behind her. She didn't know whether Wilkins was aware, though.

They had woken up at the crack of dawn, or what felt like dawn; it was hard to know in this constant shifting of graying light. Leo had the soldiers back in armor and pressing forward for the last couple of hours. She assumed his tactic was to scour the entire greenwood until they found the plant, which required a huge amount of time and effort, and judging by the deepening scowl on his face, he was probably suspecting it might not pay off.

Hours of walking and they hadn't gained much distance. It was like The Forest was intentionally leading them in circles. Usually, Arla would have followed without saying anything for days, but she didn't have the time. Jun didn't have much longer.

She marched up to the captain, her bag clanking and clattering against her back. Before she could say anything, Leo spoke. "You shouldn't burden yourself with such a heavy bag. It will slow you down."

Arla, wanting to be friendly, decided to keep her tone light and conversational. "I didn't know what we were going to face here, so

I brought everything, just in case. Fortune favors the prepared." She pasted a grin on, to show him she meant to be a joyous, helpful presence in his life.

Unaffected by her smile, Leo replied, "I *am* prepared. I have a sword." He cautiously pushed away a thin branch of leaves from their path with the steel tip of his broadsword, half-expecting it to attack him.

"Well, I have..." She pulled out a small bag of honey-covered almonds. "This."

He raised an eyebrow. "What is that supposed to—"

"The Forest is a vast place," she interjected. "Hundreds of years ago, even when this place was friendly, there were stories of children getting lost for days. When they were found, they said it was hard to know where you were because all the trees looked the same."

She pointed to the tree bark next to them where a sliding honeyed almond was making its slow merry way down the trunk.

"I've been marking the trees we've been passing." She pointed to another identical honey-covered almond sticking to another tree; this was freshly stuck, not sliding down yet like its brethren. "We've already been here."

The muscles in Leo's jaws tightened as if he suspected this all along. "We are wandering in circles."

She stuffed the nuts back in her bag and tied it up. "It's okay." She wanted him to know she was on his side and that they could work together. There was no reason to hate her. There was no reason to dislike her in any way. She would be happy and friendly and most of all, useful. "I think I can get us to the heart."

"All this time, I thought that was what I was trying to do," he replied sarcastically.

Arla continued her cheery approach. "We just have to see where the middle is." She looked up at the canopy. "Maybe from the tree-tops."

"Did your fake journal tell you that?" he asked.

Immediately, Arla forgot about her friendly attitude and pulled out her journal in a triumphant and smug huff. "I'm so glad you mentioned that." She flipped it open to the black blob illustration, showing him. "The journal warned me about the death trees, I just didn't see it. Someone *did* survive this place and they *did* write this journal so,"—she snapped the journal closed—"it seems I was right." She puffed out her chest like a proud bird.

Leo's frown deepened, but he didn't say anything further. Arla smirked, sheathing her journal back into her pocket.

That's right. Eat your words. I hope it gives you gas later.

Arla took a few paces away from him and observed a nearby tree.

Not enough branches.

She moved to another one and tested the roughness of the bark.

The rougher the better.

"What are you doing?" Leo's eyes followed her curiously.

"Finding a tree to climb," she answered. "I need a higher view."

The captain crossed his arms. "Do I need to remind you that the trees are trying to kill us?"

She gestured to the surrounding trees. "These are fine. They are friendly." She tried to sound confident. Was it working?

He grimaced, looking at the treetops. "And what exactly do friendly trees look like?"

Arla pointed to a nearby branchlet, whose leaves were soft and plump, almost like peaches, but they were a light shade of jade. "Friendly."

She walked over to another tree and pointed to another leaf, viridian with small, bulb-like edges. "Friendlier."

And then she pointed to a small bush, half dead, one side skeletal, the other side still clinging to its leaves. "Probably not as friendly." She took one step away from it in caution.

Leo caught on. "So the trees with leaves are safe?"

"Yes."

"And you got this information from your journal?" Leo's eyes followed her from tree to tree until she settled next to a large one with low-hanging branches.

"No, that's from all the books. And... mostly my gut." She dropped her bag at the base of her chosen tree and put a foothold on the side of the trunk, testing if this crevice would hold her weight, and then stepped up.

Leo's eyes widened. "You're really going to climb that tree?"

"I told you." Arla grabbed the nearest branch and pulled herself up. "I'm going to see which direction we need to go." She scrambled up to the top of the first limb, pulling her stomach over it and unintentionally making an unladylike grunt. Then she grabbed another above her and hoisted herself over that one, swinging one leg over it.

She heard Rose's voice from below, who stood next to Leo now. "You should stop her."

"She's too far up," Leo replied, folding his arms in defiance. "And I am a terrible climber, you know this." He sounded almost amused.

And then a shuffle of steps followed by Uro's voice burst through the branches below. "Princess! That's not safe!" he shouted up at her. He seemed the only one who cared about her safety at all, which she appreciated.

"The likelihood of her falling to her death is high," Rose said nonchalantly.

Well, that isn't helpful.

Arla pulled herself onto another branch. She kicked up her feet to hop to the next one, and then her knee drove straight into the unsparing wood. She hissed from the pain.

"Very high," Rose repeated in her dead-pan tone.

Not helpful at all.

Arla knew she looked awkward. She felt it as she crisscrossed her arms in ways that almost tangled herself and sometimes her foot would get stuck in a crook of a branch, and she would accidentally make a whelping noise when she slipped a couple of times. But she kept going, trying to look like she knew what she was doing.

It felt like she had grabbed and pulled at a hundred branches, each getting thinner as she scaled them until finally, with great effort and buckets of sweat, the air thinned and the greenery parted, leaving her at the top of the tree. She clung to the trunk on the last sturdiest branch that could hold her weight, facing away from the horizon.

She needed a break. Her heart raced like a rabbit's, and her biceps and forearms throbbed. They were going to be sore later for sure, but still, she felt a gust of pride inflate her lungs, making her chin tilt higher.

She did it. She had climbed this tree!

She was flushed, sweating, and tired, but she did it, and it was exhilarating.

Grinning, she was ready to claim her prize, to see the bright horizon and a clear view of the center of this vast forest, but when she looked out, her heart fell.

Instead of seeing all the trees spanning a great distance, she only saw a thick layer of depressing fog. A dark gray haze of mist and nothing. Like the entire place was in a dome with smoke trapped in it. This was why the light below seemed so inconsistent and drab; this haze was blocking the sun.

Only the closest pine needle trees within a couple of feet were visible to her. She wasn't going to be able to find the center this way at all. She imagined the captain's face if she returned and told him she saw nothing. He would look down on her with that height of his and not be surprised she failed. No one would be surprised she failed.

Her shoulders hunched. There was no other option; she had to return.

Sitting on the branch, she prepared to lower herself down when something caught her eye ahead of her at the end of a branch limb.

A glittering.

Slowly, she shuffled her feet, one foot at a time away from the safety of the tree's core trunk and towards the thinning branch. The branch groaned underneath her, warning her it would not be able to hold her further than this.

She stopped and looked out to the adjacent trees, whose pine-needled branches overlapped each other.

Did she imagine it? Was there not—

Something shimmered to her right.

Looking over, she finally saw what caught her eye.

A thin, web-like string of water beads the size of small kiwis hung on the end of a thin branch from the tree next to her. When the small amount of light refracted off the small water globe, it shimmered again. And then something shined behind it.

Another string of water beads hung from another branch just behind it, and then Arla realized there was a cluster of them hanging from the highest limbs of all the trees around her.

And they were sparkling like diamonds.

It was breathtakingly beautiful. Was this what the forest was like before it turned to poison? If anything, at least she got to see this before she climbed back down and delivered the bad news.

A plop.

Something soft and round bounced on her shoulder. It slid down her covered forearm and settled into her hand.

A water droplet rested in her palm, and it was surprisingly... soft. It was like holding a fragile egg. Its gel-like body jiggled as she shifted the weight of it in her palms.

It must have fallen from a string above her from a branch of a higher tree she could not see.

A smile crept over her face. She curled her fingers around the water droplet and then it... *giggled*.

Arla froze.

The water droplet turned, revealing two big beady black eyes. It looked up at her, full of curiosity.

She stepped back, causing the branch below her to wobble. Her body flailed as the droplet rolled around in her hand, its big, round eyes crinkling, like it was enjoying itself. Quickly, she balanced herself to a stable position.

When she pulled herself together again, she looked back at the water glob droplet thing, and it was back to staring at her.

Was this water bubble thing *alive*?

By the Whispers. Was it going to kill her?

She gave it a side-eyed look, suspicious and afraid that any sudden movement would trigger its killing instinct. Strangely, it just kept staring at her, as if it was trying to understand what she was. Maybe it had never seen a human before.

Daring to smile weakly at the creature, she said, "Hello." She was trying to determine if it was friendly or not.

The droplet's eyes widened and then scrunched up as its eyes squinted, like it was smiling too, or at least, mimicking her.

Maybe this creature wasn't a harbinger of death. Maybe it was trying to communicate with her? Talk to her in some way?

Wait. There was something here. Something she had seen before.

The water spoke to me, and it was beautiful.

Was this the water the survivor was talking about?

The water droplet bobbed up and down, like it was happy, or dancing.

The water spoke to me, and it was beautiful.

The water *spoke*.

Arla was glad no one was here to see this; they would have thought what she was about to do was crazy.

She leaned forward, hoping the droplet would understand. "Um, I was wondering... do you happen to know where the heart of The Forest is?"

The droplet stared at her for a moment and then bobbed up and down again. She was going to take that as a sign it was nodding. Relief washed over her.

"If it's not too much trouble... can you show me the way to the heart? I'm looking for a plant that heals."

The water droplet did not bob up and down this time. It just blinked at her, its big black eyes innocently gazing up at her. *Of course, it doesn't know.*

She sighed. "It's okay, let me just put you back home."

Arla reached out and hung the water droplet on a nearby translucent, sticky string. It giggled again and turned to look at her. The other water droplets on that string also turned. And the next one and the next one, until a thousand beady eyes faced her. And then all at once, their faces disappeared, turning them back into non-alive water droplets.

A faint glow illuminated from each of their bodies, brightening every second, one after another. They shone across the entire canopy, cutting through the fog, revealing an endless forest. So endless, it was impossible to know where the center was.

And then row by row, the lights pulsed in rhythm, like the echoes of a heartbeat. She could almost hear the drum-like sounds.

She gasped, remembering what she had said to Wilkins the night before.

Some past scholars described that the water was so essential it beat with the heart of The Forest itself.

It beat with the heart.

The rippling continued, but it was stronger to her left. Arla followed the wave of dimming and brightening lights until it was clear where the first wave was coming from. Far down to the west side, a light brighter than the others glowed.

The heart.

Arla clasped her hands together and bowed to the water droplets. "Thank you." She hoped they understood the amount of gratitude she had just then.

The droplets wriggled in response. She pulled her bent arms to the sides of her chest in a tight ball of excitement. This might actually be possible. All they had to do now was go in that direction.

A roar rippled through the treetops, swirling and bending the branches, shaking the strings the water beads clung to. It slammed into Arla, knocking her off the branch. Her panicked hands gripped a barked limb as she fell, letting her land on the branch below.

The water droplets quivered and then shrank, reabsorbing themselves into their threads, becoming as small as seedlings.

Arla scampered back to the trunk of the tree, away from the edge of the branches, clinging onto the rough bark. The wind thrashed and pushed on her like it wanted her to go away.

Then came the heaving pour.

Rain plummeted down from a sky she could not see. It poured over her, but it wasn't water. It was gunky and thick. The slime coated the entire branch she was on, flowing over her feet like it was trying to push her off.

She didn't need any more signs. It was time to go.

Quickly, she made her way down the branches, but the slimy rain only gushed on her harder, sticking to the tree limbs and making them slippery. In a clutter of clumsy grabs and holds, she managed to make it halfway down without losing her grip. Almost there.

The wind had stopped chasing her now, but the slime kept coming.

Her foot tried to settle onto a lower branch and her hands moved down, trying to steady her, but as she reached, her hand slipped. She cried out as she fell, and the branches dodged her as if they wanted her to keep falling with nothing to stop her.

She screamed, bracing for the impact. Strong arms enveloped her, stopping her fall. She landed on something smooth, but hard. And she realized she was once again on top of Leo.

Leo's arms were wrapped around her, his chest pressed against hers. She felt the heat of his hands around her waist, the warmth of his breath on her neck, which sent tingles of blush through her body. She scrambled up to her feet, pushing herself as far away from him as possible.

"I'm so sorry!" she shouted. She offered him her hand, which seemed to surprise him, but he didn't take it as he got up with a groan.

"I am not your landing cushion, you know," he grumbled as he brushed the dirt from his clothes.

Rose stood where Arla last saw her, still beside Leo, her hand resting lazily on the pommel of her sword. "I am shocked you survived." Nothing in her expression showed she was shocked. She was like a wall of monotone grays, just like The Forest fog. Neutral and impossible to see through.

Uro, on the other hand, was practically jumping out of his armor in relief. "I'm so glad you're okay!"

The young boy ran around her, checking for injuries, even lifting the ends of her long, damp hair to see if her back needed tending to, while still maintaining a distance great enough that he did not touch her body.

Leo inspected her too as he swung his elbow in circles, loosening the arm that took the brunt of Arla's weight. "Why are you wet?"

Arla looked down at herself, the slime still clinging to her coat and pants, and then back at Leo and Rose. Strangely, they were still dry. Whatever sludge fell from above did not make it down here. "It was raining up there and—"

She stopped herself. Time was ticking.

"It doesn't matter." She looked at them with bright eyes. "I know where the heart is."

CHAPTER 8

Arla was used to being ignored. So when Leo looked at her dumbfounded, she thought for sure he was going to tell her she was being silly, or insane, but he didn't.

Instead, he asked her, "How do you know where the heart is?"

They remained standing under the tree Arla fell from, with the slime still dripping from her jacket and hair. Sucking in a breath, she told him everything she saw up in the trees and then waited for his reaction, again expecting him to cut her off and tell her she saw nothing. That it was impossible. But again, he didn't do what she expected.

He lifted his hand to his chin, rubbing it in thought, and then said, "Well, then, lead the way."

"Me?" Arla stumbled back. "You want me to *lead*?"

Rose shot a questioning look to her captain, as did Uro.

"You said you know where the heart is," he replied, a bit annoyed.

She didn't know if he was making fun of her or not. Was he setting her up to fail? But the shock on Uro's face made Arla think that maybe Leo was being serious. Sweet Uro was kind, but even he did not look convinced enough of Arla's story to let her lead them deeper into The Forest.

Leo must have sensed she suspected him of possible sabotage because he sighed and said flatly, "You took the risk of going up the trees, so you should reap the rewards of your courage."

Was it courage or desperation?

Arla didn't know.

And didn't this captain want the credit? If it was her father, he would have taken her discovery as his own and then tell her that she didn't climb fast enough.

Hesitantly, she agreed, because they did not have more time to waste, and she was confident in knowing what she saw at least. If this was a trap set by Leo, she was hoping it would spring later when they were closer to the center, which would give her enough time to prove herself right. Arla looked at the frowning captain again, trying to read his mind, but he seemed serious.

Arla quickly changed into dry clothes behind a very thick tree, so as not to be seen. Leo had ordered everyone yards away for decency.

She put on another shirt with long sleeves, of course, but had forgotten to pack another jacket, distinctly remembering debating whether she should stuff another jacket in her bag or the thickly wrapped paring knife instead when she was packing. She chose the knife and now it permanently belonged to a murderous tree. When she was done, she scurried back to them, and they were on their way.

She led them toward the direction she remembered where the bright light shone and they followed, trekking behind her for almost another hour.

"I still think you should lighten your load; it's going to slow you down." Leo's eyes were on her bag again, which was slung behind her.

"I'm fine," Arla replied, shifting the weight of it.

She was *not* fine.

She had to admit, the backpack was getting heavy. Her legs were not used to walking this much or running, or climbing, and she was starting to feel the soreness in her calves. Maybe she *did* need to remove some things. But everything in here had saved her so far. What if she took something out now and then horribly realized she needed it later?

Leo sighed. "I will carry it then."

Arla pulled away. "I can do it," she said too bristly and then added in a softer tone, "Thank you, though."

He probably thought she was a weak High-Born too privileged to have ever carried her own bag. She wasn't going to give him the satisfaction of proving him right.

Leo's face remained neutral as they journeyed further into the woods.

The trees were getting extremely large; some trunks expanded beyond Arla's entire arm span. She prayed these were not the kind that moved because they would be crushed within an instant, if not by their branches, then by their giant roots that now half jutted out of the ground. Glancing to her right, she saw Leo eye them as well, thinking the same thing.

The ash-covered ground slowly went away, revealing small peaks of soft grass below their feet. It seemed the further in they went, the more alive and friendly The Forest looked.

As Leo kept his pace with her smaller steps, he started to make conversation. "So, this journal you have. Can I see it?"

Arla lightly touched her bag, where the book now rested. She remembered how Wilkins had made fun of the words the author wrote. She didn't want that again. "Maybe some other time."

"You've read a lot about The Forest then, in the royal libraries." Leo pushed a thin limb of leaves out of their way as they stepped between two massive bushes.

"Yes." She was surprised he remembered that. And she was even more surprised at how much he was talking to her. Was it working? Did her climb up the tree prove she was useful to him? Was she winning him over?

"What else did the survivor say about this place?"

"That The Forest likes to play tricks," she replied.

Leo eyed the grand trees suspiciously. "I don't like tricks." He put a hand on the pommel of his sword as if daring The Forest to try something. "They are lies and the only people that think they are funny are those inflicting them." He said that last part more to the trees rather than to Arla.

"That's true," Arla agreed. "And usually it's just cruel."

Leo gave her a sideways glance as if to ask, *Are you speaking from experience?* The corners of her lips curved up into a slight smile, to deflect his questioning look.

"What little the scholars told me before we left, they said the plant would look like a weed, with circular leaves with small yellow flowers," Leo said with a hint of that bitterness she heard before when he talked about the knowledgeable elders.

"What else did the scholars tell you?" she asked.

"That the plant will be at the center," he replied.

"That's it?"

Arla understood now why Leo was sour. It was unnerving how little the scholars had prepared them before sending them off to the most dangerous place in Ulsana. Maybe she could help him feel more prepared. "The healing plant was said to be only as tall as the length of one's hand." She waved her hand around at him. "It could heal anyone of any ailment, as long as they squeezed it first to release its oils and then eat it. You know you've found it if you touch the petals and it closes within itself."

She paused, surprised she hadn't been interrupted yet, but Leo kept walking beside her, his head tilted just a little toward her like he was still listening.

"...Should I keep going?" she asked.

He raised his eyebrow. "Is there more?"

"Yes."

"Then why did you stop?"

She fidgeted with her hands. "Um..." No one had let her talk for this long without telling her to be quiet.

Leo grunted in annoyance, so Arla kept going. "They said it grew everywhere in The Forest before The Darkening, but people kept picking them for every little ailment, a cough, an itchy nose, a stubbed toe. Soon there weren't that many plants left, so The Forest retreated the plant to its heart and protected it."

Leo scoffed. "I'm not surprised."

"By The Forest?"

"By the people," he grumbled. "They always want more."

Arla thought about how The Forest must have felt, all those grubby hands pulling its precious gift from the ground, something that could heal deadly diseases and bring someone from the brink of death. How long it must have taken for it to grow each plant, to feed it water and sunlight, just for someone to snatch it and waste it on a small cut or a bruised knee.

Was that why it rejected us?

Someone stomped behind them, crushing the sleeping grass. Wilkins caught up to them, shoving a leafed branch away in disgust. "Are we close?" His impatience was fuming from his nostrils. "What did your diary say?" he demanded.

"It's not a diary, it's a journal," Arla snapped back, surprised at her irritation.

"There's no difference," Wilkins snarked.

"Yes, there is. A diary is more personal with feelings and reflection. A journal is more about details of a day and knowledge," Arla argued.

He groaned. "Who cares? Are we close or what?"

Arla gathered up all the things she wanted to shout and pressed them into a box in the corner of her chest. Drawing in a calming breath, she responded, "The heart is far. It'll take at least a couple more days to get there if we walk fast."

"Then walk *faster*," Wilkins demanded.

Arla's voice grew quiet as she picked up her pace. "I'm walking as fast as I can."

She was embarrassed because she thought she was already going as swiftly as she could without sprinting. Maybe her short legs could not keep the pace he wanted.

"If we use up all our energy too early, we may not have enough left to defend ourselves if we are attacked," Leo rebuked.

"Attacked by what?" Wilkins's eyes bulged, suddenly afraid of the air around him.

"Well," Arla started to explain, "the villagers said they would hear the screams of people here constantly, but sometimes they heard different sounds. Screeching. Like animals." Her voice went low. "So there are probably creatures here that could hurt us. Maybe even... monsters."

"Monsters?" Wilkins scoffed as he kicked a layer of moss on a passing rock. "Princess, I'm sorry but think logically. There are no prey animals in this forest. What would the monsters eat to survive here? There is almost nothing."

Except us.

"So you can accept the murderous trees, but not monsters, Wilkins?" Leo replied so casually and coldly that it was borderline condescending. "I would give this place a little more respect. We are at the mercy of The Forest now, not your father's estates."

Wilkins's eyes narrowed, and his head bent forward like a hunting predator. "It's *my lord* to you."

Again, Leo ignored him, continuing forward. Arla thought Wilkins's blond hair would kindle into flame in rage. His face was so red it looked like he was boiling from the inside. If steam came out of his ears, she wouldn't be surprised.

"*Viere!*"

In a flash, faster than humanly possible, Wilkins was in front of Leo.

This is Wilkins's magic, Arla realized, remembering how fast he moved when the trees attacked, he could hear the Whispers to make him quicker.

Wilkins's finger pressed deep into Leo's chest plate. "I've had enough of your disrespect, Low-Born," Wilkins spat. "You will address me by *my lord*, as your filthy kind should."

The other soldiers behind them froze in their places. They didn't know what to do as much as Arla did.

Leo's expression remained blank.

Wilkins grinned. "That's right, you act like you don't know your place, but you do, don't you Low-Born?"

He shoved Leo backward.

Something crossed Leo's eyes, a scream for murder, but then his indifference returned. The captain did nothing to retaliate or defend himself as Wilkins pushed him again, harder this time.

"That's right, you know if you hurt me in any way, you'll lose everything. Even if I do this." Wilkins slapped Leo across the face. Red bloomed across his sharp cheek.

Arla gasped. Without thinking, she lunged and pushed Wilkins off his feet, sending him flat onto his butt to the ground.

"How dare you!" Wilkins screamed. His hands dug into the dirt and grass.

"I'm sorry! I'm—" *No.* She wasn't really sorry, was she? She straightened, fists curled. "Please don't do that again."

Wilkins shrieked. His rage was so familiar. It was the same that ran through her father. The pride-bruised High-Born shot up in a fury, like a bull on a target. He wasn't thinking anymore, he just wanted retribution. He stormed toward her.

"You can't touch her!" Uro piped up, his voice cracking. He wasn't used to shouting, Arla could tell.

But Wilkins wasn't listening. He was too caught up in his own emotions. "*Viere!*" he shouted and in an instant, he was in front of her. She braced for a hit, but nothing came.

Instead, Leo was there, his hand gripping Wilkins's arm, now twisted behind his back, and in one swift movement, he pushed Wilkins face-first back into the ground.

With bared teeth, Leo growled, "Don't you dare."

Wilkins screamed through a mouthful of dirt. "You insolent bastard! When we get out of this place, I will make sure my father strips you of everything you have! You will be shamed in front of all your soldiers! Your blood will feed my crops!"

Arla's heart was pounding dangerously fast. He wasn't lying. Leo was going to get in a lot of trouble for what he just did.

The captain's eyes cooled into a darker shade of brown. The kind that shot cold iron through your soul. "Rose, Uro, take Wilkins to the back of the brigade. He needs time to calm down."

"Yes, Captain." Rose pulled Wilkins up to his feet with the help of Uro.

A few other soldiers surrounded him and the High-Born struggled for a few minutes before realizing he was outnumbered and that any real fight would have him on the losing side. They escorted him to the back of the group. As the soldiers spread apart, Leo ordered them to keep moving forward in the direction they were going. Arla looked again at his reddened cheek.

She knew that pain.

"I'm sorry he hit you. Does it hurt?" She laced her clammy fingers in nervousness.

Leo shifted his gaze to her and for a moment, her breath caught. It wasn't gratitude or softness in his eyes, it was loathing.

"Do you think you're better than him because of what you did?" he spat.

"I—um..." She couldn't find the words.

"Pity is just as bad as hatred, *Your Highness*. And I don't need either of them." Leo marched past her, to his soldiers.

She stood in silence, her mind still trying to put the pieces together of what had just happened. She'd really started to believe he was beginning to warm up to her, but clearly, she was wrong.

CHAPTER 9

Arla was falling behind, her legs shaking from the effort of carrying her bag. After hours of walking, her sticks for legs had decided they weren't going to support her anymore; they had done enough. Her slowing pace was fine with her, as it kept her behind Leo. After what he said, she thought it was best to give him some space and some for herself as well.

She had to admit she was a little stung by his words.

You should be used to the hurt by now, she scolded herself. Sometimes she wished she was like the three-headed statue in the Endezee Garden. Something that could never feel emotional pain no matter what you did to it. Stone was cold and distant, it couldn't burn and most of all, it couldn't feel.

Distracted by her thoughts, Arla didn't see the rock when her toe slammed into it. Her body flew forward as she flailed her arms like a flapping penguin and landed straight onto her already bruised knees. The dry moss provided little cushion from the impact.

Arla! she reprimanded herself. *Do better! Be better!*

"Princess!" Uro quickly helped her up while Wilkins burst into a fit of laughter behind her, which ended with a sharp oof.

Arla turned just in time to see Wilkins holding his side as Rose retracted her elbow. Uro gently held onto her until he was sure Arla was standing steady. At the very least, she was grateful that Uro didn't hate her. She hoped that wouldn't change the more he got to know her.

"I'm okay." Arla was trying to convince herself more than Uro. Her legs wobbled in disagreement. Damn her tiny, weak bird legs.

She caught the young soldier giving Rose a glance, who nodded in some sort of understanding. Rose walked past them, up to Leo, and said something into his ear. The captain paused, dipping his chin down, before turning completely around to face them.

"We'll stop here for the day," he said, addressing his soldiers. "Make camp by the trees over there."

"No, I can keep going!" Arla shouted, surprised at the power of her voice. She didn't want to be the reason everyone had to stop.

Leo ignored her and moved the soldiers to their new campsite. "Here, Princess." Uro helped her along like she was a child, which made Arla even more embarrassed, especially since Uro was years younger than her. She was supposed to be helping them, not slowing them down.

The gray sky had darkened into a dull onyx blanket of a starless night. Fires were quickly made and some of the soldiers fell asleep immediately, which made Arla feel a little bit better that she wasn't the only one who was tired. Others lagged behind, eating their dried dinners. Wilkins, still fuming from their ordeal, had begrudgingly gone to sleep surrounded by a handful of soldiers who were watching his every move.

And Uro stayed near Arla's side. He settled on a rock across from her, worried.

"I feel great," she said in the most joyful voice she could muster.

She didn't want him to fret over her, so she tried to seem perkier than she was feeling. Uro's tensed shoulders eased, which showed her act was working. *Good.* She half expected him to leave her, since the last time he had spoken to her at camp, he was reprimanded by Leo, but the harsh-eyed captain was nowhere in sight.

Uro's eyes also seemed to be scanning for him before concluding that Leo was not watching. He looked eager to say something, so Arla just waited, laying her still-wet jacket out on a rock by the fire that flickered between them. She hoped it would dry out by morning.

"I can't believe you pushed Wilkins," Uro finally said, muffling his giggle as best he could. The brightness in his eyes made him look younger. So, this was the side of him that remained youthful. It made Arla smile.

"I can't believe it either." She suppressed her own giggle. It had all happened so fast; she didn't know where that daring had come from.

Scooting forward on his small rock, Uro spoke in a low voice so as not to be heard by eavesdropping ears. "Can I ask you something, Princess?"

"Of course."

"How did it feel?" The way Uro looked at her, she could tell he had wanted to do something like that for a long time.

Arla gazed down at her hands. "It felt right."

When she met the young soldier's eyes again, they both burst into a fit of more giggles. It was true, it did feel right, and to say it out loud made it even funnier. She didn't know why. She laughed so hard that the side of her ribs ached, a feeling she cherished, even though it was somewhat painful.

When the giggle fit ended, Uro sighed, staring at the dancing flames. His expression changed to something more solemn. "I'm worried about Leo. He's going to get in trouble when we get back. *If* we get back." Uro took a stick from the ground and poked the fire, making it roar larger. A sight that made Arla twitch a little, unconsciously touching her arms. "He shouldn't have done that to Wilkins," Uro continued. "I'm scared he'll be punished. He's always been like that, you know. Hateful to High-Borns, I mean. He's gotten away with it in the army because we're all Low-Borns and he doesn't deal with nobles directly. But... the higher in rank he goes, he might have to, and I'm afraid it will get him killed one day."

Arla had only really known Uro for a couple of days and yet she felt his worry so deeply, it hurt her too. He reminded her of her brother in a way. *Half-brother.* They both had messy black hair and snowy skin, but it wasn't the looks that were similar so much as it was the essence of him.

She imagined when Jun grew up, he would—hopefully—end up like Uro, sweet and so open with his kindness. And this thought alone was the reason she replied, "I'll do everything I can to make sure Wilkins doesn't say anything to my father so Leo won't get hurt."

"You will?"

Uro was so trusting, so hopeful. Arla had never held any power in the royal court, over anything or anyone, but she knew she had to try. She would do that for Uro because he believed she could, and strangely, she didn't want to lose that belief.

Uro leaned closer. "Tell them he only did it to protect you. Wilkins would have hurt you if he didn't step in."

Arla hesitated. Was that why Leo moved against Wilkins? To protect her? But he hated her. This was confusing.

"I will do my best."

That was all she could promise, although she felt a bit guilty that her best was probably not going to do much. Maybe she could convince Norendra to persuade her father to go easy on the captain. However slim that chance was, it was still greater than the odds of her swaying Mathus.

"Thank you, Princess." Uro smiled and continued to poke the fire that grew between them. The night had shifted into its darkest form, making the fire blaze brighter against the black that covered the air around them.

She wrapped her arms around herself and leaned towards the heat, the chill seeping through her shirt. "Uro?"

"Yes, Princess?"

She adjusted her jacket on the rock, flipping it over like a pancake to make sure it dried on the other side. "Can I ask *you* something now?"

"Of course." Uro placed his head in his palms, his elbows on his knees. He seemed giddy that someone was interested enough to ask him questions about his life.

"Why are you here?" she asked.

Uro looked at her quizzically, not knowing what she meant.

"It's just... you seem too young to be out on a job like this already," she explained.

"Oh..." he muttered. "Well... in some cases, they let people as young as ten join the army."

"Ten?!" Arla looked across at the sleeping soldiers, realizing she was too loud. She didn't want to disturb their sleep. With a lower voice, she said, "But that's so young."

"Well," Uro explained, "you start off in the stables doing chores, and then eventually become a trainee. You don't become a full-fledged soldier until you're at least fifteen or sixteen. But... the last couple of years there haven't been enough recruits. Leo told me there wasn't enough incentive to join since the army couldn't pay the soldiers much. At least, not as much as they used to. So they started putting us into the soldier positions earlier."

So it was true. Ulsana's army was dwindling. In the many years of peace between kingdoms, Mathus must have reduced his focus on Ulsana's defenses. This was what the advisors were talking about and the reason why a boy as young as Uro was able to become a soldier so quickly.

"But why did you join so early?" she asked.

"Because they feed you in the army." Uro smiled, a mask for a sorrow that dug deep into him. "My family couldn't feed me anymore, so they told me I had to leave."

His family... *told* him to leave? Like a command? Arla was horrified. Who sent a ten-year-old boy out into the streets to fend for himself? She couldn't even imagine.

"The army recruiters were so eager to have anyone, and I didn't know where else to go, so I joined." Uro grinned, trying to keep things light. "It's a good living. They give you a place to sleep and regular food. It's my home now."

"I'm sorry that happened to you." Arla meant it. She wished there was something she could have done, even if she didn't know him back then. Someone like him didn't deserve a day of suffering.

Uro shook his head, never losing his joyful mask. "It's not that uncommon. A lot of us are like that," he said. "But to be honest, I didn't do well the first year there. My fighting skills were not very good, and I really thought I might not make it, but then Leo took me under his wing and helped me get better. I was very lucky. He's looked out for me ever since. He's still looking out for me."

She glanced at the other campfire a few feet from them. Leo and Rose had reappeared, sitting and eating their stick of something barely edible in silence. "What do you mean?"

She hoped Leo wouldn't notice them long enough to finish the conversation.

"Leo wasn't originally supposed to lead this brigade," Uro explained, the fire crackling. "They didn't want him going because he's the best swordsman they have. The youngest captain in a hundred years. A prodigy with a sword. They didn't want to waste him by going off and dying in The Forest over a plant, but he volunteered to come anyway."

"Why did he do that?" Arla was now really curious, still staring at Leo, watching the muscles in his jaw tense and pull as he chewed on the stale jerky in his hand.

Uro looked down at his feet, looking guilt-stricken. "Because of me and Rose. We were ordered to go, and he said he wouldn't let us go without him."

Because he wanted to save them.

Maybe she and Leo had more in common than she thought. He had come here to save the people he cared about, and so did she. Both of them had volunteered to most likely die in this place. They were both really brave, really desperate, or really stupid people.

Leo turned from his seat and caught Arla staring. She blinked and turned away. It was over. He was going to come here and separate them. But to her great surprise, he merely turned back around and bit into his stale food. *Interesting.*

"He must really care about you two," Arla replied.

She could see why Leo would risk his life for them. Uro was kind and innocent. Rose was strong and focused. Worthy of being saved. Just like her brother. Arla, on the other hand... She wondered what it was like to be cared for like that. For someone to believe you were worth risking their life for.

"He's never said it out loud, but yes, he really does." Uro grinned. "He's not very good with words, but you know what he feels by his actions. He's the greatest person I've ever known." He said those last words with the awe of a younger brother.

"That's a big claim you're making," she teased.

Laughing, Uro replied, "We don't have much, so sticking together and watching out for each other is the only way we survive. And to have someone like him on my side? I'm lucky."

If it wasn't for his baby-face and cracking pubescent voice, Arla would have completely forgotten Uro was younger than her. He spoke so eloquently, like an adult, even better than her. Maybe because he had to grow up much faster than she did. It made sense why he sometimes acted older than he was. The same with Leo and Rose. Those who were raised starving with swords probably grew up quicker than those wandering alone in sheltered castles.

She had never had to think about starving or where she would sleep for the night, and she imagined Uro had many more nights outside than he ever should have.

"And what about you, Princess?" Uro beamed. "Do you have friends in the royal court? I'm sure you have so much fun there."

Arla almost laughed out loud. How beautiful he must have thought her life was.

"No one really talks to me in the castle."

Uro's eyebrows squished together in confusion. "Why?"

"Why?" she repeated, asking herself. "Well because I have no magic and a High-Born with no magic has no worth."

She suddenly felt stripped naked, the light breeze cutting at her like shards. Like any little thing could tip her over now. It was something she had always known deep down, but to say it out loud made it so... exposing. That was the funny thing about truth, it had a way of stabbing you in the most tender areas.

"Well, if you have no magic, then you're like us!" Uro was excited for a few moments before realizing how insulting his words would have sounded to a noble.

The last thing any High-Born wanted was to be compared as an equal to a Low-Born.

When Arla was younger, Simion had thrown her a wet rag which she instinctively caught. He snickered as he announced to his friends, "*I told you, she would make a perfect kitchen hand. Look at the way she is holding that rag. Those hands are ready to clean.*" He often told her that she might as well have been born a Low-Born and that maybe she might have been better off that way because no one expected anything from a commoner. "*You're good at being quiet and following orders, so what's the difference?*" he had said.

She had cried for days after that, believing it was a great insult to be called a Low-Born, but now, sitting across from Uro, seeing these soldiers risk their lives every second they remained in these woods... she thought it wasn't such an insult at all.

"I mean..." he backtracked, the fire throwing shadows on the creases of worry on his forehead. "I'm sorry, I didn't mean to offend you."

Arla smiled, shaking her head. "I'm not offended." She placed a hand on his shoulder. "If having no magic means I'm more like you, that would be a great thing."

Uro returned her smile, his round cheeks flushing.

CHAPTER 10

The regular gloom of the morning gray sky materialized above them like a thick murky fog. By the time Arla woke from her slumber, the fire had gone out, but she was grateful it stayed burning long enough in the night to keep her warm without her jacket. When she retrieved her coat, it was still as wet as it was yesterday.

Was the slime magic? Did it never dry? She sighed, covering it in a blanket and shoving it into her bag. The weight of the slime only made the sack heavier. Maybe she should toss it...

Her tongue smacked against the roof of her mouth, her dry throat beckoning her to get water. She reached for her waterskin and opened the cap, but when she put it to her mouth, no liquid came out. *Strange.* She could have sworn it was half-full yesterday.

She probably forgot. Rummaging through her bag, she looked for another water skin, but there were none. She didn't bring enough. *Stupid.* She should have packed more.

A rustle of bending grass told her that someone else had gotten up. She looked over and saw Leo, tightening the metal shin guards on his legs. Thinking about what Uro said the other night, she thought if this young man was the type of person who would offer himself to go into The Forest for his friends, then maybe he wasn't as heartless and bitter as she thought. Maybe there was a way she could still win him over and prove she could be a comrade, or better yet, a friend.

Arla decided she would try again, one more time.

"Morning, Captain," she chirped as he wrapped his shield into place on his back.

He didn't seem like he wanted to reply, but common courtesy won out. "Good morning, Princess."

One step forward.

"Yesterday, you said you wanted to take a look at my journal. You can still do that if you want before we get going." She handed him the bound pages.

He hesitated; he looked doubtful that she was doing this out of the goodness of her heart, but eventually, he graciously took it from her hand and flipped through the papers. As he did that, Arla thought it would be a good time to get to know him a little better and he could get to know her and soon they would be laughing together, like the friends they were meant to be.

"So, did you have any dreams last night? I usually dream about desserts. Sweet bread drenched in honey and fluffed white vanilla cream."

She was making her own mouth water. She couldn't wait to go back to the castle kitchens and get her hands on one of those airy, sweet bread filled with strawberry cream.

Leo stopped flipping the pages, landing on one that had engrossed him. Then he flipped to the next page, and then back again. She frowned slightly, discouraged by his lack of attention, but rubbed it away quickly before trying again. "What about you? Do you like dessert?"

"That's strange," he muttered.

"Desserts?" *How dare he talk about desserts that way.* She pursed her lips in defense. "Desserts aren't strange, they are the delights of the entire lands, the reason I get up on Sundays. When the bakers make this specific jello, I almost—"

"No," Leo replied. "This." He motioned to a mostly intact page. At the bottom was written: *Beware the.*

He flipped to the next page. *The Forest plays tricks.*

"Oh," she said in a sympathetic tone, pointing at the words. "It says: Beware The Forest plays tricks."

"I know what it says," Leo snapped.

"Oh," Arla startled. "You can read?"

He gave her an insulted look.

One step back.

"Why did you think I'd want to see the journal?" he asked sarcastically. "To look at the pictures?"

"I'm sorry I just meant..." She rubbed her forearms. "A lot of Low-Borns aren't taught to read."

"My father made sure I was educated," he responded curtly. His sharp eyes were glaring now as he shut the journal.

"Oh, that's surprising, most Low-Borns—" she stopped herself. It was better at this point not to talk anymore; she was just making it worse.

"If you're going to insult someone, you should do it completely." He passed the journal back to her, eyeing her with disdain. "Fully commit to it."

"That's not what—I wasn't trying to offend you, I'm sorry." Her cheeks were burning now. "I'm glad you know how to read."

Leo walked past her, muttering, "I doubt that."

Something boiled inside, rose from the pits of her gut, and bubbled to the surface. Whirling around, she lashed out, "I'm just trying to help!"

Leo stopped in his tracks, turning halfway towards her.

Exasperated, she had nothing left to do but ask the real question. "Why do you hate me so much?"

His sharp eyes darkened. He closed the distance between them, getting so close, she saw the exposed part of his armor, where his neck met his clavicle that expanded to his wide shoulders that disappeared into the crevices of the steel chest plate. His jaw set, his entire demeanor as hardened and cold as the armor he wore. In a low, husky voice, he asked, "When do you plan to drop this act?"

"What?" She was taken aback.

"I want you to know, Princess," he warned, "I see everything, and I can't be fooled by your sweet, naive persona. You act like you want to work with us and help each other, but the moment you get your hands on that plant, you wouldn't hesitate to leave us to die so long as you get what you came for."

Arla was simmering now. She stepped forward, throwing her chin up at him. "You think I'm just some selfish person who's only out for herself? How can you think that when you don't even know me?"

Leo closed the distance between them, his chests almost touching hers as he glowered down at her. "You are a High-Born," Leo snarled. "That's all I need to know."

They glared at each other, each huffing in a fire of contempt with every draw of their breath. People had called her many things in her life, but a deceptive, selfish person was never one of them, and for some reason, this was where she drew the line. She may be stupid, useless, alone, magicless, and easily ignored, but she was *not* deceptive, and she was definitely *not* self-serving.

Groans of annoyance and tossed bags sounded behind them. The soldiers were up, and they were unhappy. Arla looked to the side to see several of them scratching their necks while others smacked their lips. She saw them guzzle the liquid from their water skins down until they had nothing left. It must have been a very dry night.

She turned her attention back to Leo, ready for another fight, but he had already left her and was back amongst his soldiers, helping them pack for their long trek today. There were many reasons she wanted to hurry and get the healing plant, and never having to interact with this arrogant captain ever again had become another one.

They fell into the same walking pattern as the day before, Arla with Leo in the front as the rest followed. Although they walked beside each other, Leo kept a significant distance between them.

Good. The farther, the better.

She needed to focus on the goal at hand. Get to the heart and quickly.

She had purposefully picked up speed, ignoring her sore legs. Today, these bird sticks were going to obey her command, no matter how badly they wobbled. And at this pace, they were sure to get to the bright heart within a couple of days. She just had to keep up this pace.

But that was hard to do when her insides felt like a crackling desert. It was surprising how quickly the lack of water was affecting her. She felt like burning ants were crawling up and down her throat, threatening to set her on fire if she didn't get water soon. And she wasn't the only one, the others were feeling it too by the way they touched their necks. Even their lips were cracked and shriveling.

Some of them shook the last drops of their water onto their tongues, completely unsatisfied, while others hung onto their last few precious morsels of hydration, taking sips to conserve, not daring to share with anyone else.

Arla was still very disappointed in herself that she did not pack enough water. Of all things, it should have been the item that took up the most space in her bag.

"Give me another waterskin!" Wilkins demanded of Rose behind them. Arla craned her neck to see the noble lunging for Rose's water, but she slapped his hand away like an annoying fly.

"You will find that mine is empty as well," Rose stated.

"Then give me yours!" Wilkins shouted at Uro, who apologized that he was out too. The High-Born son of Gerald Demarcu continued to whine and complain about the lack of water, but there was no help to give him. "I cannot believe we've all run out of water!" he whined. "I swear mine was full yesterday... unless one of you bastards stole it."

He shot an accusatory look at a nearby soldier, but a quick glance at Rose's curled fist made him rethink whatever retaliation he was going to take.

An hour or so more of walking and the thirst was getting unbearable. Wilkins's earlier wailing was starting to become more understandable as others started to moan in protest at their withering throats. Dragging her feet, Arla was unsure of how long she could go on and even debated whether to abandon her bag to lighten her load. Leo gritted his teeth and hiked forward, but she could tell he was suffering too.

A dark part of her wanted to laugh at him and tell him this is what he deserved for misjudging her, but honestly, she was too drained to do anything but focus on putting one more foot in front of the other. Leo was still walking, so there was no way she was going to stop either.

She was starting to get light-headed, the graying light dimming in and out of her vision. She wasn't going to last much longer. Each toe dragged on the ground as she struggled to lift her feet. And just when she feared this intense thirst was going to take her down, the brushwood cleared, and Arla heard the sweetest sound in her life.

Rushing water.

"There's water over there!" she shouted, waving her arms, so everyone could see her.

She hopped over tangled roots and thick grass to a clearing that opened up to reveal a sparkling running stream. She almost cried at how beautiful it was. It looked like liquid diamonds skipping over rocks in an endless race. Even the sky was bright here, shooing the gray away for sunshine and warmth. She yelped in glee and threw down her bag. She shuffled inside its cloth walls and pulled out a thick cotton ball, unwrapping it to reveal a beautiful copper cup in the crude shape of a cupcake topped with a cherry.

She dipped her cup into the stream and set it on a nearby rock.

"You've got to be joking." Leo appeared behind her, his arms crossed, his skin taut in dryness. Arla knew he was talking about her cup.

"I know you think it's ridiculous, and I don't care."

She wanted to bring something that would bring her joy in a time of darkness. She knew going into The Forest would be dreary, so why not bring an object that would lift her spirits when she needed it to? Besides, it wasn't *that* heavy. The muscle in her shoulder spasmed in disagreement.

"Why are you just placing it there?" he asked.

He was really chatty for someone who hated her.

"I'm waiting for it to warm up a little."

She knew what he was probably thinking, that she was a High-Born snob who couldn't even drink water from a stream like a normal person. But it was because her teeth rattled when she drank or ate something that was too cold. She didn't want to mention it to him because having a sensitive stomach was already bad enough, but having sensitive teeth too just solidified her place as a true weakling.

"Why do you care?" she shot back. "And why are you even talking to me? Go drink some water." Arla was done with this young man, teenager, captain, whatever. She had tried to be kind to him, and he called her a deceptive, selfish person because of it. So, if he wanted to keep being rude to her, fine, she could be rude too.

He frowned. "I want to talk about that page. I have a gut feeling there is something wrong with it."

Beware the. The Forest plays tricks.

Arla rolled her eyes. "It's just a mistake. So what if the survivor wrote *'the'* twice? They probably forgot what they wrote on the previous page. No one is perfect in their writing. Unless this is because you assume the writer was a noble and therefore, they must be lying, right?"

Leo narrowed his eyes. "They could be lying. It's not entirely farfetched."

Sighing loudly, Arla got up and took out the journal, pushing it to his face. "Okay, fine, see for yourself."

Leo took it, flipping to a particular page and then flipping it back and forth. Back and forth.

Soldiers behind them jumped in the water in glee. Some cupped the liquid in their hands and drank it directly from the stream. They had not waited for their comrades to catch up to drink, who were still further back including Wilkins, Uro, and Rose.

Arla looked at her own cup, licking her lips. The water was probably warm enough by now. The sun was beaming down on it, and it *looked* warm, if that was possible. She went to reach for her cup.

"Something is wrong," Leo repeated as he pulled on a page.

She heard the sound of paper tearing and she turned back.

The page was *split*.

Arla wailed, taking the journal away from him. "You're going to damage it!" She looked down and saw the page halfway divided, but thankfully, it wasn't damaged, but... there was writing in the divide.

What?

"They are two pages," he pointed. "They're stuck together."

She lowered the journal and slowly, carefully, spread the page apart. He was right. There really were two pages. She peeled them fully apart and looked at the hidden page.

Thirst.

She flipped back to the previous page. *Beware the.*

Flipped it back.

Thirst.

She looked to the other newly discovered side. Written in bold and underlined a hundred times. A desperate scribble repeated over and over and over again.

Beware The Thirst. Beware The Thirst. Beware The Thirst. Beware The Thirst.

Her heart plummeted to the bottom of her rib cage.

"Princess..."

She followed Leo's widened gaze to her cup on the rock. Before it was in pristine condition, but now it was corroded. Its metal disintegrated with jagged holes on the side, the water pouring out of it.

The water... it was eating away at the metal.

Like *acid*.

Dread filled her entire soul with icy terror. She turned on her heels, sprinting to the others.

"Get away from the stream!" she shrieked.

They looked at her like a crazed woman, unsure of what she meant. Uro had made it to the others. His hands were mid-reach to the rushing water.

"No!" She lunged full force and tackled him to the ground.

Screaming.

Everyone was screaming.

Soldiers in the stream wailed as their legs disintegrated below them, staining the water a sickening crimson. Soldiers grabbed their throats, blood gurgling up from their mouths as their melting bodies splashed into the running stream.

Arla screamed with them, horrified.

A body thudded on the ground next to her. What was left of the female warrior poured like molten lava into the grass, the tang of iron and sweat assaulting Arla's senses.

Her face.

She couldn't see the soldier's face anymore; it was just a warbled mush of blood and a halfway-dissolved skull.

"Don't touch the water!" Rose shouted. She had finally reached them with Wilkins in tow.

A soldier's hand was dissolving, the skin falling like hot wax. Rose unsheathed her sword and sliced off the soldier's hand, stopping the acid from taking more. The soldier clutched his wrist in agony.

"Move!" Rose shouted, pushing them away from the water and into the thicket of the trees.

"Help me!" A middle-aged soldier, with short black hair and long limbs climbed out of the stream, his arms and legs gurgling into brown and pink liquid. He swung out his arms in a desperate move to reach someone, spraying water on nearby soldiers, who wailed as the water ate away at their armor and hands. Leo was running—no, dashing – towards the dying soldier, reaching out his hand.

Arla flung out her own, trying to stop him.

Don't touch him!

But Rose got to him first. She wrapped both her arms under his armpits, locking him in a hold as he pulled and pushed against her to try to get to this dying soldier.

"Please!" the man shouted, reaching out his hand as he fell to his knees, his shins completely gone now. "Please!"

Leo's eyes brimmed red as he continued to fight against Rose, but the hold was too strong, and the soldier cried out one last time before decomposing into bone and sludge. Arla lost track of them, of everyone, as her ears began to ring. Her chest felt heavy like she couldn't breathe.

Focus.

She had to focus. She couldn't fall apart just yet. Not yet. Not when she still needed to find the plant. To save her brother. To save—*Uro*.

Pulling at everything she had left, Arla twisted away from the decaying body and grabbed Uro's hand, and ran and ran and ran until she couldn't hear the sound of sickening rushing water anymore.

CHAPTER II

The sound of wailing echoed in her ears. The image of men and women, their skin melting off of them, exposing strings of muscles underneath, made Arla uncontrollably shiver. She could still hear their blood sloshing into the rushing water.

That stream... it was stained with their lives.

Arla tried to get her breathing under control, to remember she was still alive, and it was over now, but the shaking wouldn't stop. And every new breath was getting harder and harder to draw in.

There were so many others around her, crying out in shock and distress.

This was too much. Nothing could be trusted in this dead land.

Arla's breathing quickened too fast and yet the air would not go into her lungs. It would not fill her with the oxygen her body needed. The world was caving in, and she was going to be crushed underneath it. She was sure of it. Her heart raced like a wild horse, thrashing for a lifeline.

She was drowning.

Help.

She couldn't breathe.

Help me.

She couldn't get anything in. She couldn't—

Wide, warm hands covered her ears. It held her head firm, steady. Sunkissed brown eyes locked onto hers, drawing her back toward the surface, stern and determined.

Leo.

"Breathe." His tone was gentle. The most gentle she'd ever heard him speak. She was surprised he was even capable of such a comforting cadence.

He slowly drew in air through his nose and then blew out slowly, as if to show her how to do it.

In. Out. In. Out.

Strangely, it made her body mimic him, taking in deep breaths as he did.

"It's over now." His hands remained steady, supporting her. "It's over now," he repeated.

Slowly, her lungs filled again, and her body relaxed.

It was over now.

Tears lined her eyes. She was still unable to speak, but breath finally returned to her.

"You're alive," he said softly. "You're going to be okay."

She lightly touched his hand, a gesture of gratitude. His gaze softened. And for a moment, there was only them. His eyes guided her back, his nose breathed for her, his soft lips...

His hands loosened, no longer a grip of a purposeful task, but a soft hold as they slid down, cupping her cheeks. She was unsure of what this feeling was, or what was going on, but it was the most comforting and safe thing she had ever experienced. His eyes absorbed hers, and they melted together like that for what felt like a long moment.

And then a look of panic crossed his face like he just realized what he was doing. He looked away from her, breaking the connection, and let go of her face as if her skin pricked his hands.

He retreated without a word and disappeared into the crowd of beaten soldiers, leaving her confused. Did she do something wrong?

The others were no better off than she was. Some stared at the ground in complete silence, unable to comprehend what had just happened, while others jittered, untrusting of everything around them.

They had started out with more than thirty soldiers and now... now there were only ten left. A third of the brigade her father sent.

The Forest meant to take them all. She knew that now. This place of nightmares did not plan to let them leave; it wanted their blood to coat its charred ground and feed its moss and streams with their decaying bodies.

Wilkins paced back and forth, madness in his eyes. "We're going to die here!" he wailed, his voice cracking. "The Forest is going to kill us! We have no chance! We're not going to make it!" He was crying now, shaking uncontrollably. The fear festered and spread amongst the soldiers who shouted in agreement.

"We have to leave!" someone else cried out. "We have to get out of here!"

They huddled together, their eyes darting at every angle to see if there was danger coming for them again. Their captain stood, like a pillar of granite against a sea of fear. His forehead creased in a way that told the others he was contemplating.

Finally, he said, "You are right. We need to leave."

Arla shot up. "But we haven't gotten the plant yet. Jun needs it."

"I am not going to subject my soldiers to more death over one High-Born." Leo's voice was strained thin. Dark circles had formed under his eyes which made him look suddenly so solemn and tired.

"But he'll die without it."

"If we stay here, *we* will die."

"So you're going to sacrifice a child's life?" she fought back. "My *brother's* life?"

"There are more lives at stake here than just one prince," Leo argued. The vein on his temple enlarged in suppressed calmness.

Her mouth hung open in disbelief. How could he be so cold? So ruthless? A true captain of Ulsana's army would never make such a decision. "You are a soldier, bound by duty!" she shouted, pointing an accusing finger at him.

"I am a soldier because I had no other choice!" Leo snarled. "As did most of them!" He threw his hand out, gesturing to the frightened soldiers. "We are here because we were ordered by a king who let us starve enough to force us to become cattle for him to send to die!" Leo huffed, as a lingering silence blanketed over them.

Arla was speechless. His sudden anger shook her, making her step back.

The captain's breathing slowed, his rage slowly wisping away into weariness. In a strained, contained voice, he said, "I have already lost twenty soldiers. I am not letting any more of them die."

Arla's throat tightened. She had seen his face, reaching for the dying soldier as Rose held him back at the stream. Thrashing. Desperate. For everything she feared for her brother, he had seen it happen to his soldiers. Twenty times over. How terrible that must have been.

Her shoulders slumped. Slowly, she nodded her head in agreement. "I understand."

Leo blinked in slight shock and confusion. He clearly wasn't expecting her to accept his answer.

"You should go." She turned to the soldiers. "You should all go and save yourselves. But I... I have to keep going. I have to save my brother."

Because I can't fail.

If she went back now, knowing she was so close and still did not bring back the plant, her brother would die. Her father would blame her and the empty life she lived of lonely punishment would only get worse. She wasn't going back to that. Even here, where death was threatening her at every corner, she still had felt more alive and happy than she was wandering the tunnels alone in a court that despised her. If she couldn't get the plant, she wouldn't return at all. She would perish here, a better fate than returning to the life of a ghost no one wanted.

Arla readjusted her bag, stepping away from the soldiers. "I really wish you luck." She meant it. Leo was right, why should any more of them die?

"Don't be ridiculous," Leo said. "You will die within the day."

The certainty in his voice made Arla pause, but only long enough for her determination to fill her again. Without responding, she turned.

"Princess," Leo called out. But Arla didn't turn to look back. "Princess," he repeated.

She didn't want to hear him say that she was being stupid again. She stepped over a large root, readjusting her bag as she made another step away from them.

"Wait!" he commanded.

Another step. She needed to pick up the pace.

"Alright!" he shouted after her. Something in his tone finally made her turn around.

Leo remained where he was, but his body was facing hers. He looked defeated. "I will go with you."

Arla didn't know what to think or say or feel. Why was he doing this? He'd just admitted that he hated her and all High-Borns. Was he volunteering because he felt guilty? Or maybe it was because she was a princess, and he couldn't let her die without having consequences for his soldiers too. If she died, her father would surely punish them.

She opened her mouth to protest, thinking spending more days alone with just Leo would be a different type of torture, but she never got to say anything because Rose stepped forward instead. "Leo—"

"Rose, take the others and return to the castle." Leo readjusted his sword and shield, ready to join Arla.

"No." Rose planted her feet on the ground.

Leo's eyes narrowed. "That's an order."

"With all due respect," she said, "I refuse. I will not leave you here."

"I won't either," Uro squeaked beside her.

Leo opened his mouth to protest, but the other soldiers moved to join the duo. Their heads bobbed up and down as they agreed to stay, determined to follow their captain. They were glued to the dirt, daring Leo to try fighting them on this.

Wilkins shook his head. "Well, I'm not!" He pointed to the soldiers nearest him. "You five! Escort me back to the castle!" The warriors did not budge. "I order you to take me back!" he shrieked, his face swelling in shades of maroon and burgundy.

"We do not take orders from you," a soldier replied to Wilkins.

The brigade watched their captain for orders. She could see Leo was torn; he didn't want them to stay, but they refused to go.

"We are not leaving without our captain," Rose repeated. She shrugged as if nothing had fazed her. Not the stream, not the killing trees. "And like I said before, if we return without the plant, we are dead anyway."

The soldiers all nodded, cloistering together around Leo. The hints of fear still laced across their faces, but there was also a sense of determination. They stood straighter, their chins high, willing to face the unknown with Leo.

Watching them filled Arla with awe.

To be able to win the respect and loyalty of this group... To have them willingly follow you back into death... Arla wished she had that kind of leadership quality that Leo seemed to exude so naturally. The kind of aura made people trust you with their lives, but she was just a spectator, meant to watch on the sidelines as others gained their glory.

For a long second, Leo looked like he was going to order them to go away again, but Arla knew they would continue to refuse, and he probably knew it too, because he just gave a slight nod in appreciation. "Then let's find this plant and get out of here."

CHAPTER 12

They may have slipped out of the stream's deadly current, but their thirst did not quench, and Arla knew they would not go much farther without water. Many were already feeling the dangerous effects of dehydration: getting sharp headaches and becoming dizzy as they waddled forward. After only an hour of walking, they had to stop because Uro and the others became too light-headed to walk anymore. Several sat on the ground now, leaning against the evergreen trees.

The gray sky had strangely splotched, sending rays of sun beaming through the treetops, heating the air around them and making them sweat out the rest of their precious water. The Forest was playing another one of its deadly tricks.

It had taken their water and hastened their thirst, luring them to the embrace of its brook. Now that they had escaped it, The Forest must have decided to squeeze out the remaining water from them until they perished instead.

How cruel.

Arla did not sit with the others. Instead, she ran her hand down a nearby tree, whose leaves were like soft clouds surrounding a slick trunk. Too soft to climb. She moved on to another, whose wide branches seemed promising, but they were too high for her to reach without help.

Leo followed her from tree to tree, watching her. After his reluctant acceptance of his soldiers' choice to stay, he took up the habit of hovering around Arla, like a parent babysitting their untrustworthy child. He probably thought she would run off and die if he wasn't around because she was too stupid or ignorant to survive.

"You're going to climb another tree, aren't you?" he asked, keeping one eye on her and the other on the soldiers a few feet away. The way his attention kept bouncing between the two made her think of an overworked mama hen.

She tried to jump to catch a high branch but didn't even make it an inch above the ground. She was not a good jumper. "I'm going to ask the water for help," she grunted, jumping again.

"What?"

"The water droplets I told you about earlier. They showed me where the heart was when I asked. Maybe they'll help us find where safe water is." When she first thought of this idea, it was because she was daydreaming about water so much during their walk that it triggered the memory of the small, translucent globes above the trees. It also jostled her memory of the wind and sludge that came afterward, trying to push her to her death. Which still left her feeling uneasy.

A stabbing pain ran through the front of her skull. The thirst was getting worse.

She had no choice; it was either try this or wait around and shrivel up out of existence.

Arla looked around her, all the trees had such high branches, unlike those before. Were they trying to stop her from climbing them? She readjusted her feet and bent her knees lower, priming herself, and then leapt as high as she could, catching nothing in her hands. Damn her short legs and short arms and short everything.

"Here." Leo knelt on one knee, putting his hands out in front of him for her to step on. "Climb on and then I'll push you up," he grumbled.

She looked down at his calloused palms and then at his face in disbelief.

"Whatever you did before helped us, so maybe it'll help us again. Besides,"—he looked back at Uro, Rose, and the others, who were slumped in the underbrush with Wilkins laying on his back in exhaustion—"we need that water."

Arla nodded. Any assistance would be better than nothing at this point. She put a foot on his hands and steadied herself by holding onto his wide shoulders, pushing off. He threw his arms up at the same time, tossing her higher than she expected. She yelped as she folded over the first branch.

"Are you alright?" Concern laced across his features as he looked up at her.

Arla grunted as she adjusted herself. "I'm fine."

Metal rattled to the ground as Leo took off his armor below her. Now it was her turn to ask questions. "What are *you* doing?"

"I'm coming with you." He waved his hand to the left. "Move."

Arla scooted over as Leo jumped, easily grabbing the branch and hoisting himself up. If he noticed her shocked expression, he didn't show it. Instead, he looked at the branch they were sitting on and the rounded leaves that grew from it. With one hand moving to a small dagger on his hilt, he pointed to it. "Friendly or not friendly?"

Arla snickered. "Friendly."

On the ground, Leo towered with confidence that intimidated those around him, but in the trees, he was just as awkward, if not more awkward than Arla. He overused his strength to hoist himself up from branch to branch, unlike Arla who used strategic hand and foot placements to nimbly move up. She was almost twice as fast as him.

She looked down to see Leo curse under his breath as he pulled himself up over another branch, sweat beading his brow. He stopped to take a break, leaning a hand on the trunk for support. When his head hung low, the chuckle Arla was trying so hard to contain leaked out like a small chortle.

Hearing her, he gave an exasperated look. "Yeah, I know, I'm a terrible climber," he admitted, sliding a hand through his locks of waves.

It was wrong, but Arla felt good having a skill over someone. This dark-haired young man might be a force with a sword, but it looked like she was a better climber.

As he reached for another branch, he asked, "Are you sure the water droplets are up there?"

"No, I'm not sure at all, actually," she responded, continuing her climb.

"Great." She heard him mutter under his breath in the sarcastic way he did. He stomped on a branch harder than he needed to as he kept going up after her.

She hoped the droplets were up there, or else they were wasting more precious energy and water on a fool's chase. The smell of pine and cool air kept her mind off her dizziness and shaking hands. The dehydration took a toll on her body, especially now that she was using so much energy to scale the trees.

When she finally broke through the top of the canopy, she could barely see straight, the last of her water had leaked from her skin and she crawled onto the final branch, laying on her stomach to catch her breath. After she finally settled herself, she looked out, and to her great relief, the strings of droplets were there in all their sparkling glory, lightly pulsing, as if they were sleeping.

Leo heaved himself up next to her, still clinging to the trunk like a frightened woomble. She watched as he took it all in. His eyes went wide, and his mouth was agape as he absorbed all the beauty of the water beads, but a lace of stress still lingered on his face. Was he as dizzy as she was right now?

He looked down and immediately knew he made a mistake. He leaned closer to the trunk, digging his nails into its bark. And that's when it dawned on her.

"Are you afraid of heights?" she asked.

"No." His refusal was too quick.

Arla burst into a fit. She couldn't help it. To finally see the intimidating, mean captain with his knees trembling was too much for her to hold back. He didn't seem angry that she was laughing at him.

Instead, he blushed and turned away from her, hoping she didn't see, which made her feel a little bit guilty. Maybe he was embarrassed by his fear. She knew what that felt like.

"Why did you follow me if you're afraid of heights?"

He didn't answer, instead gesturing to the water droplets. "Are you going to ask them or what?"

Arla shook her head, her ribs slightly sore from the giggling. She edged a little farther off the branch, leaning over.

"Careful!" Leo shouted.

If she didn't know any better, it sounded like he cared if she fell. She gently plucked a small water droplet from its thread and stabilized herself back on the branch.

"Hello," she said softly. The droplet turned, its eyes opening lazily from its slumber. This little globe was smaller than the one before and its eyes were bigger and closer set, giving it the look of an inquisitive youth. It stretched and bobbled to stir itself awake. "I'm sorry to wake you up, but I need to ask another question."

"What's it saying?" Leo shouted, his eyes wide from watching the droplet. He looked a little pale. She didn't know if it was from the heights or the fact that a water droplet was alive in her hand right now.

Bending slightly, she said, "That's Captain Treterra. He is afraid of heights."

"Don't tell it that," Leo almost whined at her. He looked over at the other water droplets on their strings, checking if they heard her. She chuckled again. The droplet wiggled as if it was laughing too.

"Do you know where we can find safe drinking water?" she asked.

The water droplet rolled around her cupped hands. These creatures really liked to do that.

She giggled letting it tip almost to the edge of her fingers before rolling back to the center of her palms.

"I don't think it took you seriously," Leo stated, daring to edge closer to her to get a better look at the water droplet. He went as close to Arla as he could, but his trembling arm was still outstretched, ready to lunge and grab the trunk of the tree at any sign of danger.

When he was close enough to see the little droplet, he scowled down at it. "Does it even understand you?"

The droplet stopped rolling and looked up at Leo. Its eyes narrowed as it returned the captain's scowl. Leo tensed and scowled back harder, which made the droplet frown even more at him. It was a strange scowl contest.

Arla pivoted the droplet away from him. "Stop it. You're going to make it mad."

"It started it," Leo grumbled. And these were the words of a captain who led soldiers into battle? Arla inwardly scoffed.

Arla spoke to the droplet. "I would be really grateful if you could help us. We need some water soon or we'll... we will be in trouble." She didn't know if the droplet understood what dying of thirst was since it was itself made of water. Could it even die of thirst?

The water droplet slowly blinked at her. This globe creature was smaller than the other one she plucked before, so maybe it was younger, too new to understand her words. She couldn't speak to this droplet in her language, but maybe *showing* what she needed instead would work.

Arla pretended to scratch at her throat, coughed, and then acted like she was gagging as she raised her other hand in the air like a claw gripping at nothing. The droplet leaned forward, watching her intently with curious, wide eyes. Then she dropped her head and closed her eyes, pretending to be dead.

She slightly peeled open one eye to see if it understood her. The blank expression told her, it didn't. Not yet anyway. She held an imaginary cup and sipped it, and she opened her eyes and looked alert. Alive again. The droplet bounced back, shocked, and then immediately joyously bobbed with squinted eyes.

"Do you understand now?" she asked.

The droplet kept bobbing. She sighed. Maybe she needed to ask a bigger, older one. She was about to put it back when the creature started to shimmy, releasing a sprinkle of water from its body, splashing Arla and Leo in the face.

Arla looked up to see the other droplets waking up, bobbing and stretching, and then they shimmied too, releasing more showers of water from the tops of their heads. Crisp, cold drops pelted on her head, at first softly and then rapidly like it was... raining.

Arla let out a joyful cry as she raised her free hand into the air, letting the water pool into her palm. It was so cooling. She didn't hesitate as she drank, letting the water replenish her body and soul as it brought back her senses.

Leo, too, was collecting and drinking as much water as his one hand could get, while the other remained outstretched toward the tree trunk.

From down below the soldiers whooped and hollered in fits of pure glee. She let out a sigh of relief; it was raining on them too.

Looking at the droplet, she said, "Thank you." She bowed to the little one, who rolled around in her palms again in childish delight.

She nudged Leo, who grunted and bowed too, grumbling, "Yes. Thank you."

Gently, she hooked the droplet back on its thread, where it yawned and turned, no longer showing its face, looking like an innocently non-alive water droplet once again.

As Leo was having his fill of more water, Arla looked out across the trees placing their location. They were nearing the heart. Good, at least her sense of direction wasn't wrong. All those years navigating dark tunnels had really honed her ability to find her way around the most convoluted and darkest paths.

"Aren't they beautiful?" Arla said, sitting on the branch, enjoying the view of the thousands of sparkling water droplets as they continued to rain down on them. "Maybe this is what it was like before The Forest turned on us. I would have loved to have been there when it loved us."

"The Forest only loved the High-Borns," Leo said, his bitterness returning.

She didn't know why The Forest would give magic only to a select sort of people and not others. Norendra said it was because it knew whose bloodlines were superior, who were meant to be rulers, and who were meant to serve. But that never really made sense to her.

How could a place that had such kind creatures like these droplets also be so cruel as to not grant magic to everyone? Then again, it did try to kill them all twice now, maybe three times if Arla counted the rain of slime that was intentionally trying to push her off the branches the first time she climbed.

Which reminded her. Arla scooted a little bit away from the edge of the branch in case the wind and slime came again.

"If it makes you feel any better," she said to Leo, "The Forest hates everyone now."

Leo smirked. He *smirked*. The first time he had somewhat been pleased by something she said. She wanted to pat herself on the back, but she couldn't without Leo asking questions, so she would have to do it later, in private.

After some time looking out into the horizon, the beams of the sun started to dim. Maybe The Forest realized this strategy was not going to work and so it slowly hid the sun from them once again, only letting the haze of light through.

"We should start climbing down," Arla suggested as she moved to get up.

"Thank you," Leo muttered so quietly, Arla thought she misheard it. She froze mid-standing, looking at him. He fixated on a clump of trees far in the distance ahead of him. "For saving Uro."

"Oh," she hesitated. When was the last time anyone thanked her? She couldn't remember. "I didn't do anything."

"That's not true. You've done more for them than I did."

There was something in his tone, a hollowness that she recognized. A deep sorrow masking itself as a quiet lamb, trying not to be noticed in a flock of others. Maybe it was because they were alone with no one else to hear them, but for the first time, Arla thought she heard Leo's true voice underneath his hateful glares and sarcastic remarks. And that voice sounded like it needed help.

"Are you okay?" she asked.

Leo frowned defensively. "Of course I am."

Arla remembered his face when he was reaching for the dying soldier. He was breaking as Rose dragged him back. This was a man who had volunteered to come to protect his friends and his soldiers. What would that type of person feel if he saw so many of them die, unable to do the one thing he came here to do in the first place?

"I know you hate me and don't care for my opinion," Arla said cautiously, "but for what it's worth... I think you saved more soldiers than you realize. If you didn't point out the stuck page, we would have all died. This place is trying to kill us every chance it gets, and the fact that we survived this long is because of you."

She didn't know if she had said the right thing or not, but whatever shadow that hung over him lifted somewhat.

"You don't give yourself enough credit, Princess," he said, still looking out into the treetops, refusing to meet her gaze. "You saved us too."

Arla smiled shyly. Thinking about it now, she wasn't so sure if Leo really hated her. She knew what real hate felt like. It was cruel and violent and malicious, but with Leo, he had trusted her to lead and followed her and helped her more times than she'd realized up until now. So maybe it wasn't hate, maybe it was something else.

The climb down was slow and methodical and silent. Leo was fully focused on not falling to his death, and Arla was trying not to pay attention to how she could see his forearms bulge and tighten and wonder what it would feel like to touch them. It was so strange, the things she was starting to pay attention to. She shouldn't look too much. She should be like Leo, never maintaining eye contact with her and staring into some other expanse far away.

When they landed safely back on the ground, the soldiers were drenched as their waterskins swung in their hands: full. They were laughing and dancing amongst themselves.

"Can you believe it, Captain?" an older soldier exclaimed, running up to Leo. "All this water just rained on us and it's safe to drink! We had Uro test it." A couple of soldiers slapped Uro's back in jest as they drank from their water skins.

"You have the princess to thank for that," Leo replied, his voice returning to a solid, commanding tone. "Be sure to show your gratitude."

"You made this happen?" The soldier was genuinely shocked, never believing Arla could do anything, no doubt.

Arla blushed, not knowing how to take this new credit thrown her way. The other soldiers approached her, thanking her profusely. She had never received such attention before, and she didn't know how to take it. She felt weightless like she might float away in happiness. As Leo passed her, she could have sworn she saw the corner of his lips curl into a short smile. *Second one today. A record for sure.*

They had eaten and rested well that night as a single fire burned to keep them warm. The water had brought hope to the soldiers that they might actually survive, especially if Arla could speak with magical entities in the green canopy. Uro grinned so proudly at her across the fire at the mention of her name, and she returned it. Leo had stopped lecturing them on the rules of High and Low-Borns eating together, so she sat with the other soldiers, listening to their chats.

Wilkins, however, did not take up the opportunity and demanded a fire be built for him far away, which they did.

As the soldiers conversed and laughed, she took a small nibble of dried jerky. Her stomach constricted after the third bite, sending a sharp needle into her side. She winced, cringing slightly, trying to hide it as best she could. She bit and swallowed another piece. She needed to eat for energy, no matter how much this would shred her bowels in the middle of the night.

As she chewed, she caught Leo staring at her from across the flames. But she must have imagined it because when she blinked, he was already looking somewhere else, muttering to Rose.

CHAPTER 13

They had been treading the forest for days at this point. How many exactly? Four? Five? Even so, they were starting to feel like weeks. It was like this place was becoming something she was getting too familiar with as if she'd strangely always been here. A new nightmarish home she would never escape.

Maybe that's why the author scribbled so crazily towards the end of the journal and their sentences became more incoherent, proof of a deteriorating mind. It wasn't the murderous trees or the acid streams that were torturous, it was the hopelessness of feeling like you would never leave this place and wondering where the next attack would come from. What new tricks The Forest would take to wipe you out of existence.

But regardless of The Forest's efforts, they were still alive.

She looked at the back of Leo's head. Those dark, wavy locks caught the breeze. They hadn't spoken since their talk up in the trees. Every time she tried to start another conversation, he suddenly had to help another soldier carry something, or his armor needed readjusting, and he pivoted away from her. She wondered now if she had misinterpreted what had happened when they were with the water droplets. If he did intend to still keep her at arm's length because she was a High-Born.

It wasn't until much later in the day that she was finally able to corner him.

"Are you avoiding me?" she asked directly.

Leo's stoic demeanor stuttered a bit when she asked, but he recovered back into his distant look. "I do not think that is possible here," he replied.

She didn't understand him. One moment, he was complimenting her, and the next, he was avoiding her. He couldn't seem to make up his mind.

She took a step towards him, ready for an argument when a screech echoed across the trees.

In a flash, a large dark creature swooped past her and tore the trunk of a nearby tree clean in half, sending chunks of wood flying everywhere.

Spinning into the air, it flung its giant wings out on each side, blocking what little light came from the sky. It resembled a giant bat the size of at least three wagons, but instead of fur, its body was covered in blood-red scales and its claws held talons, each half the size of Arla's body.

The bat-monster shrieked into the air, diving towards her. Leo pulled her away just as it was about to rip her to shreds, slamming her against a tree. Her breath left her lungs from the impact.

"Are you hurt?!" he shouted, quickly inspecting her body for any damage.

"I knew it!" Arla pointed an accusatory finger at Leo. "I told you there were monsters in The Forest!"

"I didn't say there weren't any monsters!" Leo exclaimed. "That was Wilkins."

"Oh, right." She pivoted, finding Wilkins staring in shock at the creature soaring above them. She moved her finger to point at him, with Leo still by her side. "Wilkins!" He looked at her. "I told you there were monsters!"

"Shut up, woman!" Wilkins shouted. "*Viere!*" He shot across the ground, swiftly moving behind a tree. The creature's eyes turned to him, spotting prey.

Darkness swooped down on him. Wilkins threw soldiers in the beast's path as he dashed from tree to tree, but the creature continued after him, tossing the soldiers aside.

And then it struck.

For a moment, it looked like he was floating, but that was before she saw Wilkins's torso flying in one direction and his legs in another. He hovered like that for a moment, his eyes frozen in terror. His upper half slammed to the ground, blood pouring out of his stomach like a spouting geyser.

She covered her mouth, stifling her scream.

"Center on me!" Leo shouted.

All at once the soldiers surrounded her and Leo, forming a cluster. "Shields up!"

Circular steel raised over their heads, creating a dome defense against the flighted monster.

"Archers ready!"

Some of the soldiers pulled their bows from their backs, aiming arrows through the holes of the shields.

"On my command!" Leo looked up, dead focused on the abomination that soared above them.

For a moment, the bat-monster assessed them, waiting, and then, losing patience, it dove.

"Hold…" Leo commanded. The soldiers nervously fidgeted next to Arla, their arrows taut, itching to release them. "Hold…"

The creature extended its claws and opened its wings to slow down its descent.

"Now! Aim for the wings!" he shouted.

A shower of arrows burst through the openings between shields, tattering the monster's wings. It shrieked in pain, trying to fly away, but its wings were now useless.

It spiraled down toward them.

"Move!"

In unison, they opened the cluster. Leo pushed Arla to the side, tucking her behind a nearby tree.

The creature came crashing down onto the forest floor, sending chunks of dirt and rocks everywhere.

In an instant, Leo was there attacking the creature while it was still disoriented. One swing of his sword cut across its face. In a vile screech, it swept its tattered wing and knocked him to the right.

In the corner of her eye, Arla saw an arrow bounce off the creature's scaled side. The creature turned to Rose, who was holding her bow, her next arrow notched and ready to fly.

Arla had never noticed Rose's weapon until right before the fight; she must have strapped it to her back, or maybe she just didn't pay attention enough to her this entire time.

Before Rose could release her arrow, the creature lunged and snatched her up in its claws.

"Rose!" Leo sprinted toward her, but the creature swiped at him with its sharpened talon at the top of its wing. It may have not been able to take flight, but its powerful legs still allowed it to jump and thrash while the two front talons on its wings stabbed into the legs of nearby soldiers. There was no way anyone could get close.

Arla crouched behind the rock, hands digging into the cold, bumpy surface. She watched as the creature dragged Rose along the dirt as it struck out against the soldiers, its red scales protecting it from arrows and swords.

She wanted to help, but... she had no magic. No fighting skills. No strength. What could she do against a creature like that, except be its next meal?

Urō cried out as Rose was smashed against a tree, still in the grips of the creature. Her armor bent and cracked. It was the only thing that saved her from a death blow.

Another soldier got close to grabbing her, and that's when the monster struck, slicing the soldier's throat open with the tip of its talon. Someone cried out their name.

It's using Rose as bait to catch the others.

Arla shook her head, trying to pull herself together. She couldn't sit here and do nothing. She dug through her bag and pulled out the stainless-steel forks she stole from the royal kitchen, immediately missing her paring knife.

With one in each hand, she crawled to the creature's blind side, the ground thundering with its steps and swings as others screamed their last breaths. Dirt kicked up into her eyes as the rocky ground scratched her stomach and elbows, but she kept crawling, hoping she wouldn't be seen until she got close enough.

Rose was trying to pry herself out of the claw, but nothing was working. The creature stepped to the side, forcing Arla to roll under it.

This was it.

Now or never.

Arla slid underneath the creature, almost flattened by an unexpected footstep.

Rose saw her and looked from her face to the forks in her hands and back again. It was hard to explain the depth of disappointment on the soldier's face when she realized what Arla was trying to do.

Arla jumped and thrust the forks into the creature's unscaled claw.

It screeched, raising its arms. Arla's hand gripped the forks as she was flung side to side by the thrashing creature and Rose along with it.

The creature bent down. Its menacing eyes focused on her, making Arla's entire body freeze for a moment.

Let go. Let go. Let go.

No. If she did, Rose would die.

The creature reeled back to bite Arla's head off. She braced for the pain.

Metal and bone clashed.

She opened her eyes to see Leo's sword between the creature's teeth. The weapon held the creature's mouth open, unable to bite down.

Leo shouted, lifting up and pushing the creature's head back. The monster flailed its head, trying to get the sword out of its mouth, finally swinging it free.

If it wasn't angry before, the bat-monster was enraged now, focusing all of its attention on Leo. While it was distracted, Arla fully scrambled onto its leg, kicking at its claw, trying to get it to open.

Her foot slipped, and she accidentally kicked Rose in the face, leaving a red mark.

"Sorry!" she yelled as she kept kicking.

They didn't have much time. The creature was only going to be distracted by Leo for so long.

Rose gave her a look of somber acceptance, like a meditating priestess. "So, this is how I die then."

Arla ignored her, focusing on what she should do while holding on for dear life as the monster pivoted again, chasing Leo. The creature's wing hit him, tossing his shield away.

Panicked, her thoughts raced. *What can I do?* She wouldn't be able to kill it with its scales; only the face and feet were exposed, but even then, there was no sword for her to use. She looked down at the creature's talons, the skin surrounding them.

She didn't need a sword.

She just needed a point of pain.

In a last-ditch effort, Arla pulled out the fork from the creature's upper claw and stuck it in the soft underskin between its skin and talon. It roared and opened its claws, sending the women tumbling to the ground on opposite sides.

The beast swung around to Arla, and she could see its razor-sharp fangs as it closed in on her.

An arrow twisted in the air and struck the creature's eye.

It reeled in pain.

A gust of wind blew them off their feet as it sprung itself away from them. Arla thought it would turn around and exact its revenge, but instead, it thundered deeper into the forest, leaving them. Arla looked to see Rose at the other end, bow in hand, her face still bruised.

It was over.

Arla went limp in relief. The power that surged through her body during the chaos faded and left her feeling suddenly very tired. Rose appeared before her, still holding her bow.

"You saved my life," Rose stated neutrally like it was a simple fact.

Arla wasn't sure how to respond. "Leo helped distract the beast." Her eyes fell on Rose's cheek. "I'm sorry I kicked you. Does it hurt?"

Rose shook her head. "No. Your kicks were so weak, it didn't even leave a mark."

Arla could see the bruise turning purple as they spoke, but she didn't dare mention it.

"How did you come up with that idea with the forks?" Rose inquired. It was the first question she had ever asked Arla, which made her insides bubble up in glee.

"Well, back in the garden, I once stuck my hand in a rose bush and a thorn went straight under my nail. It hurt so much, I cried for an hour until Norendra was able to get it out. I figured it would hurt the monster too."

"Clever."

"You know, Rose," Arla said excitedly. "We haven't been able to speak much since we've been here. Maybe we can learn more about each—"

Rose turned and walked off.

Arla was flabbergasted, her mouth still open mid-speech. Arla would have been more hurt if she wasn't already bubbling from pride because, for the first time in her life, she felt she did something important.

The circle of trees and shrubbery around them was flattened and destroyed by the creature's thrashing. Tree trunks were ripped apart and injured soldiers were strewn on the ground. It seemed most had kept their lives.

Leo ran up to Rose, who lightly bobbed her chin as if to say she was fine, and then he pivoted towards Arla. "Are you alright?"

Her pride swelled inside her chest, "I am."

She was more than alright. She had saved someone's life. Not from running away or avoiding something, but from going on the offensive. She had helped defeat a creature the size of a two-story tower. For the first time in her life, she felt... capable.

Leo seemed to notice her change as his eyes glinted with amusement. "I can't believe you defeated that thing with a fork."

"Aren't you glad I kept the bag? I remember someone saying I should have dropped it, but I can't remember who…" She gave him a sidelong smirk. Her new-found confidence was putting her in a teasing mood.

"Whoever it was,"—Leo smiled—"he must have been a fool."

Arla could have almost laughed then if Leo's face didn't suddenly darken at something below her chest. She followed his gaze and saw her tattered shirt and minor scratches on her stomach, but that wasn't what he was looking at.

She kept looking and then…

Her joyous pride bottomed out into a pit.

It was her sleeves. They had been ripped open, no blood poured from them, but they exposed her forearms underneath.

Leo was looking at the multiple splotches of burnt skin flecked across both her arms.

His jaw tensed as he snarled. "Who did that to you?"

All the blood left her face. Arla tucked both her arms behind her. "No one. Nothing. It's nothing." Without another word, she turned on her heels, searching for her bag.

She needed her coat. Another shirt. Anything to cover this up.

CHAPTER 14

Arla pulled at her sleeves, making sure her scars were tucked away for no one to see. She was crouched behind a large bush, whose dark auburn leaves covered her while she changed clothes. The night blanketed her, hiding most of her anyway, but she wanted to make sure she was completely unseen when she changed her shirt.

After the attack, Leo thought it best to stay amongst the trees and shrubbery, a natural defense against any other threat that could come from the sky. It was ironic that they used to think the trees were the greatest danger and now they didn't look so menacing compared to a monster that could shred them apart without effort.

Like it did Wilkins.

Arla bundled her torn, bloodied clothes and carried them back with her toward the campfire where the others were tending to their wounds.

The soldiers were not saddened at all by Wilkins's passing. In fact, they seemed more relieved that most of them had kept their lives.

They buried two bodies that day. One was a soldier and the other was Wilkins. Many volunteered to speak good words about their fallen comrade and left trinkets on his body before they threw dirt on his mortal form. But Wilkins had no words or trinkets, just a swift burial, and was quickly forgotten. It made her feel a bit bad for him.

Even though Wilkins was terrible, he had people who loved him somewhere. She thought of his father, Gerald Dermarcu, and how devastated he would be when he found out his son was gone from this world.

Arla threw her old clothes into the fire, which burned bright into the setting sky, throwing flecks of burnt cloth into the air. The garments on her now were her last clean ones. She hoped the sleeves would remain intact. She remembered Leo's face when he saw her arms. Did he think they were hideous? She'd rather not know.

Arla stood staring at her charring clothes almost in a trance as she watched them redden and fold into themselves before going up in smoke and ash. Light footsteps approached.

"What an amazing fight you gave," Uro exclaimed as he appeared beside her, along with Leo and Rose. They were all out of their armor already, back in tunics and pants with leather braces around their wrists. A standard clothing choice for all the soldiers, it seemed.

"It was all thanks to my bag," she responded, which guttered a laugh from the young boy.

"Fortune favors the prepared," Leo replied, repeating her words from before back to her.

She smiled. "Exactly."

"Then you should be more prepared for attacks and threats like those monsters," Leo said, his expression turning stern. "You should learn how to fight."

Arla was a little taken off guard by this one. *Fight? Me?* With her noodle arms and squishy legs? Rose raised an eyebrow, clearly questioning Leo's judgment too, but the stoic soldier's lips remained tightly closed.

"My father told me it wasn't worth teaching me to fight."

"Well, your father was wrong."

Leo said it so casually like her father was some villager no one cared about. Did he forget that he was speaking about a king? *His* king? "I saw you go against that creature. You have a fighting spirit."

A fighting spirit? Arla had been called many things in her life, but a fighting spirit was definitely not on the list. She had never considered herself a fighter, but strangely she liked the way it felt when Leo said it. It made her feel like someone she wished she was.

"Besides, there aren't enough soldiers left to truly protect you," Leo continued. "Better you learn how to fight now, so I don't have to worry about you so much."

"You are... worried about me?" Something fluttered in her chest.

He realized his mistake too late. Leo's eyes moved to the trees beside her and then the sky and then the hilt of his sword, anywhere to avoid her gaze.

"Did you just admit that you worry about the Princess?" Uro teased.

Arla looked at Leo with hope. "Did you?"

"No, I did not," Leo grumbled, blushing against his will.

"You did," Rose confirmed in a dry tone. "I was standing precisely here when you said the exact words, 'so I don't have to worry about you so much.'"

"That's enough out of you two." Leo scowled at his traitorous friends.

Arla laughed, holding her sides as Uro joined in the jovial fun. Rose, who truly didn't realize they were teasing Leo, frowned in confusion. To her, she was merely stating a fact.

Arla loved it when Leo got flustered; it was just too easy to do.

"This was a mistake," he huffed, turning to leave.

"No, no!" Arla shouted between chokes of laughter, reaching out to stop him. "I'm sorry, I didn't mean to laugh." *So hard.* She didn't mean to laugh *so hard* and so loudly. "I want to learn," she pleaded.

"You do?" His tone was almost eager, like the teenager he really was rather than the leader he was appointed to be.

"Yes." She wanted to be strong, like these three, and if Leo was willing to teach her, she would do it.

Leo cleared his throat. "Alright, then." He moved a few feet away from her and stood across her eye line.

"We'll leave you two to it," Uro said as he dragged Rose away, who at first resisted his tugs but was eventually pulled away. They returned to the other soldiers, leaving just the two of them to face each other.

Leo pivoted his body, one foot in front of the other. "The first thing you'll want to learn is how to dodge attacks."

"Oh, we're starting now?" Arla suddenly felt exposed, wishing she was holding a shield or at least her bag to protect her.

"Better now than later," Leo said nonchalantly as he tightened the leather around his wrists. "Who knows what this place will throw at us next?"

Before she could agree, or disagree, Leo lunged, shooting his hand out and pushing her shoulder. She stumbled back. The touch wasn't painful, but it was hard enough that she knew he was serious about this.

"Hey!" she shouted, shocked and appalled.

"You need to dodge it," he stated in a level and serious tone. It wasn't Leo at this moment across from her, it was the captain.

"But how do I dodge attacks?" she asked.

"You look at their body language. Predict where they'll strike next."

"But how do I *do* that?" she asked again.

Leo struck out and instead of dodging, Arla instinctively pulled her arms up to protect herself. The tips of his fingers dug into her forearm. Into the wound that was still too fresh to withstand a hit like that.

Arla yelped in pain, clutching her arm. It felt like a white-hot knife sliced against her skin.

Leo withdrew immediately. His eyebrows crinkled together in concern. "Are you alright?"

"Yes," she managed to choke out.

"I don't think you are. Let me see." He reached for her.

Arla snatched her arm away. "It's fine!" she shouted too harshly.

Leo paused, his expression was hard to read in the dark, but for a moment she did think she saw something like hurt cross his face.

Clearing her throat, she said in a lighter tone, "It's really fine. Let's continue."

He didn't budge. Unsure.

"Please," she said.

Slowly, he nodded and took another fighting stance.

This was going to be a long lesson.

By the end of the hour, Arla had learned two things. One, she was not a fast person. And two, she had terrible hand-eye coordination. Leo was pummeling her with pushes and shoves constantly, never letting up, saying she needed to read his body language, to predict where he was going to strike next. She didn't know what was more annoying, his constant shoving or his constant lessons.

It reminded her of Norendra's magic practices back when Arla was a child. Non-stop sweat and effort, but unlike Norendra, Leo never told her she was a shame on her family name. He just blankly stated where she could improve, like he believed she could do it if she tried.

"The problem is you don't trust yourself," he said when the session was over. "Once you do that, I'm sure you will see progress much faster."

"This is my first lesson," she whined. "Couldn't you go easy on me?"

Leo contemplated it for a moment and then replied, "No. There is no time for easy."

Arla rolled her eyes, another gesture she usually didn't make, but she was too tired and grumpy now to care. "You're so intense." She slumped onto the ground, her back against the thorny grass. It might have hurt if her legs and arms weren't already throbbing. "Can I just have a little break? Like a short nap. One hour, maybe two." Her eyes were already drooping from the ache.

"I'll allow it," Leo replied dryly. He was joking, in his strange, intense way. He sat next to her, crossing his legs, shifting his sword to the side so he could sit comfortably.

Arla thought of how easy Leo had made it look when he was fighting those murderous trees or that monster. But the truth was fighting took a lot more energy and effort than she ever thought. And if this was just one training session that did this to her, how did someone survive years of this?

Her respect for these soldiers grew. Not only were they fighting and trekking this forest constantly, but they were doing it in heavy metal armor and holding shields and swords. She was in awe of their strength and bravery and hoped she could become half as tough as they were.

As she lay, looking up at the night sky, she was surprised Leo remained by her side.

A long moment or two passed in a silence that was slowly lulling her to sleep.

"You keep surprising me," Leo muttered under his breath.

"Hm?" She was so tired. The light breeze only made it easier to start drifting into slumber.

"You stopped Uro from drinking that water, and you stopped that beast from taking Rose. I never expected a High-Born would ever risk their lives to save one of us, but you did."

"Why wouldn't I?" Arla groggily replied. Sleep was so sweet, and it had finally come for her. She let herself dip into the deep pool of slumber.

Just before she completely went under, she could have sworn she heard Leo say, "I may have been wrong about you."

CHAPTER 15

Arla would have loved to have slept for days after her training, but such was not her fate. Two loose strings tickled her nose as she was lightly shaken awake. Groaning, she begrudgingly opened her eyes. What cruel creature was trying to wake her?

Sharp brown eyes with a strong nose bridge looked directly down at her. She groaned again. Of course, it was Leo. The loose strings in the middle of his tunic kept grazing her face as he shook her again.

"Time to wake up," he said. "Dinner is ready."

She waved him away; she could eat her dried bar of jerky later. "Can't I just keep sleeping?"

"Come on," he said. "It's worth it. Trust me."

He didn't push further, leaving Arla to decide whether to really get up or not. She would have remained on the ground forever if a delicious aroma didn't waft over her nostrils just then. And one thing Arla could never resist was the smell of food.

She let her nose lead her, still somewhat asleep as she half-crawled, half-walked her way to the campfire where Leo sat, poking at a pot in the middle of the flames. There was just him sitting on a log. The others had probably fallen asleep too. It was pretty late. A swirl of savory sea and pepper redolence floated from the pot. She peered over and saw an almost translucent soup boiling with squares of seaweed dancing on top.

Drool collected at the edges of her mouth as she pulled herself onto the same log as Leo, with her feet tucked under her, like a starving critter, perched on a tree. "What is this?"

"It's soup."

He took a spoon and carefully ladled some of the liquid deliciousness into a bowl. She resisted lunging for it by tightening herself further into a ball. Patience was key.

On the ground, around the fire, were small packets of leftover spices and dried seaweed, meticulously lined and spaced evenly away from each other.

Leo must be a very ordered person, she thought.

"Where did all these things come from?" she asked, reaching for a nearby packet of mystery.

Leo handed the bowl to her, which made her immediately abandon the packet as she grabbed it ravenously.

"We have magic bags too." He grinned.

Was that a joke? He was really becoming quite humorous.

She tipped the bowl to her mouth and drank. The heat scorched her tongue, but she didn't care. Bursts of rich bone broth and lightly spiced seaweed filled her stomach and her soul. It was the best thing she ever tasted.

"Oh my Whispers, this is so good." She hugged the bowl to her chest. "Did you make this?"

Leo nodded, trying to hide his pleasure.

Arla drank more, like a starving animal. She hadn't even noticed how little she had eaten until now. She thought she was going to finish the entire pot at this rate as she reached out her bowl, asking for more.

As he ladled another scoop, she realized her stomach wasn't hurting. Usually, after a couple of mouthfuls, it would have kicked her in pain. "Huh," she muttered, mostly to herself.

"What?"

"My stomach…" she replied. "It's not yelling at me."

"Of course, it's not. I made it so it wouldn't hurt you."

Arla looked at him, wide-eyed and unblinking.

What?

His expression remained stoic as he focused on not splashing any soup onto the ground. "Your stomach has been hurting from the dried food. That's why you haven't been eating much, right? It's because the food we brought is full of salt and sugar and garlic and things that inflame the gut, which you're probably sensitive to. My dad had the same thing."

Had. The past tense, meaning his father…

He stirred the ladle on the outer edges of the pot, causing mushrooms to pop up and then sink down into the soup. She almost leapt up in excitement. There was mushroom in this too? Arla looked down at her filled bowl. Was there a mushroom in this one? She swirled the liquid, watching for the top of a button mushroom to float up. She wanted a mushroom.

As if he read her mind, he dipped the ladle back into the pot and captured three mushrooms, and put them into her bowl. She brightened, looking down at the mushroom swimming happily in her soup. Her mouth was watering again.

"This soup won't hurt your stomach and will give you healing nutrients," Leo said.

Arla was at a loss for words. Did he make this meal... for her? He said he had noticed she wasn't eating much. Tears lined her eyes, and she felt her heart swelling.

"This is the kindest thing anyone has ever done for me," she breathed.

Leo's gaze fell on her. She hoped he knew how genuinely she meant it. How thankful she was. No one had ever paid attention to her like this.

His expression was tight like he was holding back something, but she could see the softness in his eyes, the smoothness of his brow. And for a moment, as they locked eyes, she felt the presence of a thread strung between them and they were at each end, lightly holding on, afraid any sudden movement would sever it.

"It's nothing." His voice was barely audible. "Don't think too much about it." And there it was, the sourness of his shield coming up again, cutting the thread from his side.

A crunch and a movement and Rose appeared between them, taking a seat, sitting on the thread, the last thing to smother the connection.

"Did you cook?" she asked as she grabbed the ladle from Leo.

Uro plopped himself next to Arla. "Wow! Soup!" He tried to grab the ladle from Rose, who pulled it out of his reach.

"Wait your turn," Rose said sternly, like a mother to a child. Uro pouted but listened, waiting patiently, his mouth drooling.

They ate the soup rapidly, just like she did. Maybe they, too, were starving for some good food.

Uro moaned. "This is the best soup ever! Why didn't you make this before?"

"Because we are limited in ingredients. I could only make it once," Leo explained.

"Oh? So why now?" Uro gurgled the rest of the liquid down his throat.

Leo's eyes flicked to Arla and then back to the pot. "The dried seaweed was going to go bad."

"What this needs is chili pepper," Rose added. "Lots of spicy peppers."

"You're always trying to make everything so spicy. No one can eat it like that," Uro complained.

Rose shrugged, drinking the rest of her soup. "You just don't have the strength to withstand the rage of fire that is the chili pepper."

Uro shot Rose a scowl, which made Arla giggle. These three really were like siblings. She wondered if she and Jun would interact like this one day, even when he became king. She hoped they would find days to enjoy meals together and laugh like this.

"Princess!" Uro moved his bright-eyed attention to Arla. "Isn't Leo such a great cook? He got it from his mother. She can make any dish taste amazing!"

"Oh?" Arla's curiosity was piqued, and she turned to the captain. "And where is she now?" Leo didn't respond. His lips were tight, and his brow had furrowed.

"At Bruhaul!" Uro answered. "It's a village right outside the city."

"Oh, why doesn't she work *in* the city?" she asked.

"Because the High-Born she works for won't let her leave," Uro responded. "He's actually a close friend to the king. Lesandres, right, Leo? And he—"

"That's enough, Uro." Leo's voice was strained, like a wound-up catapult, ready to pull. "The princess doesn't need a history lesson about me." He gathered up his ingredients and shoved them into a burlap bag, leaving them without another word.

Uro turned red as his face fell into a downcast expression. Rose patted his shoulder in comfort, although she, too, was frowning.

At first, Arla thought Leo would come back, but he didn't and so she drank the rest of her soup with Rose and Uro in silence.

CHAPTER 16

Arla sat alone next to the dying fire. The others had turned in for the night and Rose had taken up guard this time at the edge of the camp, leaving Arla by herself to process her thoughts. She shifted uncomfortably on the log, its hardened surface was starting to make her sore butt even sorer. She pulled open her journal. Flipping through it, she read what she could.

Many pages were either completely missing or too burnt to be readable, so she felt like she would never know the full story of what this survivor went through or why they even came in here in the first place. Were they seeking the healing plant too? Or was it for something else?

Whoever the survivor was, they were an artist for sure. They captured details of the trees and flowers in a way only a painter or a sketcher did, with every crevice and shade of light accounted for. There was one particular drawing, where they even drew the wind as penciled wisps in the air. If one squinted, the wind almost looked alive.

The survivor wrote that The Forest was angry. Angry at losing its gift.

A small tug of dread pulled at her. Did The Forest lose the plants? The gift of healing? Was it still here?

She turned the page, hoping for more clues, but instead landed on another blackened page, barely hanging on to the glue that held it in place to the spine of the journal. The ink had all but gone, but there was one sentence that was legible.

It spread so fast.

Every time she read a new sentence, Arla couldn't help but get a bit anxious. Everything felt like a warning. She knew to take these words seriously, because the last time she didn't look hard enough, it had cost many lives. So she brainstormed. What were things that could spread? A dark cloud of acid? A flood of acid? She needed to stop thinking about acid. What else?

Her brain started to hurt. She needed to rest and give herself some time to digest it. In the morning, she would be refreshed, and her mind would work better then. And so, she closed the journal, tucked it away, and lay right next to the fire, letting its fading warmth drift her off to sleep.

Someone was laughing.

A womanly, beautiful laugh.

It sounded like a spring symphony with the highest notes of a violin. Strong hands held a basket of carefully picked flowers. Its colors were so vivid, almost unreal. These beauties were like glistening rubies, the edges of their petals dipped in silver, and at its center, was a white so pure it glowed.

Arla felt so honored that this was all for her.

But it *wasn't* for her.

The hands that took the flowers did not belong to her. Those hands were golden-brown, covered in gold rings and bracelets. She wrapped her arms around someone, feeling his chest breathing against hers.

And then her vision clouded, a breath of fire and ash misted her eyes, shrouding her world in black. She wasn't afraid of the dark. It was where she lived for so long. Tunnels and sun-blocked bedrooms, the shadows of High-Borns who ignored her or berated her. Darkness was her normal. But this cavernous night felt wrong.

The ash stabbed her eyes, making her tear up.

"Hello?" she called out across the abyss.

Someone was crying far into the distance. A solemn, quiet cry.

"Hello?" Arla was quieter this time. She didn't want to frighten this person. Whoever they were. *Wherever* they were. She reached out into the darkness. "It's okay," she tried to console them.

A hand shot out, grabbing her wrist. She screamed, pulling back, but the hand would not let go. Flames burst around her, smoke filling her lungs with the taste of searing cedar. She coughed, trying to see past the haze. Panic built in her as she thrashed against the hand.

From the billowing smoke came the shadow of a face, dressed in gold and black fur. He was grinning. She could smell burning flesh, but it wasn't hers—not yet. It was coming from all around her.

And then her arm burst into flames, burning her flesh off like wax.

She screamed until her throat was hoarse and her lungs suffocated in the smoke.

Help! Someone, help me!

She was lurched up from the ground, shaken as the heat fell away and the night sky bloomed above her. The chill of the wind told her she wasn't in that hollow dark anymore. Hands held her steady. She was trembling uncontrollably, her hands clammy from sweat, her entire body cold and shivering.

"It's okay," Leo consoled her. "It was just a dream."

She looked at him. His eyes told her she was safe now. That she would be okay.

And then everything hit her at once. She clung to him, burying her face into his chest. He smelled like oak and seafoam.

Closing her eyes, she breathed through everything she had ever felt in her entire life. Everything she pushed away and everything she was never able to have. The pain in her forearms. Her father's cruel words. Her brother's graying face, losing life every day she failed to get the plant. The childish wishes she made that had never come true.

She breathed through it all, trying to settle herself as her fingers curled into Leo's shirt, tightening with every inhale.

She didn't know how long they stayed like that, but he did not move. When her body began to relax, she could hear his heartbeat against her ears. A soft thumping that seemed to be skipping a couple here and there. It soothed her and she wished she could hear this sound all the time.

It was then she realized how close they were as the warmth of his skin under the cloth radiated around her. She also realized how inappropriate this was for a High and a Low-Born to hold each other like this. What it looked like. She tried to pull herself away but was met with resistance.

For a moment, Leo's arms did not budge, holding on a second longer than he should... And then with a slight flinch, he let her go.

She looked at the ground in embarrassment. "I'm sorry. I... over-reacted..."

"You do that a lot, you know," he said. "You're always apologizing to people."

"I have a lot to apologize for," she explained. "Norendra says I wouldn't have to apologize so much if I just did things right the first time."

"She's wrong," Leo said matter-of-factly. "And she sounds like a terrible friend."

Arla snorted a laugh. She had never heard anyone say a bad word about Norendra. Usually because many feared the first advisor. Arla wondered if Leo would fear her too if he ever met her. "She's not a friend, she's my father's first advisor."

"I see." He shifted to sit back next to Arla, a respectful distance away. His legs bent in front of him as he rested his arms on his knees. "Did you have a nightmare?"

"Yes."

He paused. "Do you want to talk about it?"

"I think it was about my father. He grabbed my arm and he..." She wondered if she should tell him the full truth. If it would really matter to him. Her fingers tapped lightly on her forearm as she debated.

"Your father. His magic controls fire." Leo's eyes narrowed, his face twisting into the hate she knew was reserved for nobles. "That's how you got those scars, isn't it? *He* did that to you."

How did he know that? Or was it obvious? She looked down at her fingers still tapping away on her arm. Of course it was obvious.

She pulled her hand back to her side. "He said I needed to learn how to be obedient. He said all people are animals and they can only learn from pain."

Leo's voice darkened, like a low threat. "No one should harm you like that."

She didn't know what to say. What someone *should* do and what they *actually* did were often two very different things. "He is the king."

"He is High-Born scum," Leo muttered under his breath.

She was shocked to hear such contemptuous words from his mouth. And that he openly said it to her, the king's daughter, a High-Born herself. She knew he didn't mean for her to hear it or to say it at all because he immediately looked away from her.

"Why do you hate High-Borns so much, Leo?" she asked. Something must have happened to him to make him seethe with such hatred that now shone in his eyes. What was it?

He jerked slightly. Maybe he wasn't ready to tell her.

And then he gave a great sigh. "I was born in Bruhaul. There's a nobleman there, Lesandres, who owns most of the land and farms there. He thinks he's a king too, in his own way. He worked my father and mother mercilessly in the fields, but my mother... She's always been sick. Constant pain in her muscles, so my father took on both their work to protect her. But there was just too much to do, and Lesandres... he likes to punish, just like your father. Every yard of crops my father didn't pick, he would be beaten."

Arla felt her chest grow heavy, as Leo tightened his fists so hard she was afraid his skin would bleed.

"One day, Lesandres went too far, and my father never recovered. He died a month later. I begged my mother to leave, but she loves Bruhaul. Says it's her home. I joined the army so she would at least not have to worry about feeding me anymore and any money I get, I bring back to her."

"Why not just tell her to leave?" Arla asked. "She can live somewhere else."

Leo stared at her as if she'd said something ignorant again. "You make it sound so easy... But where would she go? High-Borns barely pay us enough to get by for a month. How would she survive without work long enough to find another home? And even if she somehow managed that, how can she know it won't be worse there than where she is now?"

Arla picked at her sleeve. She did not think of this. She had never had to.

He gave a long, frustrated exhale like he was trying to calm himself down. "Something you may not understand, *Princess,* is that there is no other life for her or for me. You will never know what it's like to live with the harsh truth that... no matter how hard I work..." His hostility morphed into a thin sheet of gloom and sorrow. "I will never make enough to free her from that place." His shoulders slumped as he stared at the ground with such hopelessness that her heart ached watching him.

Arla wanted to reach out and tell him she was sorry. That she didn't mean to say something so naive. She should have known the solutions weren't that simple. They never were. But she worried that apologizing would only make him angrier, and she didn't want him to think she was pitying him again.

So instead, she said, "Your mother is lucky to have you as a son. Someone who cares about her so much. At least, she has that comfort."

He didn't respond and that was fine with Arla. Sometimes there wasn't anything else to say.

She continued to sit with him, keeping him company as he brooded in the darkness.

After a long bout of silence, Leo finally spoke in an almost snarl. "We are told we are not worthy of a good life because we can't wield magic. That's bullshit. We are just as worthy as anyone else." He turned to her, his gaze serious but devoid of the anger from before. "And that includes you, Princess."

He got up, dusted off his pants, and looked back at her. "Don't let anyone tell you any different."

CHAPTER 17

In a few hours, they would be walking into the heart of The Forest and finally reach the yellow-flowered healing plant. Arla could hardly contain her eagerness. She also could barely contain her anxiety. Surely The Forest would be protecting its most precious gift and the princess worried about what was waiting for them there.

Arla had scoured the ripped and tattered journal cover to cover by then and had memorized all the sentences she could. All the possible warnings.

The only thing she saw that seemed disturbing was the sentence she read last night: *It spread so fast.* She relayed this to Leo and now they were both on the lookout for something that could "spread". Maybe a creature made of goop, or butter. *Butter? No, not butter.* Arla's mind had been turning to food a lot more after the delicious soup she inhaled last night.

It was ironic that the place she was beginning to create the best memories of her life was also the place she had her worst. The joy and the horror. The rollercoaster ride of emotions was exhausting, but maybe that was what The Forest wanted. To wear them down any way it could.

Even with all this worrying and danger watching, Arla still managed to get pulled into a conversation with Leo. It was a lot easier to talk to him lately.

"A week?!" Arla exclaimed as she hopped over a fallen branch on the forest floor.

Leo nodded proudly. "I had to build a metal wire fence so the critters wouldn't eat them."

"But a week is such a long time to wait!"

"If it takes that long for the sun to dry seaweed, I'll wait," he replied simply.

"Wow, you are so patient. I would have just eaten them immediately." Arla tightened her fingers around the strap of her bag that was now slung across her shoulder.

"That is why the wired fence is there, for critters like you."

Arla playfully frowned at a chuckling Leo. A few days ago, Arla would never have believed she would be able to make the unpleasant captain laugh. Leo and joy seemed like completely opposite things, but seeing him so relaxed and smiling, maybe it was possible. But Arla noticed Leo's constant cursory glances at the trees and sky and the tight hand on the pommel of his sword. Despite their interesting conversation, he was still ready for an attack.

"Why did you pack all those spices and dried seaweed and mushrooms?" she asked.

"The same reason you packed that gaudy cup," he responded. "I wanted to bring some joy."

Arla rolled into another soiree of laughter.

"What are you two laughing about?" Uro hopped between them, putting a hand on Leo's shoulder to stabilize himself. "I want to laugh, too."

Leo shrugged the young soldier off in jest. "It's too late, we had fun without you."

Uro's mouth tilted down in sadness, making Arla feel bad for him, but it was also so amusing to see him pout in that way. She would have said something comforting if she hadn't just then rammed her knee straight into a nearby rock.

She yelped and covered her injured patella with her hands.

"Are you okay?" Uro's forehead creased in worry.

She choked back embarrassed tears. "Yes, I'm fine." She glared at the rock and then at her knee.

"What did I say?" Leo lectured. "Always be aware of your surroundings."

"Yes. Yes. I know," she grumbled. She needed to be better about this, or else she would lose both her knees. She pointed at the rock with a warning finger, almost like a promise that she would have her vengeance. Or be better about avoiding it. Whichever route saved her knee. As she glared at it, she noticed something fall gently onto the undaunted rock.

Its various layers of ruby-shining petals gleamed along its silver edges.

A flower?

Why did it look familiar?

She heard the soldiers gasp in awe. Ahead of them was a line of silver-barked trees, as smooth as porcelain, and above their crisscrossing branches bloomed exquisite crimson petals with snowy centers that seemed to glow.

"Wow," Uro gaped.

There was something about these flowers…

And then Arla remembered.

They were the same ones in her dream. Someone had gifted them to her. Or no, gifted it to another woman.

A glowing warmth spread through her, drawing her to the flowers, which seemed to be calling to her. Their soft petals promised love and devotion. And they weren't just calling to her. Other soldiers were pulled to them, their eyes glazed with the look someone would give to their beloved. A slight breeze picked up, loosening the beautiful blossoms from their branches. They were like floating jewels, twirling and spinning in the air.

A woman giggled in her ear.

Arla reached out her hand to touch a floating flower that descended gently her way.

It looked so soft.

So inviting.

A low shout rang out.

From her peripheral, Arla saw Rose clutch her hand. A flower had settled into her palm, blackening the skin as it slowly embedded itself into her flesh and disappeared underneath. The soldier held tightly to her wrist, just staring in shock at what happened.

Arla snapped out of her daze. *This is another trick.* When she looked around her, there were thousands of ruby flowers descending above them, like gentle, dangerous snow. The soldiers pulled up their shields, covering them from the snowfall of petals.

Arla pulled her bag over her head.

"This way!" Leo ordered, pointing over the hill, where the flowered trees ended. It wasn't too far, only a few feet, and they could make it without being touched by another flower. Luckily, the burning petals did not eat through their metal shields.

And that's when the wind picked up.

Like a hurricane, the air whipped around them, knocking shields away from the soldiers' grips and slapping the flowers against their faces and hands. The plant absorbed into them, leaving scalding black marks on their skin. They shouted in pain as they hurried away.

Arla could barely see from the wind whipping her hair across her face. She tried to keep her bag over her, but it wasn't enough to shield her.

A flash of red and silver steered toward her.

She put out a hand to protect herself.

Leo's wide hands wrapped around her waist, swinging her around his body, drawing her into his own hips and chest. He tucked her between his shield and his own form guarding her against the sweeping petals.

He bared his teeth as a flower seared into his neck, burying itself into his skin and disappearing, leaving only a solid splotch of blistered, angry black. Another landed on his hand, which also left a nasty mark.

She called out his name, but he didn't look at her, instead, he turned toward his soldiers and shouted, "Keep going!"

They slugged through the tornado of burning flowers.

Leo held onto her, pulling her along, making sure no petal touched her. Finally, they stumbled over the hill and past the trees and spilled into an ocean of tall white cotton-like plants. The wind stopped chasing them as if it could not reach past the line of trees they left behind.

The tall cotton plants hovered over them by at least a foot or two, like sunflowers at their tallest height. They were so packed together it was impossible to see past their stalks.

All of the soldiers stopped, prepared for the alabaster flora to do something.

Time passed and the cotton plants remained harmless, gently bobbing in the breeze.

Arla let out a breath, judging it was safe, but Leo was more cautious. His entire body strained as he listened and watched everything, looking for danger. His grip was still strong on her waist.

"I think it's over." Arla tried to sound soothing, to calm him and the others, especially Uro, whose breathing still hadn't slowed. No one moved or spoke, still looking out between the stalks. "Leo..."

Hearing his name must have drawn him back because he finally turned to her, his nose slightly grazing her own, which made her breath hitch. His eyes were blazing for blood, but when he found hers, the darkness ebbed away back to a soft hazel.

Despite her stopped heart, she managed to say, "I think we're safe now."

Leo slowly slipped his hand from her waist, leaving her curiously missing the warmth he took with him. When he turned, Arla saw the pulsing, charred skin on his neck.

"You're hurt." Without thinking, she lightly placed her fingertips on the base of his collar, just below the swollen skin. He jerked back, surprised by her touch.

"I'm sorry." She raised her hands in innocence. "I—I have something for that." Swinging her bag around, she fumbled through almonds, forks, and cloth to pull out a roll of gauze and a jar of translucent goop. Lifting the jar, she said, "It's for burns."

Leo's eyes widened and then crinkled as he smirked. "Why am I not surprised your bag would have the exact thing we need right now?"

A wave of warmth went through her as she smiled at him, which seemed to soften him up even more.

He motioned to the others. "They'll need it more than me. Let me help you."

He took the jar and motioned for her to follow as they went around to each soldier, dressing their wounds.

Everyone had been burned. The flowers had not spared any of them, except Arla who was covered by Leo. But the injuries were not life-threatening, just "a little irritating" or "slightly stingy" as some of the soldiers described. They would heal quickly, unlike her own burns on her arms, which were created by magic and scarred deeper.

One by one, she and Leo covered the wounds of the others. And as she placed the gauze, they would thank her for helping them. It filled her with such joy. She had never been so appreciated as she was now, healing those who needed it. Arla decided she liked the feeling.

Only when all the soldiers were cared for did Leo allow her to look at his neck and hand. The jar was almost empty, but she had made sure to use only what was needed so that Leo would have enough at the end. She knew he wouldn't put himself first above the others. Despite his standoffish demeanor, she had concluded that Leo really did care for the people he was in charge of. She had seen it over and over again, during the battles and moments of doubt and fear.

He winced as she spread the ointment onto his wound. "Sorry," she apologized, trying to be as gentle as possible.

"Nothing to be sorry about," he said. "It's actually kind of cold."

"It's the peppermint oil. It's supposed to numb the pain a little and cool it down." She ripped a piece of gauze and placed it over the wound, smoothing the edges down with a sticky mixture that would hold it in place. "It took me a while to figure out the right measurements, but I cracked it."

"You made this yourself?" he asked, astonished.

She nodded. "The physician had some too, but they were getting tired of me taking so much."

"Why did you need so much ointment?" he asked.

Arla hesitated.

He looked at her with understanding. "For your arms. That's why you brought it. You still have a fresh one that is healing."

Arla just smiled at him, hoping it would be enough to stop the conversation. Mercifully, he did not push any further.

She looked down at Leo's hand, at the second burn. She thought his hand was very elegant, like a musician's; his fingers were long and slender, but they still looked like they could crush whatever they chose to grip. She dipped her hand under his. His palms and fingertips were callused, which felt like sandpaper. And even though his hand was larger than hers, she was surprised at how perfectly it fit in her own. Like a piece falling into place.

What a silly thought.

She spread the ointment on the top of his knuckles and palm, making sure to cover the entire wound. She focused on wrapping up his hand, bending her head very close to the wound, refusing to look up at him. She was afraid he would see her blush over something so stupid as holding a boy's hand. She held plenty of the other soldiers' hands when she bandaged them, so she didn't know why holding Leo's was any different.

It's not any different, she told herself. *It's not any different at all.*

As if to prove it to herself, she gripped his hand harder, to finish the drying process of the glue and then she hastily flung his hand away, like it was just an object.

"We should keep moving," she said, still not looking at him, pretending to be occupied with putting her empty jar back into her bag in the most perfect place possible.

She heard Leo stand up and clear his throat. "I agree."

CHAPTER 18

They were almost there; she could feel it. They pushed and pulled at the tall stalks, which barely bent enough for them to squeeze between, but they did not stop. *Stay strong, Jun,* she thought, hoping her brother could hear her somehow. *I almost have it.*

With a final push through the tall plants, they broke into a small clearing. And finally, after all those days of camping, fighting, and running for their lives, there in the middle of the soft grass was a bundle of weed-like plants growing in the shining sun. Their small yellow flowers were as bright as the beams of sun rays that pierced through the gray haze above them.

Arla shouted in relief and joy. She barreled toward the plants. She was so close. Jun was going to be saved. Everything was going to be okay.

But just as her foot hit the edge of the circle of plants, a sudden spray of black fog jetted from the ground like a geyser. Arla stumbled back, watching in dread as the thick black mist covered the plants and tumbled towards her like a wave.

She scrambled backward as the mist curled over her feet.

Acid?!

No, the mist didn't do anything, but she wasn't going to wait to find out if there was an after-effect. She raced back to the soldiers who now stood at the edge as the black fog overtook the clearing but stopped just at its border.

What is this?

Leo cried out.

She whipped around to see the captain grip his neck. His face contorted in pain as he collapsed onto his knees and hands.

"Leo!" she shouted as she ran to him. "What's wrong?"

His skin was pallid and cold from sweat. She peeled away his hand to see raised thick black veins flowing out from his covered wound. Panic overtook her. Why was this happening? Was the wound infected? She peeled the gauge back to see the mark still on the skin, turned black and pulsing out veins under the surface, like an ugly web.

He coughed, spitting out blood. This type of pattern wasn't an infection... It was one of poison. The flowers were poisonous.

Pulling at his arm, she said, "You need to get up."

But he didn't hear her, his eyes squeezed shut in agony like he was using all his energy to fight off the pain he was feeling now.

Metal hit the ground behind her as another soldier collapsed, clutching where the flower had burned them. And then another and another. Until they were all writhing on the ground.

Heart racing, Arla knew she had to get them away from the mist, in case it spread over the clearing boundary and did something worse.

She gripped Leo's wrists and dragged him as far as she could take him, her legs trembled from the effort. Swiftly, she returned for Uro and Rose, trying to be as gentle as she could while hauling them across the dirt, rocks, and broken branches. One by one, she got all of them, her arms aching from pulling so much weight back and forth.

The poisoned soldiers twisted in agony, crying out in pain. Some were choking on their own blood while others were twitching, shouting at visions no one else could see. It shook Arla's soul, hearing them plead to the Whispers to end their torture. Arla tried to feed them water or keep them on their backs, but nothing helped.

She tiptoed past the screaming men and women until she got back to Leo. Looking at him struck fear into the greatest depths of her being. His face had turned a sickly purple, and rings of red-rimmed his eyes. He was gazing up at the black sky above. His strength left him with every breath. It was unnatural how fast this poison worked through the body. She had only left him a few minutes...

It spread so fast.

The journal had warned her, but it was too late. She crouched next to the captain. This was all her fault. She was the only one untouched by the flowers, thanks to him. He was here because of her.

Leo turned to her, shivering. It was the weakest she'd ever seen him, and it terrified her.

"You need to go," he said. His voice was strained like his lungs were struggling to take in air. "Save yourself, leave this cursed place."

She shook her head. There was no way she was going to do that. How could she abandon them when they risked their lives to get her here?

"I'm sorry I was such an ass," he wheezed. "You didn't deserve it."

"It's okay." Tears brimmed her eyes.

Leo didn't seem to hear her as his eyes closed. Arla cried out, shaking him, but he did not wake. She put her ear to his nose and relief washed over her. Breathing. He was still breathing.

She looked at all of them writhing on the ground. Some had already gone deathly still. Uro was clutching onto Rose's hand, bloody tears rolling down his cheeks as he bit his own tongue from the uncontrollable convulsing the poison was forcing his body to do. Rose squeezed tightly back, as her own breathing dragged between inhales. She was looking up at the sky, staring at nothing.

Was this how it was all going to end? Sudden and swift without hope? They were all going to die here. And so was her baby brother. Arla had failed them all.

She hugged her knees together, curling up into a ball. Maybe she should wait for the poison to come to her too. Or some other force The Forest would inevitably send to kill her.

The mist hissed behind her, still cloaking the tree lines and clearing that held the healing plant. It had stripped the trees around it from their leaves, turning them sickly and skeletal, like the trees that killed so many soldiers around the border.

She could feel the malicious force radiating from the fog.

Weren't they warned of this? The Forest was a place of death. What made her think that she could truly survive it? Because one person did? Maybe they didn't. Maybe they had died and the journal was just found, tossed out by The Forest.

She felt so helpless. She didn't know how to remove the poison.

What could help them? What could save them from the brink of death?

She looked into the abyss of inky mist.

There was still one thing that could help them survive...

Her heart thrummed against her chest as she slowly uncurled herself. There wasn't any other choice. The healing plant was in that fog She had seen it and she had to get that plant no matter what, not only for her brother but for them.

Don't be stupid. You can't do this.

She forced herself to stand up straight, her shoulders pushed back.

You will die.

Her legs shook violently, begging her not to move anymore, but Arla snapped at them to obey.

She allowed herself one breath and then she sprinted into darkness.

If Arla had thought it was dark before, it was nothing compared to the utterly empty black hole she was in now. There were no sounds of wind or water. No living thing seemed to live here at all. The crunching of her steps against the ash and crumbled rock underneath her feet was quickly absorbed by the surrounding fog.

The mist had transformed the clearing into its own world.

The darkness was oppressive here, hanging over everything like a thickness.

She stepped carefully and as quietly as she could, trying to remember where the plant was when the mist sprayed. She reached out her hand and moved it back and forth, floating the obsidian air from side to side, giving her a short view ahead of her.

The darkness can shift with motion, she observed.

A branch snapped behind her.

Arla froze, holding her breath.

Her ear strained to hear any movement behind her, but there was only silence. She let out a breath, but her body refused to stop shaking, forcing her to lean against a tree to steady herself.

She kept moving, keeping her hands out in front of her to grab onto trees and branches, using them to pivot her toward what she thought was where the plants were.

Keep moving, don't stop to think, she told herself. *You have to find the plant.*

She kicked the mist away at her feet, to see if she had stumbled upon it yet. Nothing. Just more ash.

Letting out a huff of frustration, she was about to move on when she heard a low growl reverberating above her.

Arla's heart dropped.

A puff of air pushed down on her head, spreading the fog around her, revealing more of the ground. Trembling, she looked up and found herself staring straight into bloodshot eyes.

Before she could scream, the monster struck out one of its long, serrated legs, slashing her across her arm and leaving a yellow slime on the open wound. She cried in agony as the yellow liquid sizzled at her skin. Faint smells of sour spit and rotting skin hit her nose.

She dashed behind the jagged trunk of a nearby tree to hide.

The monster dropped from the treetops and landed on the ground with a giant thud, swirling the mist. Its hideous skeletal bat-like head sat atop a ten-foot-high insect-like body. It let out another low growl, opening its mouth that took over most of its face, revealing knife-like teeth. Each of its six legs tapped the ground like it was feeling around for something.

And that's when she realized this beast has no eyes. It was trying to sense her, either through scent or movement.

Wincing in pain, Arla clutched her arm, careful not to touch her cut where the acid was still eating away at her skin. She looked around trying to find a place to hide, anywhere that would fit her. And that's when she saw it.

The yellow-flowered plant.

It was just a few feet away from her. If she could just run fast enough, she could grab it and then sprint back, hopefully losing the creature in the trees.

I can do this.

She took a couple of deep breaths and bolted for the plants, but the monster was too quick.

It tripped Arla's leg and tossed her into a tree.

Her lower side ribs cracked against the bark. She let out a gasp, tears blurring her vision as pain boomed across her entire being.

Her head felt light, drifting away for a second.

The sound of the creature clicking its tongue returned her consciousness back to The Forest floor, where she lay, clutching her ribs. She could barely breathe. The bat-headed abomination lingered in front of her, snarling. Was it toying with her?

She wasn't going to give up. Not when everyone depended on her. She had to try.

She crawled away from the creature, toward the plant. Her broken ribs dragged across the forest floor sending pain across her entire body, but she still clawed her undamaged hand into the dirt and pulled herself forward. Serrated edges slashed at her calves, erupting screams from her throat.

The creature screeched and knocked her sideways again. While her body was still in the air, the beast stabbed its poisonous leg into her shoulder, skewering her to a nearby tree.

She let out a guttural scream.

It was too much now.

All her world felt like torment. Memories flashed in and out of her mind. Jun's smiling face. Her father's disappointed snarl. Uro laughing. And Leo. The way he cupped her cheeks as he breathed with her. In and out. In and out.

Blood dripped down her shoulder. She grabbed the creature's leg, futilely trying to pull it out, but she was no match for the creature's strength. Her body was growing colder. Her mind was fading.

Death was coming for her.

Please. Please. Let me go. She pleaded with anything that could hear her. *Let me save them. I need to save them. Please. Let me do this one thing.*

The creature clicked its tongue again as it opened its acid-dripping jaw.

Something stirred beneath them.

It wrapped around Arla and seeped into her chest, filling her entire body. She felt it crackle through her arm and into the creature's leg.

The creature recoiled, pulling its leg out. Arla fell to the floor on her knees, depleted. The monster twisted and bent in unnatural ways, its bones cracking. The unseen force encircled her like a tornado, snapping the trees in half.

A flood of words in a language she couldn't understand invaded her ears.

A high-pitched cry scattered the words away. She covered her ears, unable to bear it.

A strong hand grabbed her chin and lifted her face. Arla looked up and saw a woman. Just a little older than herself. Short black hair whipped about her face, and her golden-brown skin seemed to radiate, breaking up the shadows around her.

Everything about this woman was refined, regal, exploding with color and sunlight. Everything except her eyes, which held the deepest sorrow Arla had ever seen.

The Woman opened her mouth. *"Ithen-a it-arel vic-ni-hana yu-olith."*

A surge flooded into her body, piercing the very core of her being. Her limbs screamed as if they were being broken and healed and rebroken endlessly. It was unbearable. And then a deafening crack split inside her.

Something opened within Arla, sucking in everything, and then the pain blipped away. A blinding light cut across the entire forest, and then darkness sucked back in, shriveling up whatever the light touched.

And that was the last thing Arla saw before everything went black.

CHAPTER 19

It was an armada of clamoring screeches. Shouting and hissing things she didn't understand. It rose and rose, piercing her ears, threatening to burst her skull open. She couldn't take it. It was too much. She shouted into the abyss, but instead of her voice, it was another inhuman screech tumbling from her mouth, filling the world with permanent night.

Arla snapped awake, screaming.

She shot her hand to her shoulder, expecting an oozing wound and more pain, but there was... nothing. She looked down. Her shoulder had completely healed. Her pants and shirt were torn and still stained with blood, but where there was once a gaping wound now lay soft untouched skin.

Soft gray ash lay around her and the mist was nowhere to be seen, leaving Arla alone in the clearing. And there clutched in her balled-up fist, was a handful of yellowed flowered plants.

It was real. She had gotten it!

Just as soon as the joy came, did the panic quickly replace it. How much time had gone by? She dashed forward, surprised at how nimble and strong her body felt like she hadn't almost been shredded apart by a nightmarish monster just moments before. She was an inch away from death. How did she survive that? She couldn't think about it right now. She needed to get back.

When she made it back to the group of trees, her heart froze, hearing the unsettling quiet where the soldiers lay. There was no more screaming or moaning of pain. Just rows of pale, rigid bodies, all deathly still. And at the end of one of those rows was the captain.

She slid next to Leo, whose eyes were closed. She touched his face, feeling the cold of his skin on her fingertips. Pulling off a chunk of the healing plant's leaves in her hand, she crumbled it, releasing its oils.

Please, please let this work.

She dropped the leaves into his mouth, making him chew them by pulling at his jaw.

She waited.

And waited.

And waited.

Not daring to think the worst. Her legs were growing numb from sitting on them, but still, she did not move. And then...

Leo's eyes flew open.

The color returned to his face as he drew in a slow deep breath like he was waking up from a light slumber. Arla cried in relief then, throwing her arms around him, which he hardly seemed to feel as his eyes were still clearing.

Never had she felt so grateful and light as she did then. Like a pile of stones had lifted from her chest, allowing her to breathe again. Tears welled up as she held back a sob.

Leo was alive. He was going to be okay.

Knowing he was safe, Arla moved quickly to Uro, then Rose, who both awoke just as Leo did. Slow and confused. She dashed to another soldier, but his body had already grown too cold. It didn't matter, she pressed the plant into his mouth, forcing it down his throat. And then she went to another, the same process. And another. And another. She shook each one, pressing her head to their chests checking for a beating heart, waiting for them to return. But they never came back.

She was too late for them.

Collapsing into a seated position, she let the tears flow freely and silently down her cheeks. Arla mourned the ones she could not save.

I should have been faster. I should have woken up sooner.

She didn't know how much time passed when a hand fell on her shoulder.

Leo's skin had returned to its full healthy tone. The caked blood on his shirt was the only evidence that he had been sick at all. She saw the sorrow she felt reflected back in his own weary expression. There used to be thirty of them and now there were only four left.

"We should go," he said, his voice a dam against the flood of emotions he must have been feeling in his soul. Even now, he was trying to keep his composure. Maybe for her, or maybe for himself.

He helped Arla up to her feet. He was right. She had a brother to save. Time was running out. She placed the last remaining plant in her pocket, making sure it was secure, and grabbed her bag. Rose and Uro, still dazed from their return from the dead, wordlessly followed.

Arla expected The Forest to strike them again the moment they had hope that they could survive it. She waited for the trees to swoop down and clobber them to death, or for a new monster to chase them, but strangely, nothing stood in their way as they ran as fast as they could the way they came. It was so peculiar. Arla even thought she saw the trees move out of their way like they wanted to help them leave too.

What was even stranger was that although it took them days to trek The Forest to the heart, it only took them half the day to reach the edge. Had the paths changed? It was like this place was shifting and stretching at will, doing whatever it wanted. Something was surely going on.

She wasn't the only one who thought this.

"It's too easy," Leo murmured.

But all questions were dropped when the tree line broke and they stepped out of the borders of the darkness, Arla couldn't help but tear up as the open sky greeted her. Uro bent over and kissed the soft green grass underneath his feet, laughing in joy.

"It'll take three days to return from here," Rose stated. "But longer without horses."

"Wasn't there a village nearby?" Uro asked. "They had horses."

"West of here," Arla remembered, her sense of direction still intact.

When they arrived at the humble village, Uro managed to persuade some of its people to relinquish their horses. Rose and Leo were truly lucky to have such a lovable, friendly boy who could convince someone of anything with his genuine smile and humorous outlook on life.

They thundered across the plains on their newly borrowed horses as hard as they could until they were forced to rest for the night at a local inn in a town Arla did not recognize. It was only when they were seated for a warm dinner that they finally gained the will to talk.

"What happened in there?" Uro finally asked, ever curious as he scratched his healing arm. The black marks on their skin from the poisonous flowers had faded into a light pinkish hue the shape of the flower that burned them, which Arla predicted would disappear completely over time.

Arla didn't really know how to answer his question, mostly because she didn't really understand it herself.

"Your clothes were bloodied and ripped, but you had no wounds," Rose said. "How is that possible?"

Another question Arla couldn't answer.

Uro looked like he was about to ask her a thousand more things, but Leo cleared his throat, interjecting, "It doesn't matter. It's all over now."

Arla lowered her head, grateful for the end of the queries. It was still so difficult to wrap her mind around what she saw. *Was it even real?* Regardless, she hoped Leo was right that it was over. For the rest of her life, she never wanted to think about The Forest ever again.

For the next two days, they rode their horses as fast as they could go until they finally galloped over the final hill and saw the full view of Ulsana's main city come into view.

Ulsana had the largest lands compared to the other kingdoms, and its city was also known for its great size. It was built on the side of the great Opala Mountains. A walled city of marble and granite with elevated tiers of homes and streets that slanted upward toward the top where the castle stood. Its ivory towers held the flags of Ulsana's crest that bore an image of The Forest with twin swords crossed between its trees. It was a true sight to behold.

Arla clutched the plant in her hand. Only a few leaves remained, and she didn't know how much would be enough to save her brother. They have been gone for more than a week. What if her brother had not made it?

As they raced to the city walls, she felt the mood change among them. Leo, Rose, and Uro grew stiffer and spoke less, mentally putting on their soldier roles like armor. By the time they reached the main gates of the castle, they were off their horses.

"We'll escort you until the royal guards get you," Leo said, his tone serious and distant.

"I'll come find you all when my brother is healed," Arla promised. She didn't know if the three of them wanted to see her again, but at least they would know that she did not intend to forget them.

"I'll be waiting!" Uro said, his face beaming.

Rose gave the young boy a slight shake of her head.

They were no more than a few feet from the castle when the guards rushed towards her. "Princess?!"

They seemed surprised at her presence. Had they even known she was gone? She didn't bother to question them. Instead, she readjusted the bag on her back and dashed past them, through the gates.

Right before she crossed the entirety of the front courtyard, she turned once to the trio, mouthing 'Thank you' as she disappeared around the corner.

She went halfway through the hall when Norendra turned into it. Her teacher's eyes widened.

"You reckless, flimsy girl!" Norendra shouted, charging for her, the skirt of her long dress whipping past her heels. "Where have you been?!"

Arla pulled from her pocket the last leafed remains of the healing plant, the yellow flowers long wilted. Norendra stopped in her tracks, mouth agape.

"I went to get this," Arla responded.

CHAPTER 20

T he doors of the throne room flew open as Norendra nearly tackled her way through the king's advisors, making way for Arla to trail behind her. Her former teacher only stopped when she finally got to the short steps before the throne. Mathus stood from his chair with Ametha by his side. It was the first time Arla had ever seen her father look shocked as he gazed at the plant hanging from Arla's hand.

This was the moment.

"Father," she began, full of pride. "I got the healing plant."

Ametha wailed in joy as she rushed towards her, but Mathus got to her first. His eyes were wide, and his face was taut as he reached out, his arms wide and open. Arla opened her own. Finally, the embrace she had wanted all these years. This time away must have made him realize how much he truly did care about her.

"I went to The Forest to get this for Jun. That's why I've been gone," she explained, tears brimming in her eyes.

The plant was yanked from her hand as she was pushed back.

"What took you so long?" Mathus growled, tossing the plant to a nearby guard in the corner. "Get this to my son, now!"

The guard bowed quickly and dashed out of the room, followed by a still-crying Ametha. Mathus's attention went back to Arla, who recoiled from his cold gaze. "You've been gone for almost two weeks," he spat down at her. Arla backed an inch away, feeling the temperature in the room rise. "You wasted precious resources having guards out looking for you. Norendra suspected you left for The Forest with the soldiers. What a foolish thing to do." He took a step toward her. "First, you dare leave without my permission. Then, you take weeks to come back here with that plant. Jun could have been dead by now."

Arla's voice caught in her throat. She didn't know what he expected her to say. Did he want her to apologize? Did he want her to grovel at his feet for forgiveness?

Arla had risked her life to save her brother and all her father could do was berate her for taking so long?

Something deep rattled in her then, a loosening of disappointment crept from every corner of her chest into her core.

Mathus snapped his fingers for his advisors to follow him out of the hall. None of them stopped to welcome her home or ask if she was injured even though she had just come back from the most dangerous place in all of Ulsana.

She was small again. An insignificant decorative piece that collected dust in a neglected corner of a sun-deprived storage room.

And as she stood there, forgotten, she finally understood the truth.

It was never going to be enough.

She was never going to be strong enough. Smart enough. Fast enough for her father. No matter what she did, he would always belittle her and make her feel like she wasn't worth the air she breathed.

A slow heat burned within her. All those years she clung to the hope that he would throw a kind word to her. Like a starving dog to its master. And for what?

She *was* stupid. Stupid for wanting his love.

Footsteps shuffled beside her. Not everyone had left the hall. Gerald Dermarcu, Wilkins's father, hovered near the door. There was a question on his face that Arla did not want to answer.

"Gerald," Norendra called to him. "Your king has ordered you to leave with the others."

"Of course." Dermarcu bowed low and hurried out of the room, leaving only Norendra and Arla in there. They stood quiet for a moment. Norendra's eyes looked her up and down, accessing her. "You were reckless for leaving."

"I know," she said curtly, tightening her grip on the strap of her bag. It was the harshest she'd ever spoken to Norendra. She didn't want to hear any of her former teacher's scolding today. She was tired, and her chest felt heavy. Without giving Norendra the chance to reply, she marched out of the hall.

⁂

Arla was relieved to see her old friend again. The stone beast crouched firm, its outstretched claw welcoming her back home. She smiled, touching the top of its center snake head, feeling the coolness of the rock. She sat on the bench, alongside the stone creature, leaning against it. Above her, Jun's nursery window was taking in the afternoon sun. Multiple figures stood, pacing back and forth. They must have given him the plant by now.

Arla rubbed her forearms, a little worried the plant may not work. What if it had decayed? Or lost its effect away from The Forest? Who knew how it really worked? There was nothing to do but wait. So, she sat there, as the sun lowered against the horizon. The figures drifted in and out of the room. She strained her eyes to see if there was any sign from their body language of good or bad news. And then, a crowned figure raised her hands. Ametha. Was it joy or sorrow?

Arla wanted to shout up from her bench, asking for an answer, but they would not be able to hear her. So, she kept waiting. And then someone opened the window and Arla heard the most beautiful sound in the world. A baby's cry wailing into the wind. It was a strong cry, one of demands and life.

"Looks like the prince will live."

Arla twisted around to see Simion and his hollow eyes gleaming at her. "Hello, Simion." She turned to face his lanky figure, never letting the royal scholar out of her sight.

His hands were clasped behind his back in his usual elderly-like posture. "I just wanted to stop by to congratulate you on not perishing in The Forest. Although, I had hoped a funeral would have happened. The food is delectable at funerals."

"It is cruel and treacherous to wish for the death of a royal," Arla spat.

A flash of surprise crossed the scholar's face that melted into intrigue. He curved that snake-like mouth of his into a smirk. "Well, Princess, I dare say The Forest has had an effect on you."

"I don't know what you mean."

"Something is different."

"I am the same," Arla argued.

"No..." Simion seemed to be studying her like he did his books and theories in the libraries. "I don't think you are."

CHAPTER 21

No one knew how Arla got into Jun's room the first time, so it was no different the second time she entered without permission. When night fell and everyone had gone to sleep, she snuck in, pushing the tapestry to the side. His crib had been changed, something more decadent and larger; maybe he had grown since she last saw him.

She tiptoed towards the wood-carved bassinet and saw a flash of rectangles on the ground. Leaning a little to the side, she expertly avoided the corner of a newly placed large chest that was probably put there after Arla had left for The Forest.

Patting herself on the back, she congratulated herself for dodging something so expertly and saving her poor knee, just like she was taught by Leo. *Be aware of your surroundings.* She gave the wooden chest a smug look, wanting it to know she had conquered it.

As she stepped away, still looking confidently at the chest, her stomach caught the back of a heavy chair. It dug its knobbed ends into her soft belly, causing her to cough out a spurt of pain. She folded over the chair, clenching her fists.

So close.

In the bassinet, Jun gave a soft grunt acknowledging her presence. She peeled herself off the chair and peered over his crib. There he was. Bright-eyed and awake, Jun rocked side to side, smiling up at her. He looked so healthy, just like when she last saw him. So perfect.

It was only then that she let herself completely cave into her relief as tears flowed silently down her cheeks.

"I'm so happy you're okay," she said, patting his round belly. He giggled at the touch.

She had done it.

For the first time in her life, she had helped someone and succeeded in doing so. Everything she had gone through was worth it just to see that he was safe. She giggled with Jun as she tickled his feet, watching his tiny, clenched fists rapidly swing back and forth.

She heard movement down the hall, a warning that she needed to leave. Arla tucked Jun into his blankets. "I was never here, okay?" she said, putting a finger to her lips to make a hushing expression.

Jun just stared blankly up at her as if to say, *How would I even tell anyone?*

And just as quietly as she entered, Arla left.

After her baby brother's full recovery, life returned to normal in Ulsana. Well, as normal as it usually was for Arla. She was still ignored by the royal court and still ate alone with her stone beast. Before, this would have sunk Arla further into a void where she would want to curl up and sleep forever in, but now, it didn't bother her as much.

Let them have their parties and dinners without me. Her longing to join them had faded because now they weren't the only ones who mattered. Maybe Simion was right. Maybe something *had* changed in her.

As early as she could wake up, Arla had gotten dressed in her bed chambers and sprinted down her tower and out into the front castle courtyard. Before The Forest, she would rarely leave the castle because there was nowhere she really wanted to go, but now she did, and today she was headed straight into the city.

Just as she was about to pass through the main castle gates, a female guard stopped her. "I'm sorry, Princess, but you aren't allowed to leave the castle grounds."

"That's not true. I've always been able to leave," Arla affirmed.

"Not without someone to escort you and only with the king's permission," the soldier replied. Was this a new rule someone had dictated because Arla had run away before? Whoever made this policy certainly wasn't her father, who couldn't care less.

A sudden suspicion pulsed in her heart. Was it Norendra? Why would she care if she was gone?

"Well..." Arla started. "I *do* have the king's permission, and *you* can escort me."

She hoped the guard would believe her lie. She let nothing show on her face as she stared at her, trying to embody the stoic confidence of Rose and the friendly innocence of Uro.

After a moment, the guard nodded and told another to take her place. The gates opened and they were on their way.

The city was bustling with life today. Merchants wheeled carts of goods from all over the land, trying to sell to any passerby. Women dragged their rowdy children by the hand, or the back of their necks, across busy cobbled streets as they ran their errands. Ulsana's city was loud and always bustling with activity and its people were opinionated, noisy, and constantly arguing, only growing silent when someone more powerful walked among them, like her father.

Most of the city's properties and markets were owned by the nobles, but it was the Low-Borns who worked and cleaned them for minimal pay. They were allowed to work here, but their lodgings were in the lower parts of the city. She imagined the calves of all Low-Borns living here were strong because the city was built on a hill where they had to live at the bottom and climb up to the top to work every day. The High-Borns had no such issues as their homes rested neatly and comfortably at the top nearest the castle.

Arla winded down the streets as they curled lower and lower. Some Ulsanans recognized her but did not bother to say hello. Even with the people, she was a disappointment. Everyone hoped the royals would wield magic because it showed strength against the other kingdoms. Arla's lack of it made the entire kingdom look weak and threatened their way of living, no matter their status.

The guard seemed to recognize this path as they descended to the lower ends of the city and blocked Arla just before she turned a corner. "This is as far as you should go, Princess."

Truthfully, Arla had never gone down this deep into the main city, mostly because she never had to. There was nothing for her here, no one she knew, but now, there were people she wanted to see. Three, in fact.

"Where are you trying to go?" the guard asked, already suspecting.

"The army training grounds," Arla stated.

The soldiers of Ulsana trained and lived in the middle level of the city, between the Low and High-Born living spaces and that's where Leo, Uro, and Rose would be. She wanted to see how they were doing.

"You are not allowed there," the guard declared. "Let me escort you back to the castle."

"Why not?" Arla put her hands on her hips. "I want to visit my friends."

The guard's mouth hung open. "Princess, that is inappropriate. You cannot mingle with any Low-Borns, let alone soldiers."

This was another truth that Arla had ignored during her cooped-up days in the castle. The thing she had completely forgotten in The Forest. The thing Wilkins shouted at Leo for and why he never dined with them.

Here, in Ulsana, the two classes did not mix. They only communicated transactionally, for business, or for services. They were not friends. They were not confidants. They were nothing to each other other than lords and servants and that's how it was supposed to be.

In The Forest, that separation blurred because they were fighting for their lives and had little resources and no society to hold them back, but here in their home, the wall had returned.

Arla looked at the street behind the guard. She could try to run past this woman... But if she did that, what trouble would that cause the guard? Would she be punished for losing the princess?

"Of course," Arla feigned a laugh. "I was only joking. It was a dare my friend in the royal court told me I had to do. He said, 'Go to the army training grounds, steal a shield, and bring it back as evidence.'" She tried to laugh harder to make it seem real. "I guess I'll have to fail this one again." She shrugged. "You're right, let's just go back."

The guard looked relieved. And so, they climbed up the steep hill, back to the castle, where Arla thanked her for being a good sport about the joke and scurried away back to the Endezee Garden and her statue.

She sat on the cold stone bench again, thinking of how she could see her friends. It could never be in public. She would have to send them a secret message. But even if she did that, where would they meet?

She looked at the monstrous statue's main snake head. "Any ideas?"

It responded with silence. Like always. She rolled her eyes, almost turning away when a loosened leaf slowly floated into the beast's hand.

How pretty, she thought. And that's when she remembered a place she had found when she was young, a place the tunnels led down and through where she was completely alone with just her and the stars and critters in the grass.

She hurried back to her bed chambers and pulled out a sheet of paper from her table, quickly scribbling a note and not signing it, in case it was lost. She would give this to the guard tomorrow. No. A different guard. No. Any guard would become too suspicious. She would tuck it away in the supply shipments that went to the army training grounds. Yes. That was it.

She knew where the shipments were packed. And she knew who packed them. So she would pass it to a servant who went down to the shipments and have them tuck the note away. No. The note would be tucked in a bag of innocuous apples that she would tell the servant to put in the shipment. Yes. It was a simple plan, with a few convoluted moving pieces that were sort of complicated when you thought about it, but it was no matter! She could do this.

That night, after explaining to the servant what she wanted, Arla retreated to her room, where she lay in bed, having only to wait. She didn't know how long it would take, but she hoped Leo, Uro, or even Rose saw the note.

If Rose saw it, Arla hoped she did not throw it away thinking it was a trick. She barely knew Rose, and she suspected Rose liked it that way, maybe because the female soldier predicted that their familiarity would not last after The Forest. But Arla would not allow their relationship to just disappear like that. She had worked too hard. They had gone through too much for her to just abandon them now. Or maybe she was more afraid they had abandoned her.

She had come to consider the three of them to be her friends, but she did not know if the feeling was mutual. When she had seen them tease each other the moments before they entered The Forest, she had felt jealous. She wanted to have what they so clearly already had – someone to care about her and when they all sat drinking soup together that one night... she thought maybe they accepted her, or at least that maybe Leo did. And she wasn't willing to let go of that thread.

That night she thought out every possible scenario of where the note could have gone. The apples could have rotted and soaked the note, making it illegible. It could have dropped out of the bag on its journey. Someone could have eaten the note accidentally in their voracious appetite for crisp fruit. The possibilities were endless. She should have packed the note with papayas, as no one would have eaten the papayas, because they were the worst.

Arla tossed her sheets off her bed, having fully given up on trying to sleep.

It was no use.

And then... a quiet whispering echoed in her room.

She froze, her skin prickling.

Slowly, she sat up.

"Hello?" she said in a low voice, afraid to shout in case it would cause a stir.

The chattering moved under her door and across her walls. And then a clear voice echoed behind her, she twisted around, and a gentle hand cupped her face.

A woman, *The Woman*, looked at her with her dark eyes, pleading.

Her body lurched down into a cold darkness, to a place she had learned to fear above all others. The Forest's obsidian trees surrounded her, their sharpened edges itching to pierce through her. Arla burst into a cold sweat. What was she doing here again?

The thick mist descended on her, covering her vision, suffocating her. And then in an instant, it dispersed, opening up to reveal The Forest completely changed. Where skeletal trees once were, was an oasis of lush evergreen trees, almost sparkling under the light of a thousand blinking stars above them.

The ground trembled with the sound of hooves rushing toward her. The Woman let go of her face and ran in the opposite direction as horses broke through the bush and chased after her.

Arla shouted, "Wait!"

The horses rushed past her, like she wasn't even there, and disappeared into the darkness. Then Arla heard a scream so loud it shook her skull.

The trees collapsed into themselves all around, almost crushing her.

She lurched back to her room, facing her bed frame.

Arla gasped, her heart pounding against her chest. She scanned over the entire room.

Nothing.

No one was there. She had never left her bed. She was sweating, but her feet were clean, with no dirt or mud.

Was it a dream? The vision felt so real.

That face... she knew that face. It was The Woman she saw right before she fainted. Why was she seeing her again?

She tried to calm down, telling herself nothing happened, but it didn't help. Arla dove further under her blanket, hoping it would provide some protection or at least comfort. It was just her imagination, right? Her ears strained to hear the voice again, but nothing came, and after a long, long time, her exhaustion finally caught up with her and she drifted into a troubled sleep.

CHAPTER 22

She was standing in a lush, beautiful forest. The sun's rays peeked perfectly through the tall trees as the birds chirped happily around her. Her toes settled into the cool, soft, evergreen grass beneath her as the breeze gently danced across her skin. It was wonderful. She heard the sound of young, joyous laughter ahead of her. There were two voices, a woman and a man.

Her curiosity led her toward them and in the mist, she could make out two figures dancing.

The woman's figure stopped, noticing Arla's presence. The mist cleared a path between them, and Arla recognized her instantly. The Woman from The Forest was holding a bouquet of the poisonous ruby flowers that fell from the trees.

Smiling at Arla, The Woman reached out her hand, inviting her to dance. For some reason, Arla wasn't afraid. She felt she could trust this person. She stepped towards her, ready to join her, when something snapped between them.

Darkness flooded The Forest, withering everything it touched. The Woman continued to reach for Arla, trying to speak, but instead of a human voice, it was the sound of a language she did not know.

She desperately kept trying to say something to Arla, but the more she spoke, the louder the wind was, until the darkness covered everything, silencing her. Arla shouted out to her, but it was too late.

In a jolt, Arla sprang up from her sleep. Her hand felt the moisture of the morning dew on the grass. She looked around and gasped.

Instead of her bed, Arla was lying on the side of the main road outside the city walls. The same road they took weeks ago to The Forest. The grass underneath her was blackened and dead like a wound on the earth.

A sharp pain stabbed her head as a flood of words she couldn't understand thrashed in her skull. There were thousands, clamoring on top of each other, demanding to be said out loud.

She gritted her teeth. "Stop it," she begged, but the noise kept coming in waves, crashing into her, threatening to shatter every fiber of her being. They gnashed and pulled, forcing her to her knees.

They wanted her to speak to them. Release them.

She resisted, but the pain only grew, threatening to crack and splinter her head apart. So she relented and blurted out the loudest one.

"*J'en-ath gurth-u dal.*"

The ground in front of her shook violently and then split. Dirt spewed in all directions and from the splintered ground, a large claw with sharpened razor tips sprung out from the depth that opened up.

Arla screamed as a monster emerged from the earth. Its large skull was wide like a fan until it narrowed into its muzzle, scaled all around in pure black. It growled, showing its crooked rows of razor-sharp teeth oozing with crimson spit. Four powerful legs held up its lizard body that ended with a long tail with knife-like edges on its spine. For a horrible minute, it looked to the sky and its surroundings and then its glowing red eyes turned and focused on Arla.

The beast roared and thundered towards her. Arla shrieked and bolted, running as fast as she could, back towards the castle. Memories of the sickly yellow bile creature and the winged demon jostled in her brain. The Forest had sent a beast to kill her.

The creature was almost at her feet. She was never going to outrun it. She was going to die here.

She tripped over something. A rock?! And fell flat on her face. She made to get up when she felt a gust of air as a clawed foot landed next to her own. Shaking, she rotated herself around, face to face with the creature. If she was going to die, at least she would die facing her enemy.

It snarled at her, its spit falling, landing on her shoulders. She flinched thinking it was acidic, but the saliva did nothing. She peered into the monster's eyes, and something flashed in them. A sense of knowing. The beast did not move to eat her or tear her apart. It just... stared at her.

Arla's chest heaved up and down, struggling for breath.

The creature did not budge.

Why wasn't it moving?

Slowly, she got up. The beast still stood frozen, but its blood-filled eyes kept following her.

The hissing returned to her mind like a thousand floating bats, each wanting their turn. But one bumped up against her skull that somehow told her it should be the one said next.

She didn't know what made her trust it, but she did. And so, she repeated the words it said in her mind. "*Sodu.*"

The creature backed up and laid down on its hindquarters, bowing its head.

Arla stopped breathing.

It was listening to her.

She couldn't think or move; she didn't know what was happening. This wasn't possible.

She inched toward the beast, which made no movement. She put out her hand, knowing it was insane, knowing it could be a mistake, but she did it anyway. She placed the tips of her fingers slowly and carefully onto the creature's scaled nose. It felt like a thousand ice needles prickled up her palm and into her arm. Colder than anything she had ever experienced. She pulled her arm back, afraid of what it would do to her. But nothing happened. No burns. No throbbing.

The noises continued to tumble into her head. Her audibly speaking two of them encouraged the others to keep coming. To say them all.

Her head started to throb, blurring her vision. The world was tilting, and her feet felt like they were going to sweep out from under her.

The fan-skulled monstrosity jerked its head in agitation and its red pupils constricted into a thin blade. It lowered its head, stalking towards her; its movements were no longer peaceful, but predatory.

Her dizziness swirled as she half-collapsed onto the ground, unable to back away. The words in her head rumbled into one, the bigger it got, the more it drained her energy, making her too tired to fight it. If the beast was going to kill her, it would be easy.

And just when she thought she would faint, a sudden current washed all the words in her head away. The creature groaned, frozen in mid-prowl and then its body shivered and broke apart into a million flakes of ash, disintegrating and blowing into the wind, like it was never here at all.

Her headache suddenly disappeared, and the shouting in her head quieted. She reached out her hand to where the beast vanished. *Is it dead?*

There was no one there to answer her questions. All she could do was watch the ash fly away.

Arla trembled at what this meant. What it would do to her. To everyone.

Because now, Arla Seojin had magic.

CHAPTER 23

The wet grass soaked the bottom of Arla's dress as she paced the meadow, trying to work out all the thoughts running through her mind. The clearing was in the softest ground anyone could ever walk on and its diverse plant life amongst the tall and short grass was home to plenty of critters and bugs.

It was a solitary place just outside the city walls that many people had forgotten about, who usually favored the northern part of the lands that expanded with villages and farms. Because the southern side remained mostly untouched and unvisited, it thrived in its natural state of woods and meadows.

She had found this particular meadow during her tunnel journeys as a child, where she stumbled upon an exit door that led down a winding path straight to this beautiful place from the rear of the castle and through the city walls.

She used to play here by herself for hours before slinking back for supper. It was a great place to ponder and debate things with herself and now she was using it for a secret meeting.

Before last night, she was more nervous about whether the trio would find her note and come meet her here. If they got the message or would agree to come. But *after* last night, when she discovered she had magic, there were other things to be nervous about.

She kept pacing, hoping to burn off some of this anxiousness, when she spotted a dark shadow approaching her. Her heart leaped. Was it—?

And sure enough, there was Leo. His sharp face and dark wavy locks were highlighted by the moonlight making him seem almost majestic.

The moment she saw him, all her worries melted away. A strange feeling, but comforting. When he finally approached her, she tried to read his face, but as always, it was well masked with a layer of emotionlessness. He and Rose were really good at that.

"Hi." She smiled.

He was so different from her. She was not the type to wear a mask. It was hard for her to restrict any emotion from her face, but she wondered if she should learn. If she did, she would definitely ask him for proper lessons.

"Hello, Princess." His voice was like running your fingers through liquid velvet, smooth and deep. His lips were soft and curved slightly at the ends.

She inwardly sighed as she realized he was smiling. Good, he was glad to be here at least.

Leaning to the side, she looked past him. "Where is Uro and Rose?"

"I wanted to come first. In case it wasn't safe." His tone was back to the captain he was. Full of caution and seriousness.

She understood. They couldn't be sure if the message was from her or someone else. Leo was only trying to protect his friends.

"I'm glad you came," Arla said, motioning for him to follow her through the meadow, which he did. "How have you been?" She was eager to know they were alright. What did everyday life look like for a soldier?

"I've been well. Uro and Rose have been training with me. Nothing out of the ordinary." He turned to her, a softening in his face. "And you?"

Arla wanted to ask more about his life. About the others, but the stress of what she discovered yesterday was building and the moment he looked at her, she couldn't help but spill everything to him. She told him about the dreams and the magic she had discovered. Even through his cool exterior, Arla could see Leo was surprised to hear that she had suddenly gained the Whispers.

"Every time I hear a voice, I just jump," she said, picking at her forearms again.

"How do you know it's magic and not something else?" he asked as he strolled beside her, both of them walking in aimless circles. His brow was furrowed, deep in thought while he processed everything she had told him. Unlike Uro, who would have asked a million questions, Leo was more thoughtful of his words, mulling every detail over until he had something important to say.

"Norendra said that Whispers are how you use magic," she continued. "And I think it's those voices. They say it's how The Forest speaks to us. How it allows us to use its magic."

He just stared at her, blankly.

"You don't believe me?"

"No. I do believe you," he assured her.

They continued their aimless walk as Arla waited for Leo to say more. The crickets had transitioned into ribbits of frogs as they headed toward a small stream. Ever since The Forest, she had been hesitant around running water, suspicious of its motives, even though she had played in this one before for years as a child.

"Do you think whatever happened to you in The Forest caused this?" Leo finally asked as he watched for jumping frogs.

"The monster that came up from the ground looked like the ones that attacked us in The Forest, so I think so."

Another pause as they stood by the edge of the thinning stream.

"Are you going to tell your father?" Leo asked.

Arla sighed. "I don't know. If I had discovered this before The Forest, I would have run to him and showed him everything, but now..." Now she wasn't sure what she wanted from her father. The longing for her father's attention had faded, maybe because she was focused on other things.

"Do you hear them now?" His eyebrows furrowed as he looked at the empty air above her head like he believed the Whispers were physical things that hovered around you like flies.

She shook her head, biting her lip. She was scared of what this meant, of what this would do to her. She remembered how she couldn't control what she said. What if it happened again? What if she accidentally hurt someone in the process?

Leo sighed, running his hand through his hair, making one dark auburn strand fall over his forehead. "I don't know much about magic, but I will help you as much as I can," he said. "I know how difficult it is… to go through things alone."

Tears welled up in her eyes. Arla couldn't help but be touched. "Thank you, Leo…You're too kind to me."

He looked away as if he was uncomfortable with watching her face. "I don't think the world has been kind *enough* to you."

She laughed lightly. "You're like a snail. Hard on the outside, but soft and gooey on the inside."

He gave her an incredulous look. "Snails are slow and ugly."

"Exactly."

A full, open laugh vibrated through Leo's chest and wrinkled the corners of his eyes. It lifted Arla's own chest and made her feel taller than she was. She really enjoyed seeing joy in his face like that.

When the laughter faded, they stood in silence for a while, staring at the running stream. She wondered when she was supposed to speak next, or if she did, would she say the right thing?

When she couldn't stand the quiet anymore, she finally asked, "So, what do you want to do?"

"Excuse me?" Leo seemed startled at the break of quiet. He may have preferred the soundless standing.

"Well, I thought we could spend time together." She scratched her head, hoping it didn't sound too weird.

Raising an eyebrow, he said, "I thought you called us here because of a dire situation, like your magic problem."

"Not at first. That just happened last night after I sent the note."

He cocked his head. "You wanted me to come here, so we could just… do nothing?"

Her eyes widened. "Yes. No. Well, it's nothing, but also *not* nothing either." She slightly kicked the grass on the ground, avoiding his gaze.

He looked at her deeply, his dark eyebrows slightly furrowing in trying to read her mind before a look of understanding finally settled on his features.

He blinked a couple of times, thinking. He seemed to be debating whether to leave or not and then finally he responded, "Okay. Let's spend some time together then."

The night moved on as the moon tracked along its path and the duo sat on the grass, talking incessantly. It was strange to talk about everything and nothing at the same time and still enjoy the company.

Well. It *was* enjoyable until Leo said something truly nasty.

"Ew!" she gagged.

Leo frowned at her in a playful way. "You said you wouldn't judge."

"But they smell so bad!"

"They are delicious," he defended.

Arla had known that there were dishes that served cooked larvae with darkened salty sauce, but she never thought anyone truly loved the flavor.

"My turn," Leo reminded as he twisted toward her.

"Wait, how many questions are we at?" Arla counted with her fingers. "Ten. So we each have only one more."

It was a game she had seen others play in the courtyards of the castle. A simple back-and-forth of asking questions to get to know someone better. She had always hoped to play it with someone.

"Alright." Leo nodded. He was sitting across from her in the grass, his legs crisscrossed beneath him. "What do you want for your future?"

Leo was not one to ask simple questions, was he?

"Um," Arla pondered. "I don't know."

"You don't know what you want for your life?"

"I..." She thought about what she truly wanted. "I want to spend more time with Jun and... eat meals with my family..." It was simple, she knew, but it was what she truly desired. She knew he meant what grand things she might want from life, but it wasn't what she wanted.

A saddened look crossed his face before he nodded in understanding. Did he pity her?

"And you?" she asked, trying to move on.

Throwing his arms behind his head, Leo looked up in thought before responding. "In a perfect world, I would leave the army and become a farmer, like my father was, and my mother would not have to work again. I would grow new crops and make dishes no one has ever tasted before."

Arla loved this dream, it sounded delicious. She scooted forward in excitement. "Maybe I could be your official taste tester. That could be my future."

"It would be a popular position. You would have to pass the tests," Leo said.

"I will prove to you that I'm the best choice!" Arla was gripped with determination.

He nodded. "We shall see, Princess."

Arla hesitated. "Can I ask you a favor?" Leo arched his eyebrow, a signal that he was curious and ready to listen. "I know we're not supposed to talk or do anything in public and I understand that. But... At least in private, can you call me by my name? Not Princess. Or Your Highness, but my name."

Leo leaned back and contemplated the complicated dangers of calling a royal by their first name. Finally, he responded, "In our kitchens, the spices are very bland and common. They do not flavor the foods the way they should. But the royal kitchens have every-thing imaginable. If you were to supply me with certain ones, then I will consider your request."

Hope filled her. "Okay, I can do that. Name whatever you want! I'll sneak it away and bring it to you here." She wondered if she sounded too eager. Too late now.

He smirked. "Then it's a deal... Arla."

Hearing her name slip from his lips was the sweetest sound she'd ever heard, filling her body with a warmth that could light a fire. Sweeter than the frogs and flies that sang into the night air around them.

"Okay, my turn." She crawled closer to him, intending for a tougher question. "How did you become captain at such a young age?"

This question was easier for him to answer.

"I believe you can grow and train to be successful at anything if you apply the right principles," he replied, ever so seriously.

"Oh?" she said. "And what are those principles?"

Leo slanted forward, a playful look on his face, like he was telling her a secret. "First is: focus."

Arla scooted even closer, dragging the bottom of her skirt along the wet grass. She needed to know these secrets. "Yes? And second?"

He was smiling, which felt endless to her.

It was then that Arla realized how close they were. They were so close that she could feel the heat radiating off him. Even on this chilly night, her body felt like it was burning up.

"Wha—What's the second?" she sputtered, trying to ignore the constriction in her chest.

An inch. His nose and lips were only an inch away from hers. Leo must have noticed what little space was left between them too because there was a shift in his gaze like he suddenly realized something. His jaw tightened as his hand curled into a fist. Could he hear how fast her heart was beating right now? They both sat there frozen, not daring to move further in or away.

And then in a hushed voice, he drew out a breath, "Discipline."

Keeping his fist clenched, he slid away from her and climbed to his feet. "I think it's time for me to go."

She didn't argue as she rose as well. He was right, it was time for them to go back home.

CHAPTER 24

Arla tucked the journal into a wooden box in the back of her armoire, careful to lay it gently on its side so its pages would not tatter any more than they had. After the entire journey through The Forest, it had become more damaged than when she found it, which radiated a deep guilt within her. She had apologized to it multiple times already, even though she knew it had no real feelings.

As she carefully closed the lid of the box with a click, she wondered if she would ever find out who this survivor was and why they didn't tell anyone about their findings. She also wondered if they were even still alive. She hoped they were, so she could thank them and tell them that their words had warned them when nothing else did.

Arla closed the double doors of the armoire, the afternoon sun beaming into her room. She had nothing to do today, which was typical. She went through the same motions she did before her adventure, wandering the halls and reading in the library. Her mood for books about The Forest had waned since she had lived the experience, so she opted for historical reads today.

The dull routine reminded her of what Leo had asked her the night before.

What do you want for your future?

Despite how cruel and terrifying The Forest was, it was also the place she had felt the most alive. Under the dark canopies, people actually spoke to her and wanted her opinion. She helped others and saved lives. She had a purpose and a place, but now that she was back home, she was no one again, ignored and left to live in the shadows. She had hoped it would have changed when she entered the throne room with the healing plant in her hand, but clearly, it was a fool's dream.

With those depressing thoughts, she wandered the stone halls again until the sun had risen halfway through the sky. Maybe she should just eat something, just to have something to do. At this seemingly logical suggestion, Arla pivoted towards the kitchen.

That's when she saw the guards. Instinctively moving out of the way, Arla was surprised to see the guards change direction so that they were still heading towards her. Confused, she leaned against the wall to let them pass, but instead, they stopped right in front of her.

She blinked at them in puzzlement. Since when did the guards look for her?

"Princess, your father requests your presence in his study," the leader of the guards said.

This was new.

Her father's wide, strong body sat behind the great oak desk that resided in the back center of his study. The chair he sat on was custom-made for him and yet it still looked too small for her father, who was still a very intimidatingly large man at forty-five years of age.

She stood before him, her hands fidgeting with the hem of her sleeves, waiting for him to speak. He never greeted her when she arrived or even looked up to acknowledge her presence. Instead, his attention remained on a slew of papers on the desk, with some already crumpled in his hands.

After what felt like a lifetime of silence, her father finally signed the last of the papers and lifted his eyes to hers. "I have made a decision about your future."

She didn't like the sound of this.

"You will move to Lerindor and train to become a Sister of Hemdalve."

The world slipped sideways.

Air knocked out of everything, pressing hard against her chest.

A Sister of Hemdalve was a woman who studied and surveyed The Forest. They did not protect it or go inside of it, they merely watched it for any changes, no matter how small. A completely facetious role acting as a mask for what it really was: a place to discard unwanted women. And he was sending her there. To be tucked away into obscurity and forgotten permanently.

"You leave tomorrow," he stated.

She didn't hear the rest of what he said. His mouth moved, but the words did not reach her ears. Her father was sending her away from everything she ever knew.

Guards appeared on each of her sides, ready to escort her to her room.

"Why are you doing this?" she asked with trembling lips.

"It's for your own good," he simply replied, having already moved on to the next pile of papers, like his business with her was over. He wouldn't say it, but she knew why. He was tired of her lurking presence, reminding him of what she was: a shame to his bloodline, a symbol to others that he, the great king of Ulsana had produced a child with no magic.

But now that he had a true heir, he didn't need to keep her around anymore. A hand wrapped tightly around her arm, tugging at her through the door.

No!

Another tug came, harder this time, but her feet remained planted. "Please, Father, I won't get in the way. You'll barely notice me around if that's what you want," she begged. "Please don't send me there."

But he didn't respond, he just kept shuffling his papers. He waved a hand for the guards to take her. A sharp yank and her feet skidded backward as she was lifted from the ground.

"Let me go!" she shouted.

A flash of something.

Arla was back in The Forest.

A woman screamed as hands wrapped around her arm and torso, lifting her from the ground. She was reaching for something. Her golden-brown hand stretched out in front of her, but the vision was blurred by Arla's—no, The Woman's—tears. Arla felt her heart breaking, shattering into pieces. A pain so great, she thought all her bones would snap.

And then the Whispers came.

They stampeded into her mind, thrashing and scurrying around, trying to find a crack to push through. They seared into the back of her eyes, making her shut them in pain. The guards pulled her through the door.

No! Stop! she shouted, but when she opened her mouth, different words tumbled out instead. *"I'et lamel al'para-tet!"*

The stones from the walls fractured and fell out like teeth as vines burst through every crevice they could find, wrapping themselves against the walls, snaking down to the ground. The leafy plants rose, tangling into themselves until they created the body of an antlered blob that was too big for the room. Its head hit the ceiling, crumpling part of the plaster above it. The moment the monster realized it was alive, it roared, shaking the books off the wall shelves and swinging its vine arms, ensnaring the guards' feet, pulling them to the floor. They immediately let Arla go, drawing their swords at the thick vines.

Arla covered her own head to dodge the thorny arms of the creature that whipped around wildly with no target.

"Hal'en!" Hot red fire looped around the monster, searing its vines body into burnt ash, layer by layer, until it was completely gone.

The guards gathered themselves, some scampering to their feet in embarrassment and awe, wondering where the creature had come from. And then, as if through slow realization, they turned to face her.

Arla shook. She didn't know the words would do that. Her father, who was standing up now, finally cast his eyes on her. His mouth agape, his eyes wide.

"You," he breathed. "You have magic."

There was no escape from the truth now.

"How?" He meant, how could this be possible.

"I don't know," she replied. "It happened in The Forest…"

"The Forest," he muttered to himself. "It grants magic once again…"

"Please, don't send me to Lerindor," she begged in a small voice, still shaking.

"Shhh. Do not worry, you are not going anywhere." He went to her, putting his hands on her shoulders. It was so oddly gentle and kind. When she dared to look up, she realized he was smiling at her. Actually smiling.

There was something deep within her that told her not to believe the glint in his eyes, but Arla buried it back, not wanting to listen. Pride and hope filled the space it left behind, and she smiled back at him, tearing up with joy.

"At last…" he said. "My real daughter has arrived."

CHAPTER 25

A bright beam of sunlight cut across her face. Arla awoke with a start, her thick hair in knots as she lay twisted in her blankets. An elderly woman, at least in her fifties, stared right back at her.

"Good morning, Your Highness."

Alra blinked repeatedly, making sure she was seeing someone real.

"Time to get up. You have a busy day today." The elderly woman placed a wrinkled, thin hand under Arla's and gently pulled her from the bed. Two girls, younger than Arla, were dusting her armoire and vanity table in her bed chamber. The thick curtains to her window were open, letting in the morning sun.

Was she imagining things? Arla hadn't seen any servants in her room since she was a child. What were they all doing here? A new pair of servants arrived through her front door, without even knocking, and carried in a bulky wooden trunk inlaid with gold flecks. The elderly woman who had woken her guided Arla to the bathroom. Like a dazed fawn, she followed, barely hearing what the old woman was saying. Arla did not understand.

Arla halted her steps. "I'm sorry, but what is going on? Why are you in my room?"

The old woman gently smoothed out her cotton skirt. "Your father ordered us to get you ready today. He wants you to join him in the dining hall for breakfast."

"For breakfast?" Arla was dreaming. She had to be. In the last six years, she had never been invited to dine with her father, and now... She remembered how he'd held her shoulders yesterday. *At last, my real daughter has arrived.*

Could it be...?

Arla was washed and scrubbed from head to toe and was a little embarrassed when the water turned a bit murkier than she would have liked when she soaked in the rose-infused bath. Rough sponges exfoliated her skin until it was soft and subtle, like a child's. The young servant girls did not miss any spot except for her forearms, which Arla had asked them to leave alone. Getting those layers of scar tissue grated with the coral-like sponge they were using was not something she wanted to experience.

The elderly woman, who eventually introduced herself as Linuth, brushed her hair until it shined in a way it hadn't for years. And when she was finally all clean, Linuth asked, "So, which dress would you like to wear today?"

Another servant held up a bright coral dress, adorned with crystals on its hems for Arla to look at. It flared out like a lampshade at the bottom, and its neckline swooped low in the way the other court ladies had theirs. It was the newest style, and Arla had ten to choose from in this mysterious trunk the servants had brought.

"Do you have one with long sleeves?" Arla sheepishly asked.

Linuth's eyes flashed to Arla's scarred arms and replied kindly, "Of course, my lady."

Staring in the mirror, Arla had to admit she looked… beautiful. At least, by her standards. The ultramarine dress she chose cinched around her waist that made her straight figure look curvier than she had ever seen it and the makeup… it was light and brought out her flushing cheeks. Her lips were painted a sheen roseate that made them look plumper and her usually dull, pale face was glowing, having absorbed all the lotions they had rubbed into it after the bath.

Arla was no longer a clown in a dress that was too big for her. She was… she seemed… like a true princess.

Linuth nodded in approval. "May we escort you to breakfast?"

It was odd not to jump into the cracks of the walls toward the shadowed tunnels she was so used to traveling to get from place to place in the castle. Where she used to slunk alone in those hollow passageways, she was now surrounded by an entourage of ladies in waiting that made way for her down the hallways to the dining hall. *This is what it must feel like to be important.*

She didn't even need to reach for the brass handles of the dining hall. Guards opened it for her without a word.

Sunlight beamed over her as she entered, glittering the copper plates and silver cups that waited on the dining table, and there sitting at the head of it was her father. Mathus looked up and, to her greatest shock, acknowledged her presence. He didn't look away or grimace, he just gave her a quick, apathetic expression and then went on to eat from his plate. Her heart overfilled with such joy that she thought for sure it could flood the entire room.

To his right was Ametha, dressed in a beautiful ivory gown, who was in the middle of sipping her cup of water when her eyes caught Arla's entrance. The princess waited for the look of disdain, but it never came. Instead, there was another expression on the queen's face: calm approval.

To the king's left was Norendra, with her tight braids and her plain black dress. Only her expression did not shift when she looked at Arla. Her thin lips were permanently fixed in a straight line as she motioned for Arla to come sit next to her.

She moved as gracefully as she could, tucking her dress to the side, so it didn't get caught when the chair was scooted back in for her. She prayed to the Whispers that she didn't mess this up. To her great relief, her dress did not catch, and she managed to sit as gracefully as a swan on the thick wooden chair.

Norendra's judging eyes saw her accomplish the task and had no other conclusion to make other than that Arla prevailed. Arla suppressed a grin.

It was strange to be sitting so close to them. It felt like she was floating, the entire room made of light and dreams as she breathed it in. She wanted to ask where Jun was, but she was afraid that if she spoke, it might break the spell. Besides, her father had always said he never wanted to hear her talk unless spoken to, so she wasn't going to ruin this moment by angering him. She didn't even dare to reach for any food.

Norendra pushed the chopsticks beside Arla's plate closer to her. "Eat," she commanded, gesturing to the baked chicken in the middle of the table and the serving bowls of rice noodles with vegetables and various black dipping sauces.

Arla's mouth watered, wanting to dive into them all like a rabid animal, but instead, she graciously cut a small piece of the chicken and put it on her plate.

She took it into her mouth, and it instantly melted, making her want to roll her eyes back in ecstasy. She daringly reached for a few more helpings, along with a bowl of noodles and some fermented cabbage and—oh, and the cut lettuce drenched in citrus dressing on the side as well. *Might as well finish it with another bowl of noodles,* she thought, so she wouldn't have to reach over Norendra twice to get it later.

And that's how Arla ended up with a full plate and two bowls beside her, enough to feed three people. Hopefully, no one would notice. She made sure to eat slowly to not seem like a starving child.

"I'm glad you are enjoying the food," Ametha finally said. Arla almost choked on her noodles. Did the queen just speak to her?

"I am," Arla dared to reply.

Her father stabbed a piece of chicken with his knife and tore into it. "How did The Forest grant you magic?" Mathus was not one for small talk.

She quickly put her chopsticks down, along with the spoon. "I'm... I'm not sure. I was going for the healing plant and then the wind picked up and I saw—" Arla felt something pull at her, drawing her away from the words she was about to say. "I saw complete darkness and then I woke up with the plant in my hand."

Mathus exchanged a glance with Norendra. "The monster you summoned. There has never been any magic like that before. It is... interesting." He stabbed another piece of chicken. She could have sworn she heard wonderment in her father's tone. "I want you to show the people your magic as soon as possible. We shall hold a ball to debut it. Let the word spread that the Princess of Ulsana is from a strong bloodline." And then her father cracked a smile. He looked proud.

She forgot about the food and the dress and everything; this was a dream, she was sure of it. A wonderful, beautiful dream.

"With all due respect, Your Highness," Norendra cut in, "I would advise waiting at least until the princess has an understanding of her newfound abilities before presenting her to the people. If she unleashes her magic and cannot control it, it may show more weakness than power."

Mathus contemplated this for a moment by chewing on the chicken, slowly, as they all sat in silence waiting for his decision. It felt like ages. Like he was intentionally being slow to show how much power he had over them. That he could make them wait all day if he wanted to.

When he finally swallowed his bird, he responded to his most trusted advisor, "I agree. You will train her as you've done before for her debut in a month's time." He turned to Arla. "And I trust she will gain control quickly if she is deserving of her title."

There was a tinge of threat to it, but Arla didn't care.

She stared wide-eyed at her father and gave a slight nod to tell him she would not disappoint him. She would never disappoint him again for the rest of her life if she could. He seemed to accept her answer as he leaned back, placing a napkin on the table.

Ametha and Norendra immediately dropped their chopsticks and spoon and placed their napkins on the table as well. When Arla reached for her spoon for a drink of her soup, her teacher gave her a sharp nudge in her side with her elbow. Norendra's stare bore into her until she realized what she was supposed to do. She put her spoon down and placed her napkin on the table as well, to show she was done eating. Because if the king was done, everyone was done.

Her stomach cramped, twisting and churning. The rich food, as delicious as it was, was going to be too much for her gut again. She ignored the sharp throbbing that was most definitely going to grow until later in the afternoon.

"Arla."

Arla swiveled her head to realize her father had just addressed her by her name.

"You are going to accompany me on my judgments today. It is time you understand what a ruler does, so when your brother becomes king, you can assist him as Norendra does me."

She could almost scream in joy at that point. Her father wanted her to join him in a royal duty. She couldn't believe it.

In as calm a voice as she could muster, she responded, "Yes, Father."

A tug from within drew her away. Telling her to be careful, but she waved it off. It was just her fear getting in the way of her being happy. This was everything she ever wanted, and now, after all this time, she was going to get it, and nothing was going to stop her from having that.

All those years of hurt and pain. It wasn't her father's fault. He was just trying to push her to be strong. To trigger the magic out of her. He had so much responsibility for presenting a powerful front, and any weakness would have hurt the entire kingdom. He was just doing his duty. If anything, Arla could understand what it was like to do something drastic to protect what was important. He was a king, and kings protected their kingdoms.

It was all in the past now. Like Simion said, it was about the future. No more forests. No more pain. The future would be happy and full of hope and love. Arla was sure of it.

CHAPTER 26

They were in the throne room again. The same room Arla had decided that she would risk her life to go to The Forest. It felt like a lifetime ago. The fall leaves had turned and abandoned their places on the trees and now the windiest days of it were almost over as the season got ready to turn to spring.

Arla had heard that other kingdoms like Nysenia had bitter seasons where the water froze and white powder fell from the sky. Luckily, Ulsanans' experience of cold was not as drastic, where a thin layer of fur over themselves was enough to keep them warm during the worst of nights. The water may have been frigid, but it never froze.

Today, the throne room played host to the judgments of her father as he heard the qualms of High-Borns who had trekked from all corners of the kingdom to ask for his final judgment. Hundreds lined up before the king as he sat like an immovable statue on his giant royal seat. Even though her father was a large, formidable man, the throne was larger still.

Guards flanked the turquoise and golden inlaid walls, to remind the nobles to behave. Norendra stood next to her father, close enough to be heard if she spoke softly, but far enough away to pay respect to his space. Arla, on the other hand, was seated far behind and to the other side. Mathus wanted her to listen and observe, but not interfere, which was what she intended to do.

The only company she had was the large portrait of her father and the first king hanging on the wall beside her. Her father's portrait was significantly larger and portrayed a younger version of him, with the same scowl and harshness that endured years after this painting. The other was of the first original king, and it was older and more faded, but the majesty of it still remained.

She didn't know anyone could look colder than her father, but in this painting, King Namkil Seojin looked like a fierce warrior who probably took more lives than he saved during his time. He had the same black hair as she and Mathus did, but while her father's was mid-length to his shoulders, this king's hair was shorter, closer to his head with a little bit more bounce to it.

It was said that it was his harshness that allowed Ulsana to thrive in the first place. To keep this large amount of land from the other rulers required an iron hand and more bloodshed than Arla was willing to fully comprehend. He was the one who fought to keep The Forest as part of Ulsana's territory during the splitting of kingdoms. His army was a lot bigger then. This grand win was the reason why his portrait remained permanently displayed next to every new portrait of the current Ulsanan ruler that hung beside him, being continually replaced, while he remained.

"Some have disappeared completely," someone said.

Arla moved her attention back to the matter at hand. She had become so lost in looking at the painting that she had forgotten she was supposed to pay attention. A female noble, dressed in deep sapphire, was addressing her father. The deep wrinkles under her eyes showed she was holding a great weight and losing sleep over it.

"I do not know where the workers went, but they cannot be found, and the ones who remain..." She looked like she was about to cry or scream, but Arla couldn't tell for sure. "They demand higher wages, or they will not work." She lowered her voice. "They are threatening to retaliate if they do not get their demands."

The king's shoulders tensed. Norendra's face twisted into a sneer of disgust.

"These Low-Borns are getting more unruly by the year," her father said. "I will send my soldiers to you, and they will dampen this insolence." Mathus waved at one of his guards, who came running. "These commoners must be taught to know their place."

The noblewoman teared up. "Thank you, my king. You are too gracious." She bowed so low, Arla thought her head might hit her knee.

Mathus nodded before saying to the guard, "And when you return, bring me back the hand of the leader of these Low-Borns who demanded these higher wages."

"My king, don't the workers need their hands to do their work?" Norendra asked in a light manner.

"That is why they were born with two hands," the king replied. The gleam in his tone made Arla shiver. Was this her father's sense of justice?

Norendra nodded, a hint of a smile on her lips. "A clear message, indeed."

The king smirked as he motioned for the next dispute. This time, two noblemen shuffled towards him, keeping as far apart from each other as they could. Arla could feel the animosity radiating from both of them. They were around equal age, probably in their forties, while one was tall with dark baggy eyes, the other was shorter with a square chin and bald head.

The short one spoke first. "My king, this nobleman and I have farmlands that share a border. I grow wheat and barley, and the seeds of those plants have blown over to this man's land." He pointed an accusatory finger at the tall High-Born next to him. "Those plants have wrongfully grown on his land, and he means to profit off them, but as they are *my* seeds, I believe I deserve those profits as my own."

"Your seeds blew onto my land!" the tall one shrieked. "How could I have controlled what they did?"

The short, bald-headed nobleman scowled. "It doesn't matter how they got there; it is *my* property!"

The tall one turned to Mathus. "Your Highness, it is my soil and water and care that grew the plants. I believe I deserve the crops for my labor."

Mathus seemed extremely bored with this squabble, looking at them both like children quarreling over nothing. He raised his hand and quickly made a judgment. "The crops belong to the one who owns the seeds. Thus," he addressed the bald man, "Lord Lesandres will have the profit."

Lesandres? Why does that name sound familiar? Arla thought.

"But Your Highness! That is—that is not fair! This cannot be!" The tall one was cracking, his demeanor devolving into a temper tantrum.

Her father's eyes narrowed into slits. "You dare challenge my judgment?"

A shocked hush fell in the line of waiting nobles as all eyes turned to the king.

"Your Highness, I would lose more than half my crops," the tall man pleaded. "It wouldn't be enough to feed my family and my workers."

Mathus leaned forward and spoke in a voice that reeked of violence. "Do you question my judgment?"

"...I meant no disrespect." The nobleman was shaking now. He looked to the others for support. "I just wanted to be heard."

The king leaned back on his throne, more relaxed, but Arla's grip still tightened on her chair. "And you are heard," Mathus said in a calm voice.

The man smiled in relief, allowing himself to let his guard down.

"But you disrespect me. And I cannot let that go unpunished." Mathus raised his hand in the air. All the color drained from the nobleman's face. Arla's heart pounded against her chest; she couldn't watch this.

"Please," he begged, backing away from the king, trying to find an escape.

In an emotionless tone, Mathus spoke. "*Hal'en.*"

The man screamed as flames twisted up his arm like a living snake, melting his skin from the bone like candle wax. Everyone was frozen in place, pretending not to hear the blood-curdling wail that filled the room. With a snap of Mathus's finger, the fire snuffed out, leaving only a charred nub where the High-Born's arm had been. The tall noble immediately fainted from the agony. No one rushed to help him.

Arla resisted the urge to throw up as the stench of burnt flesh filled her nose. Guards quickly dragged the unconscious man away and then... everyone acted like nothing had happened. Lesandres smiled widely as if he had just seen entertainment rather than a man losing his arm.

Arla clutched her lower arm. She had made a mistake. Nothing had changed. Her father was as cruel as he ever was. He would never stop burning.

No. That was in the past. This is different.

She was valuable to her father now. He wasn't going to hurt her like he had just hurt this nobleman.

Those times are over. They have to be.

But what about the others?

Lesandres bowed to her father. "Thank you for your judgment, my king. I would be remiss if I didn't offer you a meal at my estate. We are just outside the city, and I have plenty of fine wine and food grown from my lands. I would be eternally grateful if you would honor me with your presence."

The way this nobleman was complimenting her father, she could practically see him kiss his boots with his words, and Mathus, no matter how brutal he was, also had an ego that loved to be doted on. And so, her father agreed.

"Princess Arla will be joining us, as well," Mathus stated without consulting Lesandres.

She was *invited*?

The nobleman nodded. "Of course, my king, anything you wish."

The travel procession was readied and left within two days of the invitation. Her father and Lesandres led the march down and out of the city grounds with Arla and Norendra trailing just behind them on their own horses. They had made it only halfway down the city hill when the street was blocked by a small crowd of people circling something.

As their horses trotted closer, she could see it was a dispute between a middle-aged woman and a man in drab cotton, colored in washed-out brown. A cart had fallen over with grains of rice mixed with bags of garbanzo beans. The two merchants seemed ready to tear each other's heads off.

And there in the middle stood Leo in his soldier's armor, trying to stop the situation from getting out of hand. Arla's heart lurched a little. This was the first time she had seen him in public.

"Look at these Low-Borns, fighting like rats for scraps," Lesandres muttered to no one in particular.

"Make way for the king!" a guard shouted.

The merchants quickly forgot their squabble as they saw the procession, immediately stepping out of the way. Arla didn't know whether to acknowledge Leo or not. Whether she should even look at him because if she did, would that get him in trouble? Would it be obvious they knew each other?

She chose to err on the side of caution and not to look and she would have easily passed him without any issues if her father hadn't stopped his horse right next to the dark-haired soldier.

"You are the captain who went into The Forest." Her father's words were statements, as he looked down at Leo from his horse.

"Yes, Your Highness." Leo's tone was devoid of any emotion. Like a hollow shell.

"He is quite young for a captain," Lesandres observed. "Still, he must have some skill to succeed in bringing back the plant for you, Your Highness."

Leo's eyes flashed to Lesandres, and a raging flare shot through his face. Whatever mask he was wearing instantly wore down when he saw the bald nobleman on his horse. That's when Arla realized who Lesandres was. *Of course.* Leo had told her in The Forest. This was the nobleman who his mother worked for, the one who had labored his father to death. No. *Beaten* his father to death.

"I sent him with thirty soldiers," the king said lazily. "And he only came back with two. I would not call that a success."

Leo's jaw twitched.

"For them, the measure of success is quite low. Most of my workers are happy just to be fed," the nobleman said. "Are you like that too, boy?" He raised his voice like Leo was stupid, clearly not recognizing who he was. "Are you grateful to at least eat as well as our gracious king allows? You must be. Better than eating scraps like a pig."

Leo's face remained expressionless, even, and cold, like the ice mask he wore when Arla first met him.

"Oh, come now, it's just a joke, young captain," Lesandres smirked. "Isn't that right, Princess? Isn't it funny?"

Arla wanted to push the ugly man off his horse. Maybe she would do it, just tackle him to the cobblestone and wrestle him down until he apologized. But then she noticed her father watching her from the corner of his eye. This was a moment that would solidify to him which side she was on.

She forced a smile. "Yes, it is funny."

"What about it is funny, daughter?" Mathus pressed.

Arla hesitated. It was a test. She let the silence waver for too long. "The joke was funny."

"What, specifically, was funny about the joke?" He was in no mood for clever words.

The air tensed. Arla suddenly wished she wasn't there. She wanted to jump into the secret tunnels in the castle and disappear into the shadows where she couldn't be seen, but her father continued to stare at her, waiting. The silence stretched for an excruciating length until Arla knew she could not avoid it anymore.

Without looking at Leo, she finally breathed out, "Low-Borns are filthy and poor. That is why they are just like pigs."

She made the mistake of glancing at Leo. Something cracked in his face. A flash of pain. And then the cold wall froze over again. His eyes never met hers, but she knew what she did.

Her father was satisfied with the answer as he turned his horse and marched off, expecting the party to follow him. Arla kicked her horse lightly to follow, not daring to look at Leo again as she passed him.

CHAPTER 27

Lesandres's castle was just outside the city walls; it was smaller and less grand than the king's but still boasted the same design and even materials down to the same stone. Arla wondered if that was on purpose. Maybe the nobleman wanted to emulate her father's home, or maybe he even fancied himself a sort of king in his own lands. That's what Leo had said about Lesandres, and she thought the captain's judgment was exactly right.

The stable boys helped them off their horses and they were quickly led past the wooden gates to the main banquet hall, where tables were filled with an overabundant number of plates and bowls loaded with meat pies and fermented fish. Lines of green beans slathered in various chili oils and boiling soups of sour flavors welcomed them.

The feast had begun rapidly with her father at the honored front of the main table along with Lesandres and his family. Arla was seated at the end, barely able to hear the conversations between the two men. Norendra ate in silence beside her, having chosen this spot over another beside her father, which surprised Arla.

Watching her father's icy demeanor melt with every new wine glass, he almost looked human. He laughed and ate, slamming the table with his fists in fits of jovial satisfaction. It was so strange to see him this way, as she had only been subject to his contempt and coldness all her life. The nobleman joked and continually complimented the king, who took it all in stride. Lesandres knew how much was too much and would always reel it back when he saw any indication of annoyance on her father's face. It was an art form and quite interesting to see this nobleman work.

The servants were also different here than the royal ones back at home. They seemed thinner and more tired. Arla looked at each and every face, trying to see if any of them could be Leo's mother. Did she work in the kitchens or amongst the dining servers?

Lesandres shooed away a server when they tried to bring out a new plate, "What did I say, idiot? No more food. Bring out the wine." His tone of contempt made Arla remember how they had treated Leo earlier. How *she* had treated Leo.

"Norendra," she started, "why must we be so cruel to them?"

Who had decided that Low-Borns were less worthy than High-Borns and put them in service roles?

"You know this answer, girl," Norendra replied in her signature curt manner as she sliced into the meat pie in front of her. "They have no magic, and their weakness threatens our power."

The dim candles across the walls and tables barely illuminated the food in front of her, which made it even easier for Arla to ignore it, having lost her appetite. Her hands lay heavy on her lap. "When I had no magic, I was still treated better than them. I was no less worthy than they are."

"No, you are much more worthy now," her teacher retorted as she took a small sip of wine.

"Because I have magic?"

Ignoring her, Norendra continued to speak. "We treat them this way to remind them of what they are. We must always keep them in their place."

"Must we?"

Another roar of laughter and merriment came from down the table, where her father and Lesandres ordered more wine from the servant girls.

"Stop talking nonsense," Norendra warned in a low voice. "If we have children with these Low-Borns, new generations would have weaker ties to magic, until it becomes completely lost to us. That is why fraternizing is outlawed between classes. High-Borns must be with High-Borns to protect and preserve magic. It is our duty to uphold our way of life."

The law against Low and High-Born relationships was nothing new to Arla; she had heard it over and over again. The reason they could not interact was for fear that it would turn into something real, like love, something that could lead to children. There were stories of these forbidden unions that always ended in exile or execution.

After dinner, Norendra commanded Arla to follow her outside, far from Lesandres's castle, to the edge of the woods. The fall chill demanded she wear a coat, but it still did not keep her warm enough. The stars shone brightly above them as tall oaks and walnut trees created a wall between them and farmlands on the other side. She watched the trees suspiciously. Arla still couldn't look at them the same way.

"Why are we here?" Arla's teeth clattered as she wrapped her arms around herself. She should have brought a thicker coat.

Norendra, unaffected by the cold, or anything in life, replied, "Training. Your magic involves summoning unnatural creatures, and since you cannot control them, it is safer to practice in a wide-open area, away from others."

This was honestly the last thing Arla wanted to do. She wished to sleep. Her eyelids were growing heavy from the meal she just ate, and the warmth of the fire inside made her want to curl up into a soft blanket and nibble on a warm cookie. A sharp wind blew under her dress, chilling her legs to remind her that she was not going to be comfortable as long as she was out here.

The last time Norendra had pulled her in for a lesson was almost three years ago. After Mathus had given up, Norendra held out hope for another three years that Arla's magic would appear until finally quitting for good. On that last day, Norendra had calmly put down the lesson book and left the room, muttering, "Such a shame" as she closed the door behind her.

And now her former teacher stood in front of her, taking up the task once again.

"The first step is to learn how to summon your Whispers to you." Norendra circled her. "This can be done by having a calm mind and sturdy attitude. You must create an environment in your head that sets up a space for them to come in. Like opening a door."

Arla remembered when the Whispers cluttered into her head as if a gate had lifted and a tidal wave crashed against her skull. It was not something she wanted to experience again.

"And how do you deal with the pain?" she asked.

Norendra's thin eyebrows angled downward. "What pain?"

"The pain of the Whispers. The scratching and shrieking." Another cold gust blew across her body.

"Whispers are not painful," Norendra looked at her like she was weak. "They are soft and subtle, quiet. Like floating orbs in your mind. That is why they are called Whispers."

"But mine don't feel like small, quiet voices," Arla argued, trying to get her hair out of her face from the jostling air. "They're screaming at me. And there are so many of them. It's like a hundred voices are yelling at me at once."

"They are *yelling*?" Norendra paced a bit, thinking, the deadened leaves underneath her feet crunched at every step. "Could it be?" she muttered to herself. "It was said in the olden times, High-Borns could hear the entire language of The Forest. Whispers that allowed them to do grand things we cannot even imagine today. But ever since the Darkening, we're only able to hear a handful of words at most, disjointed phrases here and there. It's a fraction of the power our ancestors held."

"They're not saying just one or two words. Each of them is shouting full sentences," Arla paused. "Do you think I'm hearing the entire language?"

"I cannot be sure," Norendra answered. "But if you are hearing full sentences... then you would be the first High-Born in hundreds of years to do so."

A chill trembled down her spine. Arla had just thought that maybe because the Whispers were new to her, that she was just not used to what they sounded like. But now, she wondered if The Forest had given her more than she thought.

"Come." Norendra motioned for Arla to stand in front of her. "There is only one way to find out what you are capable of now."

And so, the lesson began. Arla was told to stand straight and keep a calm, open mind, calling the Whispers to come forth. Her legs were shaking from the cold, and it felt like the night had stretched infinitely in front of her like it would never end, yet she remained still, her eyes closed, listening to the rustle of leaves above her and the far-off bleats of woombles.

Patiently, she waited, but nothing happened. Arla sighed, opening her eyes.

"Can't you just tell me the words I have to say?" Her patience was thinning.

"It doesn't work like that," her teacher lectured, "Whispers can only be used by the person who hears them. That is why each of us cannot take the Whispers of another, even if we hear them from someone else."

"Okay, well, I remember one of the words, so I'll just say that one."

"Foolish girl. You may know the words, but if the Whispers do not tell you themselves, if they are not ready and at the tip of your own tongue, then you cannot use them. Even when I say *Benai*, my magic will not come because the Whispers have not readied themselves to me to use them. We are always at the mercy of the language."

Norendra raised her hand toward a tree. "But if I open the gates and I summon the Whispers to come to me in my head." Her fingers curled. "*Benai.*"

Arla's moonlit shadow stretched and lengthened, rising up from the ground like a floating cloak, a shadow whip, waiting for Norendra's command. "Then, it works."

Her teacher moved her hand in the air in an s-like pattern and the shadow moved with her. Closing her hand in a fist, the shadow whip dropped back into the shape of Arla's silhouette on the leaf-covered ground. "You must take control of them, Arla," she said.

Maybe that was the problem. A part of Arla was afraid to speak her Whispers. She didn't know what the magic would do, what terrifying new creature would burst from nowhere.

"What if it hurts someone?" she whimpered, her lips trembling, from cold or fear, she wasn't sure.

Her teacher folded her arms. "The magic will find a way to come out regardless. Better you learn to control it now, or it will control you and cause more damage."

Arla knew Norendra was right. Her lack of authority over her magic was probably going to get more people hurt than not trying to control it. She tried to think of why she would want to master it, to help motivate her. If she did, it would be to protect the people she cared about. Jun. Leo. Uro. Rose. She opened one of her eyes to see Norendra staring hard back at her. Maybe even protect Norendra, if she had to.

A faint noise came echoing into the dark. A small opening. She could feel it. But as fast as it had come, it shuddered out.

Breathing in deeply, Arla spoke out to the Whispers, wherever they were. *Come to me.*

They stampeded into her head, clawing at her skull. *Speak me. Speak me*, they begged. Arla clutched the sides of her head, squeezing her eyelids shut. The sharp pressure threatened to rupture her brain.

"There are too many of them," she cried.

Norendra's voice cut through the noise. "Command them, Arla."

Through the mess of tangled words, Arla tried. *Calm down. Settle and I will speak to you*, she promised. At first, they did not listen, almost enraptured by their own mission to crack out of her head.

Calm down.

They flurried in twisting cyclones in a panic.

I will let you out if you calm down. Calm down.

The more she repeated herself, the more they seemed to slow. To believe her.

Calm down.

The loud clanging became a crowded whine, still loud and overbearing, but not as painful as it was. She let go of her head, the throbbing still there.

"Good," Norendra said. "Now say the word."

Word. Her teacher still assumed there was only one. She turned inside her mind, a parent amongst thousands of hungry children.

Only one, she said. For a moment, she thought they might rebel, start shouting and screaming and threatening to hurt her again, but they didn't. Instead, one glowed, lighter than the rest, and suddenly snapped into place, the first slot of a jumbled barrel of coins with one hole.

"*Ceradas bival-ahala.*"

The wind picked up, rustling the branches above. From the tree-tops, a clicking noise hovered above them. An unnatural thing. One spindly, serrated insect-like leg pierced into the tree trunk as it hung from its branches. And then another dug into the bark, and another as it climbed down.

The blood rushed out of Arla's face.

She knew this creature.

Six giant legs crawled from the canopy followed by its skeletal bat-like head. It ducked its hideous head low as it landed on the ground, showing its rows of knife-like teeth.

Arla's entire soul went cold. This was the beast that almost took her life in The Forest, and it was back to finish the job. She wanted to scream, but her body remembered the acid burning her skin from the edges of its legs and froze, unable to move.

"Command it," Norendra hissed. Her teacher's face had paled too, having never encountered a monster like this before.

Arla shut her eyes. This was no time to crumble. She needed to try and push past the horror she felt. The creature took one step towards her. *Stop.* It took another step. *Stop!* It did not obey. Instead, it only grinned its teeth, ready to bite.

"I said stop! I order you!" Arla screamed. The creature lunged for her, outstretching its poisonous legs, ready to slice her in half.

"*Hologan.*" Norendra's words raised shadows from the ground which split into a thousand sharpened daggers that struck the beast on its side.

It screamed in rage as its acidic blood splurted against the trees, dissolving the bark from their trunks.

"*Benai.*" Shadow whips wrapped around the creature, holding it down to the ground by the neck. The beast struggled, trying to free itself but could not, and with one flick of Norendra's wrist, the shadows snapped the creature's neck, taking the blood-red fire from its eyes. The monster slumped and then crumbled into ash, floating away in the wind.

Arla's chest raised and lowered rapidly. She couldn't believe her magic summoned that monster again. Was it trying to kill her?

To her surprise, Norendra was also breathing heavily, her mouth agape. "I have never heard of someone speaking a full sentence in the language of The Forest. This power... it is too great for you to bear. I do not know if you can handle it."

Norendra closed her mouth, returning to the grim thin line it always was. She could see the conflict in her teacher's face and the fear, which wasn't reassuring to her at all. "I don't know why The Forest gave you this magic," she muttered. "But whatever the reason, we now have to deal with it."

It made Arla feel like a burden again. Even when she had magic, it wasn't good enough for her teacher because it was problematic and Arla was too weak to control it. *I didn't ask for this, you know,* Arla wanted to say, but it was too late for that now. She had it and it needed to be "dealt with", as Norendra had clearly said.

Arla suddenly felt light-headed as she fell to her knees. Dizziness consumed her, and before Arla could ask what was happening, Norendra was already answering her.

"Magic takes a significant amount of energy. You'll grow to endure it for longer periods of time." Norendra spun around, expecting Arla to follow her. "Soon, you will also understand what exactly each Whisper means. It will be clearer to you then."

I hope so, Arla thought as she struggled to get up again because right now, it felt like she never would.

CHAPTER 28

Their visit to Lesandres's home was brief. After a whirlwind of more food and lessons with Norendra the following two nights, they finally returned to the comforts of the castle. And by then, Arla was thoroughly exhausted. Norendra was just as merciless in training as she had been when Arla was a child.

The one thing she did enjoy was how often she got to dine with her father. Although they never sat directly next to each other or conversed, the very fact that she was allowed in the same room filled Arla with such joy that she thought she would be brought to tears many times. And when they settled back home, she was still continually called to join them at every meal. Every morning, she would wake up, fearful that this was the day they would tell her it was all a cruel joke and she was never to dine with them again, but, to her greatest relief, that never happened.

This particular morning, Arla was dressed again in fine clothing and placed in her seat next to Norendra. *Her* seat. It sounded too good to be true. The fact that she had sat in this chair often enough to know it was designated for her.

Ametha sat across from her, this time holding little Jun in her arms. Usually, nannies were tasked with feeding her baby brother and making sure he was taken care of, but Ametha had insisted he join her for breakfast today. She was intent on being a more hands-on mother than the other queens before her.

Ecstatic to finally see Jun outside his crib, Arla wanted to reach out and squeeze his chubby small hand, but she resisted. Looking at him squealing happily in Ametha's arms, she wondered about her own mother. If she had ever held Arla at the breakfast table the way Ametha held Jun before she passed away. Everyone had told her that her mother was kind and warm-hearted, and how devastated everyone was that she passed away shortly after giving birth to Arla. She had always wanted to ask for more details about it, but her father forbade anyone from speaking her name out loud or talking much about her at all. The only thing she ever got out of him was a scoff and a few curt words about how weak or soft-hearted she was. *A stronger woman would have survived*, he had said.

"How are the lessons progressing?" Mathus asked, not to Arla, but to his first advisor.

"They are going well," Norendra relayed. "Her control is getting better, if not slightly clumsy,"

Arla had learned to stay quiet and merely eat during these meals while Mathus and Norendra conversed about her progress. Ametha had learned this lesson too as her stepmother kept trying to feed Jun a spoonful of rice. Arla bit into a decadent, greasy mixture of fried dough filled with wilted cut cabbage and salty beef. It was pure heaven and yet her stomach still churned from the impact of the meal.

Too much salt and sugar.

Leo had said she needed to stay away from that stuff if she wanted to save her stomach. Thinking of the captain made Arla feel a pang of guilt she wasn't willing to face, so she turned away from it, focusing on taking another bite of the dough. She was happy now; she wasn't going to ruin it by feeling bad, right?

Needles pricked her abdomen, agonizing her stomach. It was too much.

Flagging down a nearby servant, Arla asked, "Is it alright if I could have seaweed soup?"

"Seaweed soup?" the server repeated, a little confused.

"Yes, with some mushroom in it maybe?" she sheepishly asked.

The servant bowed. "Of course, Princess."

"No." Mathus's voice boomed across the table. "The princess will eat whatever is on this table and learn to be grateful for what she has."

"I'm sorry, Father," Arla lowered her head. "I am grateful, truly. I just... my stomach just hurts, and I think the soup would be better for it right now."

His eyes narrowed in utter disgust at her. "Your stomach hurts? Are you a *child*? What person gets pain from simple bread? Your stomach does *not* hurt, and you will eat what you are told to eat." Mathus ripped a loaf of bread with his teeth. "Do not bring your weak nonsense here."

Was he right? Was she really just being weak? She should be able to eat anything and withstand it.... shouldn't she?

The rest of the breakfast was a blur. Arla no longer paid attention to what they were saying, instead staring at her filled plate she couldn't eat anymore because of the pain. *Why am I like this? I should be stronger. I should be able to get through a simple meal. Right?* She remembered how Leo had made the seaweed soup. He knew she was suffering, even when she didn't tell anyone, and he didn't make her feel weak or stupid.

Who was right? Her father or Leo? Was she weak or was she something else?

We are just as worthy as anyone else. Don't let anyone tell you any different.

He was so kind to her...

She remembered his face, trying to hide his hurt when she said he was a dirty pig. Admitting it even happened pained her too. And then she realized why he held a mask of ice on his face. If you expressed nothing, then no one would ever know they hurt you.

But somehow, she was able to get past the mask and she *did* hurt him.

And she had no excuses for it, except for a childish desire she wasn't sure she should hold onto anymore. Why did she hurt the person that cared for her over the person that so clearly didn't? She curled her fists under the table, a familiar self-hatred returning to her cheeks.

She waited until her father lifted the napkin onto the table to tell everyone they were done. When no one was looking, she swiped another fried ball from the plate and stuffed it into her satin dress, the grease instantly staining the fine fabric in her inside pocket. That was fine. She suddenly no longer cared if the dress was ruined.

The plan was simple, in its own convoluted way. She put a note in a bag of newly made arrows and sent a servant down to place it in the supply wagon that would be delivered to the soldier training grounds. The note was in code, one that Arla had agreed with Leo in the meadow after their long questions game.

They had thought the first note she had sent was too obvious and suspicious, so this time, if she needed him, she would send a note containing a list of the supplies, but hidden within the inventory note would be a date and time of where they should meet next. And because the list was addressed to Leo and he was a captain, it wouldn't be too odd to have these things sent to him from time to time.

He assured her that he would get it.

And so, two days later, she waited in the meadows for him to appear with the moonlight to guide him. But that night came and went, and he did not arrive. She thought maybe he had not received it, so she sent another bag of arrows with another note. And waited in the meadow and again he did not appear.

Standing alone in the short grass, with the rushing stream behind her, Arla started to suspect that he *did* receive the notes but had decided not to come.

This will not do.

Stopping back in the castle, she snuck into the servants' quarters through the winding underground tunnels until she stood in front of a large wooden closet that looked like someone hastily nailed it together with left-over planks of wood and broken nails. Slowly opening it, she found what she was looking for.

The kitchen staff usually had their own everyday clothing but changed into different ones when they cooked and served nobles, which they typically washed and put into this closet. Arla grabbed a simple cotton dress with a stained kitchen apron to wrap around herself. She threw over a tattered cloak and brushed out her curls that Linuth had painstakingly formed with a hot iron that morning.

Looking into her reflection in a nearby window, she was almost shocked at the transformation. Without proper fitting clothes or the fine satin of her usual everyday wear, Arla truly did look Low-Born. Maybe this is what everyone would look like if they didn't have access to the finest clothes and makeup to elevate their appearance.

She raised the cloak's hood over her head and slinked into the tunnels that twisted and turned until it led her right out of the castle walls, unnoticed, and into the main streets. Guards that had stopped her before were looking to protect nobles, not common kitchen staff, and so they paid her no mind as they assumed she was leaving after a hard day's work.

Arla had never ventured outside the castle at night into the city. She would hear horror stories of young maidens not knowing where they were, which streets and corners to avoid, and being attacked. To prevent herself from stumbling into the wrong parts, she stayed in the areas that were the most crowded, even if it increased her likelihood of being recognized.

The evening streets in Ulsana's main city were surprisingly still full of life at this hour. Many older men and women were stumbling out of taverns, drunk and singing. Other youths were racing around, throwing rocks and whatever else they could grab at each other. It wasn't so much violent as it was just… life being lived. Elderly women chatted around small fires in stone-lined circle fire pits and merchants who had just closed up were still sweeping out the trash that had collected in the front of their shops.

Arla followed the main street down and then jutted off to the right, where the crowd leaned out until it was just a few of them lingering. Young and old in chainmail hobbled toward and away from Arla's destination, inebriated already. Arla dodged them easily and finally found herself in front of the great iron gates of the soldier training grounds.

The front double metal doors were wide open, allowing the soldiers to leave and enjoy the night's delights, but guards flanked each side, still a line of security between the homes of soldiers and the common people. Her chest fell, knowing there was no way she was going to just waltz through.

She was hoping the lessons with Norendra were enough for her to pull off what she was about to do. Under her breath, she released her magic. "*I'et lamel al'para-tet.*"

Thin vines slithered out of the cracks between the street cobblestones. The Whispers scrambled over each other as Arla struggled to keep the evergreen shoots in her control. She curled her fists, demanding the vine follow her lead, but it didn't seem to hear her. She wanted it to create some noise, a distraction for the guards to run to, but the more she pushed it, the more the vines fought back.

Listen to me! she demanded.

The Whispers scoffed at her, pummeling against her skull in waves. The vines snaked around a guard's ankle. *No!* she directed. *Don't do that!* It yanked back the guard onto his back. The other guard shouted, running to his fallen comrade. Others hollered, wondering if they were being attacked or if the guard just slipped.

It wasn't her original plan, but it would do.

In the distraction, Arla slipped past them, through the threshold of the gates, and just as she was about to get away, her vine thrashed and wriggled out of control, whipping her off her feet.

She landed with a large *oof* on the hard surface, letting out a grunt. The fall sputtered the Whispers away and the vine immediately broke apart into ash.

"Hey!"

The guards had spotted her.

She crawled forward before taking off into a full sprint. Cutting across the main square, Arla slid through an opened door, tripping into the stables. The horses whined in her presence and the guards heard. Spinning on her heels, she pivoted to the other end door and flung it open. Then she jumped back and dove into a pile of hay in the corner, burying herself into the harsh straw. The ends of them pricked her skin as she dug herself in, cutting into her hands and face.

She heard the guards rush in.

"Where—?"

"Over there!"

They shot past her and through the open door. Only when she couldn't hear their footsteps anymore did she spring out of the hay.

Coughing from the dust, she pulled out as much straw from her clothes as she could, but getting them all was impossible.

A bit frustrated with her lack of control over her magic, Arla wished she had trained harder. She hadn't perfected anything with her newfound power. So far, she had only succeeded in summoning it, but not getting the Whispers to follow her. That was for future lessons, she hoped.

The barracks came up quickly, built an inch or two above the ground, each with three or four stairs letting you into the main doors. There were so many of these wooden homes, rows and rows of them. How was she going to find Leo? And even if she did, these homes were shared by multiple soldiers, so how was she going to get him alone?

From her peripheral vision, she saw her pursuers again, crossing the way. If they turned their heads now, she was going to be found. Dashing past the barracks, she saw a smaller wooden home. Not thinking what it was, she burst inside. Slamming the door behind her, she listened against the door for any pursuit. Did they see her?

Their footsteps rushed past, not suspecting this palace at all. She leaned closer, making sure they were far away.

"Who are you?"

Arla spun around and gasped.

Standing in front of her now, holding one towel in his hand in mid-ruffle of his wet dark brown hair, was Leo, and he was missing his shirt.

A chiseled chest glistened from the bath's moisture and Arla's eyes lowered to a toned abdomen that met the waistband of his thin sand-colored pants. Searing heat inflamed her ears and chest. She quickly looked away, seeing that she had accidentally tumbled into a bathhouse.

"I said, who are you?" Leo's eyes narrowed, violence in his voice as he slowly lowered the towel. The muscles in his arms rippled, showing signs he was ready to grab her if he needed.

Arla had forgotten she was wearing a hood. Before he sprung, she backed up and released the cloth from her head, "It's me!"

Leo's eyes widened and for a minute, he was horrified before he snapped back, "Arla, you can't be here."

He pulled her hood back over her face and took her by the elbow and hurriedly pulled her outside the bathhouse, still shirtless. She felt his barely dried chest, moistening the cloth against her arms as he led her in a direction she didn't know. His hurried pace did not stop until he pulled her inside another structure.

When he took the hood off her, she found herself in a small clay hut, with a firepit embedded into the wall, already lit and burning. Multiple levels of shelves of jars lined the walls, each containing leaves, spices, and other random things a kitchen usually had. There was a hole at the top, no doubt to let the smoke out, and one window behind her, which Leo now covered with a small, tattered, makeshift curtain.

"Where are we?" she asked, struck by the small, quaint feel of the place.

"The brick oven room. It's where we prepare some of the meals. No one comes here at this time, so we should be safe." Leo checked once more through the window for anyone who might have seen them and then shut the curtain for good.

"Were you going to cook something?" she asked, alluding to the already lit fire.

"I just come here to get privacy sometimes," he stated, putting his hand to his hips, which showed how broad his shoulders really were and heightened the muscles in his biceps. Like an aspiring sculptor, Arla studied whatever exposed skin he had, marveling at—

"What are you doing here?"

Arla shook her head, telling herself to focus.

"I wanted to see you. I sent you notes to come meet me, but you never showed..." She took a deep breath. She had to tell him. "I'm sorry for what I said to you that day in the streets. I shouldn't have said it." She brought her hand to her heart. "I swear, I didn't mean any of it."

Leo looked down at the ground for a moment and then back up at her, his expression hardened, but not angry, just... something else. "Then why did you say it?"

She lightly touched the end of a nearby shelf, tracing her hand along the edges of a jar that was filled with a light-yellow powder, it looked like ground garlic.

"My father was watching me and... I wanted to make him proud. When I went into that forest, I wanted to save my brother, but... I also hoped that it would make my father accept me. I wanted him to look at me the way he looked at Jun and when he found out I had magic, he finally did, and I didn't want to lose that... I still don't," she admitted.

Giving Leo a pleading look, she hoped he understood. "I know it's stupid and silly, but I still want his acceptance. Have you ever known something was foolish, but your heart still wants it anyway?"

Arla was learning Leo's subtle changes in his face, the feelings that leaked out through his mask, and the more time she spent with him, the more it tended to leak. And right now, in the flickering light of the burning fire, he still wore a grim, stoic expression, but his eyes showed her... longing. His chest heaved slowly like he was trying to control his breathing.

In a quiet voice, he answered, "Yes."

She smiled. "You're very important to me." She swore he stopped breathing for a moment. Was he okay? "You, Uro, and even Rose. You're my friends."

She drew something from her pocket and offered it to Leo. It was a handful of peyrun seeds; if crushed, they let out a delicate aroma of lemon and pepper. It was the thing Leo had asked for in the meadow.

"I want us to keep being friends." Her hands were sweating a little, moistening the seeds in her palm. "Please, forgive me," she uttered, barely audible. For some reason, tears welled up in her eyes. To have hurt Leo with what she said and how cruel she was, she didn't deserve forgiveness, but she still couldn't help but want it.

Leo gave her a pained expression. He moved his hand as if to reach out, but he settled it back down to his side. "Don't cry," he implored in a soothing tone.

Arla blinked back tears, frowning. "I'm not crying."

He sighed, scratching the side of his head. "Everything is always more complicated than I wish it was." Noticing her hair, Leo reached over, strangely careful not to touch her skin or get too close, and pulled out a straw from her long, tangled black strands. "You look like you've been through something," he said softly.

She laughed then; he had no idea.

"Well, you look undressed," she blurted, which she instantly regretted. Now he knew she had recognized his naked chest.

He blushed and looked away. "I was... interrupted."

"I'm sorry about that too." Her voice pitched higher than she wanted it to. Why was she feeling these tingles in her gut? Had she eaten something too greasy or fatty before she came here? Was her stomach acting up again? She brushed it aside, leaning forward. "Does this mean you forgive me?"

"Yes." Leo crossed his arms. "But I demand double the spices now."

Arla grinned. "Of course."

"I'll take those seeds now." His cool hand reached out in a cupped form right underneath hers. She tipped her hand, releasing the seeds to him, grazing her fingertips against his palm. He flinched but did not move his hand. The touch of his skin to hers sent a spark through her fingers, up her arm, and down to her core.

He gazed at her, longer than he ever had, and in that half-dark room, where no one else was there to watch them, it seemed like he let his guard down long enough for her to see something new in his expression. The thread grew taut between them, its end pulling at her heart and lungs and everything. She stopped breathing, feeling the wave of it. It was only for a few seconds, but the intensity at which he looked at her caught her off guard. It was a look she had never received from anyone.

As if knowing it was too much, Leo broke eye contact as he gingerly slid his hand away, along with the seeds. As he put them in his pocket, he said, "I think you should return to the castle before it gets too dark. I'll escort you…" He looked around him. "Once I find a shirt."

Pulling her hood back up, Arla passed the rows of barracks and outhouses outside undetected as Leo led her down a secret exit toward the back of the training grounds. He walked her as far as he could without arousing suspicion and luckily, no one recognized her in her kitchen maid clothing.

"You know, that won't be the last time we might run into each other in public," Leo said.

He was right. She didn't want to hurt his feelings again with insults, though. "If my father asks, I'll just create a distraction. Maybe I'll fall off my horse and cause such a big commotion that he might forget about it."

Leo didn't seem enthused by her idea at all. "Or if you are forced to insult me in public, just call me a snail, and I will know that you are not trying to truly insult me."

Arla chuckled. "I think that is a great idea, snail."

The amused look on Leo's face made her glow with pride, and she wanted to keep putting a smile on this captain's face.

Before Leo turned to leave, Arla grabbed him by the sleeve, "Can you come to the meadow tomorrow night? I have a surprise. And bring Uro and Rose too!"

Leo seemed to hesitate before he agreed with a nod and slinked away.

CHAPTER 29

Sweat beaded down Arla's forehead as she crouched close to the dirt below. *One more time.* She drew in a big gulp of air and blew it back out onto the small pile of twigs and shredded leaves. The small string of smoke wavered and then finally burst into a small flame. *Yes!* Arla thrust her arms into the air in glee.

I did it! I built a fire!

Kneeling back onto the back of her heels, she put her hands on her hips in a stance of pure pride. When she first arrived at the meadow, the sun was beaming high above her, basking her in the warm glow of its afternoon rays, and now it was saying goodbye as it melted into a semicircle of orange and pink. It had taken her hours to build this fire.

She quickly blew short breaths into the flames, willing it to live. She pulled out more hay from her large cotton bag and threw it on top of the flames, which made it roar to greater life. A ring of stone circled the now-growing fire which she had made when she first arrived. She had found an open spot in the meadow away from the taller grass that bordered it, to prevent the flames from being seen and catching against any underbrush that could lead to a disaster.

It was more difficult to build a fire than she originally thought. Maybe because the meadow trapped moisture within its grass and vegetation, but mostly because this was not a skill she ever really learned. She had seen Leo and the others do it plenty of times in The Forest, watching them smack rocks together, or rub sticks of wood.

They made it look easy. It was not.

With great effort, she pulled a large cast iron pot from her trusty bag and rummaged around for the other wrapped ingredients. She had invited her friends to join her in the meadow, and she was going to surprise them with a delicious dinner; just as Leo did for her in The Forest. She couldn't wait to see how surprised they would be that she could cook too.

By the time Arla was done, the night had set deep, and she was tired and hungry and sweating so much that the underarms of her shirt were embarrassingly moist. So far, she had accidentally spilled the pot three times trying to balance it on top of the fire, lost her ladle in the boiling soup twice—she really should have brought the bigger one—and burned all her fingertips at least four times. She had forgotten that cast iron got just as hot as the raging blaze that heated it.

But she was done now, and that's all that mattered. Just in time, too. As she peeked her head above the tall grass, over the hill, she saw two figures approaching. She leapt from her spot and waved them over, afraid to leave the fire unattended.

From the thicket of the grass, Leo and Uro appeared. A thick long-sleeve tunic wrapped around the captain's chest and arms, hiding away the rippled body Arla remembered from the night before, which she now was trying to banish from her mind. Uro wore a similar tunic, no doubt from the influence of his brotherly friend.

Arla and Uro bounded towards each other, squealing in glee. Uro stopped a respectful distance about to bow, but Arla swept him into her arms, hugging him tightly. The young soldier was shocked at first, but then returned her embrace. When they pulled apart, Uro burst into a string of unstoppable chatter.

"Princess! What have you been up to lately? I heard you went to a party at a nobleman's home! Was it fun? Did they have dancers? Music?"

She guessed Uro did not know it was Lesandres's home she had dined at, or else he would have not sounded so cheerful. Arla looked up to see Leo standing stoically behind him, his hands in his pockets. Arla smiled and he smiled back, a small hello.

"It was tiring," she admitted. "I didn't really speak with a lot of people. What about you?"

"The soldiers have been non-stop asking us about The Forest. I still get asked a million questions a day!" Arla could tell Uro loved it. "I told them about the killing trees, the stream, the red flowers, everything! You might not believe this," Uro grinned from ear to ear, "but I have gotten quite popular with these stories."

"Oh?" Arla lifted her eyebrow, turning her attention to Leo. "Have you been telling stories too?"

"No," Uro answered for him, making a pouting face. "Leo hates talking and crowds and attention, but that's okay, that's why they ask me instead."

"Of course," Arla laughed. "I'm sure they want to hear the stories from someone fun and not a grumpy captain who frowns all the time."

Leo's mouth tugged down into a scowl.

"Ah," she said. "There it is."

From the rush of Uro's talking, Arla had almost forgotten there were supposed to be three of them there. She looked behind the two but saw no one else.

"Where is Rose?" she asked.

"Rose isn't coming," Leo replied.

"Why not?"

Leo glanced at the ground. "She is... busy."

"Oh," Arla replied. The way Leo said it, Arla could tell Rose wasn't reluctantly busy. She did not want to come. Rose, an enigma forever. She did not want to be Arla's friend, did she?

Uro, clearly trying to change the subject, said, "Did you make us something? It smells good!"

Arla immediately perked back up. "Yes! I made noodle soup for you all!"

The aroma of spicy pepper, onion, and a tinge of sesame oil led them to the boiling pot that was ready to be served. Leo bent over, observing the floating pieces of meat and onion roiling around the pot. "How long did it take you to make all this out here?" He sounded impressed.

"Not long," she smugly replied as she poured bowls for each of them. "I wanted to thank you for everything you've done for me."

"Can't wait!" Uro was practically drooling as he took his bowl.

Leo glanced at the bag on the ground and snickered. "I'm glad to see your bag again. I have missed it."

She patted the cloth like a domesticated cat. "I think I'm too attached to it now. My legs have gotten stronger since I've been carrying it around, I feel like it's my good luck charm."

Leo nodded, understanding. "The things that challenge us the most help us grow the most."

Arla giggled as she handed him his bowl. "I didn't know you were a philosopher."

"I'm not," Leo responded, blushing as he accepted the food.

Arla was in the middle of ladling her own bowl when she saw Uro take a big spoonful and put it into his mouth. His eyes widened, filling her chest with pride. He was now enjoying the beautiful taste of—

Uro spit out the soup onto the ground beside her.

She froze mid-ladle.

Leo threw him a death glare.

Horror struck the young boy's face as he realized what he had done. "I'm so sorry! I didn't mean to spit it out. I just—It was instinct! I—"

Was something wrong with the soup? Arla dipped a spoon into her bowl and put it into her mouth. She swore her tongue shriveled back behind her throat when it tasted the sour, bubbling mess. Arla gagged and spat it out. By the Whispers, it was terrible.

Her face flushed in embarrassment. How could she not realize it was so bad? She should have tasted it as she made it. To be honest, she did not use a recipe, she just assumed she could follow the actions of the cooks, put ingredients in boiling water and flavor would naturally occur. How wrong she was.

"I'm so sorry," she panicked. "We need to throw this away, bury it where no one can find it."

"It can't be that bad," Leo said, putting the soup in his mouth. His jaw immediately tightened, locking down so he wouldn't spit it out.

It was a whiff of decaying fish, that's what the soup tasted like, and Leo was feeling all the flavors of it on his tongue right now. With the greatest effort she'd ever seen any human being use, he swallowed it down, the veins of his throat throbbing from the attack.

"Mmmm," he lied as he took in another spoonful.

"Leo..." Arla said, reaching out her hand to take back the bowl. "You don't have to eat it. It's terrible."

"No, it's not," he said through clenched teeth as he took another swallow. The vein in his forehead was bulging now, threatening to pop. He half coughed, half gagged through his third spoonful. "It's great," he rasped. "Thank you for making this for us."

They watched in utter horror as Leo finished his bowl, one painful slurp at a time, finally tipping the rest of it back with one final gulp.

Watching Leo, Uro looked like he might cry, because he knew he had to drink the rest of his bowl too. Before he made the decision, Arla grabbed the bowl from Uro and poured the toxic liquid onto the ground, where it couldn't hurt anyone ever again. She shot a glance at Leo, who was bent over, exhausted from his effort, sweating more than she had earlier building the fire. She was truly worried he had lost a year of life from what he just did.

"I…" Leo strained, "I can go for another."

"No!" Arla shouted, she kicked the pot, spilling the rest of the vile soup which killed the plants it poured over, like liquid death. Leo looked relieved as he slumped over again.

Arla didn't know whether to laugh or cry. On the one hand, she was touched by his determination to make her feel better about her terrible cooking, but on the other, he looked so pathetic having been defeated by soup. She reached into her bag and brought out a small cotton handkerchief. Bending onto a knee in front of Leo's stooped form, she offered it to him for his profuse sweating. "Are you okay?"

"I'm fine. Great dinner," he huffed as he took the handkerchief. "Your fingers," he said. "You've burned them." He was staring at Arla's fresh wounds on her fingertips. He was always noticing things like that. Small details about her. Like an eagle, he never missed a thing.

"Oh, yes, who knew that cast irons get hot on fires right?" She tried to laugh it off. Her body had a habit of burning. He reached out and grazed the tip of his index finger on the tip of hers, gliding across her fingers all, checking them.

A shrieking light blinded her senses.

When she looked up, she was no longer in the meadow, but in a barn.

Her arms weren't covered anymore, and the scars were gone. Instead, her usual pale forearms were now darkish brown that led to a hand with long fingers where her own short ones should have been.

In front of her was a young man, a bit older than Leo, who looked nothing like him. He was pale with fine golden locks and ocean eyes that sparkled in the light. He was holding her hand and lifted it to kiss each finger. But it wasn't her hand at all. It belonged to another woman she did not know. She thought to pull her hand away, but she had no control. It wasn't her anymore.

And then just as fast as the image had come, the night sky returned, and she was back in the meadow. She gasped from the shock. It was like being jolted back into her body. Leo's hands were clasping hers now.

His great brown eyes looked at her with concern. "Are you okay?"

"Yes," she replied uneasily. "I'm alright."

Leo held her there as she regained herself. And when she stopped swaying, he reluctantly let go. Out of the corner of her eye, she could see Uro staring at them like he was solving a riddle, which he seemed to have solved because a knowing grin spread across his face.

As the night wore on, she tried not to think about what she had just seen. These visions were getting more and more real, to the point where she was thinking it wasn't mere hallucinations or temporary dreams. She had a feeling it was more than that. The Woman was there in her mind and she was trying to tell her something.

But she would ponder on this another time.

"I can't give up the salt," Arla confessed. "Where will the flavor come from?"

Leo was trying to convince her to eat blander foods to heal her stomach, but Arla couldn't imagine a life without flavor.

"I'm not saying to live without flavor," Leo argued. "Just mix it in your daily meals as the others. I will write down the recipes to give to your cooks. Just tell me what stuff you like to eat, and I can make a healthier version for you."

"You don't have to... do that." Arla blushed. Why was he always trying to help her? She didn't deserve it.

Uro, who was a ball of chatter at the beginning of the night, now simply sat and watched them talk to each other. She had the sinking suspicion he was observing them with great amusement.

Eventually, the subject of Arla's magic came up, in which Uro quickly jumped back into the conversation. She suspected that Norendra's way of training wasn't working for her as evidenced by her inability to control any of them every time she summoned a creature or vines.

Arla tried to find other ways magic wielders might have controlled their Whispers by reading books, but they did not help either. They all said the same thing: that Whispers were meant to be controlled until they were submissive to you. But the more she tried to stronghold the Whispers, the more they fought back in a fury, dodging her control.

"Maybe it's not about control," Leo suggested. "When I lead my soldiers, I'm not trying to control their every behavior. They are human, each with their own beliefs and skills; it is impossible to control everyone to do your bidding, and it usually doesn't work."

Uro nodded. "It's true, Rose doesn't listen to Leo a lot. Like when he told her she should come here, but she refused. She thinks that you—"

"I just show," Leo continued, throwing Uro a warning glance, "that I will fight alongside them and hope that they trust me enough to lead,"

Darkness crept over his face. No doubt he was remembering all those soldiers he led in The Forest and how they had chosen to follow him even though he told them to escape. They had all died for that choice. Arla could see it haunted him still.

But it was their choice. Arla remembered how in awe she was that one person could command such loyalty. What it took to build that type of relationship. Maybe she needed to build that with the Whispers.

"You're right," she said. "I need to communicate with them."

"Let's try it now," Uro chimed in.

"But..." Arla started to refute.

"You can't keep running away from it," Leo said.

Arla frowned, insulted. "I'm not running away." She remembered the clicking of the six-legged monster as it climbed down the trees, and it sent the same frozen fear through her.

"Prove it, then," Leo smirked, crossing his arms. He was trying to get under her skin on purpose, she knew that. She also knew that she couldn't avoid it forever. She wasn't willing to let the fear get the better of her.

She stuck out her tongue at him and pushed him slightly to the side. "I will. Just give me some space."

Arla closed her eyes.

Leo and Uro were silent, waiting for her. In the quiet, Arla could hear the light wind rustle along the tall grass around them and the crackling of the fire as it started to wane.

I am here. She spoke softly into her mind, trying to clear the other clutter and thoughts to make room. *Please don't send me the six-legged monster.* The gate opened, and a rush of Whispers streamed in.

She remembered the water droplets and how they helped her because she had tried to speak with them, like living creatures. Maybe she had to communicate with the Whispers like that too.

Hello.

The Whispers clattered and shuffled around, like hungry guests at a dinner party with no catering.

Hello, she said again.

A few of them turned towards her, recognizing her voice. It was a small win, but a win, nonetheless.

She approached the ones that settled in her mind. She could hear their words, like faint whisps coming off of them. She bent over, trying to get closer.

Can we work together?

They glided away from the others, who were still scrambling to free themselves, nibbling at the edges of her skull. One, in particular, shifted from a thin wisp into words, forming on the tip of her tongue, letting her taste the flavor of mud and earth. It was trying to tell her what it was.

A creature of mud?

She hesitated, wondering if it was wise to release a monster in the meadow without Norendra to stop it if something bad happened. Probably not. Turning inward, she asked, *Will you listen to me?*

It did not reply.

"We're here," Leo said. "If you need us."

The comfort of his voice bolstered Arla. *Let's try this.*

In a soft voice, she let the Whisper go. *"Mo'tek en rela'io."*

The ground ahead of them caved into itself and liquified, turning into bubbling sludge. A large head, dripping with mud slowly lifted from it, along with the rest of its lizard-like body. Bat-like wings flanking its spine quickly dried as the creature fanned them out. Its face was that of a lizard, with two serpent tongues.

It hissed at Leo before turning to Arla, recognizing her. It was as if the Whisper she had spoken had transformed into this creature. It knew her. It had lived in her head.

Arla just stared back, but this time instead of being afraid, she felt like it was a part of her. Something she knew. It turned its completely black pupils at her with a look of cool apathy, so different from the rage of the six-legged monster she summoned with Norendra.

Uro and Leo stood in awe at the mud beast.

"What now?" she asked them.

"Maybe try telling it something to do?" Uro suggested, his mouth still agape.

Would you like to roll over? she asked in her head. The creature continued to just stare at her, not understanding or hearing. *Do you know what I am saying?* Mud oozed down its unmoving legs.

She took a deep breath. *Let's work together.*

Bending to the ground, Arla got on all fours, her hands sinking into the liquified dirt. Still staring at the creature, she bent low and rolled over like a dog, getting mud on her back. Uro and Leo stifled their laughter watching her do this. Even the clamoring Whispers in her head seemed to snicker.

It was a little embarrassing, yes, but if she were to take Leo's advice, she would have to prove to the creature that she was also willing to do what she asked it to do. That's how one built trust, wasn't it?

The creature shifted. And then another Whisper floated to the top of the pile, and she let it out.

"*Ferfan.*"

The creature lay on its belly and rolled over, splashing giant waves of mud into the air. Brown sludge slapped onto her face and covered her entire chest. It smelled of old water and fish, but still, she brightened in excitement.

She shouted to the boys, who were also covered head-to-toe in mud. "Did you see that?!"

Without thinking, she ran to the creature, patting its muddy body. It pulled away and she slipped on the muck it left behind, landing straight on her side. It gave her one last huff as if it was annoyed and melted back into the pool of earth it had come from.

She sat on her butt, completely drenched and extremely excited, but also, very tired. Calling this magic was very exhausting.

Uro cried out as he jumped in the air. "Wow! Arla! That was amazing!" He wiped sludge off his shoulders, shuddering from the touch. "I'm going to rinse myself off in the water," he announced as he dashed off to the nearby stream, away from view.

Leo patted her shoulder. "Great job."

Surging from the high of having commanded a monster that could have shredded her easily, Arla felt like the most powerful person in all the land. She grabbed his wrist and threw him into the mud, covering him with more brown muck. He blinked blankly twice, a little shaken.

Smiling, she replied, "Thanks."

A playful twitch tugged at his lips. "Oh, so because you could make a monster roll over, you think you can overtake a captain?"

"Didn't I?"

He laughed, so loudly it bounced against the grass. She loved the sound of it. The mud had got into his hair, tousling it into a messy scuffle, even like this she liked the way he looked, but mostly how bright his eyes were at that moment. She could barely feel the mud now drying on her clothes and hair, she only saw him.

She leaned forward, not thinking, and pressed her lips on his. They were warm and soft, like pillows, and it made her want to explode into a thousand strands of starlight. And then her senses came roaring back.

She pulled herself back, in dread.

Oh no. She didn't mean to... She wasn't supposed to...

He looked at her intensely, like he was torn between two warring sides in his mind.

"I'm sorry," she quickly said. This was wrong. She shouldn't have forced a kiss on him. She shouldn't have—

In a swift motion, Leo's hand pulled her towards him by the waist, molding his body against her own. His soft lips welcomed hers, sending a tingling electric bolt across her entire being. For a moment, she was shocked, but then she wrapped her arms around his neck, pulling him closer to her, trying to merge herself with him, even though the mud on her hands made everything slippery.

The feel of his mouth on hers was warm and intoxicating and so... right. His hot tongue slipped between her teeth and hungrily tasted her as if he had wanted to do this for a very long time. It was all-consuming. She never wanted it to end.

The grass crunched behind them. "Leo, Princess!" Uro's voice called out.

They pulled away from each other, facing opposite directions. Uro stopped in his tracks as he came upon their probably strange demeanors, still dripping wet from his jump in the stream. Arla became suddenly very fascinated with the edge of her sleeves, picking small clumps of muck off of them.

"Are you two alright?" the young boy asked.

Arla got up first, sludging through the sticky silt and out towards the stream. "Of course!" she said as cheerily as she could. With her head held high, she didn't look back, afraid to make eye contact with anyone as she marched into the cold water, praying it would bring her back to her senses.

CHAPTER 30

The dreams were getting more intense and more frequent. So much so that Arla knew when she was in them, as she was right now. The Forest spread around her, but it looked different. Instead of the hollowed skeletal trees, there were lush, vibrantly-colored oaks and cypresses of various shades of green and white speckled with purple flowers. It was magical how the leaves swayed in the wind, but across this serene background, the sound of hooves beating against the ground rumbled beneath her. Except she wasn't really there, either. Instead, she was high above, just floating amongst the wind.

A woman screamed, "Run!"

Arla was suddenly in another body, with the same dark skin tone and gold jewelry hanging from her wrists as she pushed against the trees, trying to outrun the horses behind her. Hands grabbed the back of her dress, lifting her into the air momentarily before dropping her face first, sending her into darkness.

"No!" Arla sprung up in her bed with the force of her shout.

Linuth startled, dropping a basket of soaps from her hands.

Arla was back on her bed, drenched in sweat.

"I'm sorry." Arla crawled out of bed, picking up the soaps from the rug.

"No need to apologize, Princess." Linuth graciously took the soaps from Arla's still-shaking hands and put them in the woven basket. "I wanted to bring you a more gentle soap this morning, for your arms…"

Arla smiled at the elderly woman, grateful. She was starting to get used to this routine of her bedroom window being opened for her and the servants bathing and dressing her. There were times she wished she was left alone to sleep in like before, but she didn't dare say any word against them, lest they tell her father and he called her ungrateful again.

She *was* grateful. Truly, really grateful.

"Princess, your father requests your presence in the Great Hall this morning," Linuth relayed. "And then you will dine for lunch with Ametha at noon." The elderly woman was always stating her schedule as she picked the dress Arla was going to wear that day.

She nodded. It was a relief not to have to make choices this morning since her mind was still preoccupied with her dream. They were becoming too frequent to be ignored now. It couldn't be explained, but Arla felt something was going to happen if she didn't address these visions soon. She hadn't told anyone about them yet, because she was afraid they would think she was insane.

But maybe Leo would believe her.

As the servants brushed her hair, Arla's thoughts turned to the Ulsanan captain. She lightly touched her lips. They had kissed. Really kissed. What did that mean? Why did she do that? She had become overcome with a feeling she had yet to pinpoint when she lunged for him. It was an overwhelming feeling of wanting to be close to him, to know everything about him, to hear his heartbeat in her ears.

These feelings... she had never felt them for anyone before. Was this what it was to care for someone as more than a friend?

She remembered how his rough hands traveled from her abdomen to her lower back and up to the base of her neck into her hair. The intensity of his kiss made her think he had unleashed something he had been holding back for a long time. But who really knew?

And then the questions came. Did he regret what they did? Did he think it was a mistake? Her heart froze in dread, at the possibility that Leo thought it was a mistake. She cupped her face into her hands. How was she going to face him again?

"Princess, are you well?" a young servant girl questioned.

Arla spoke through her hands. "I hope so," she mumbled.

The Great Hall was mostly empty today. The tables were pushed to the side and her father, dressed in bright silver and black, stood in the center, guarded on each side by big, bulky guardsmen, while the walls were lined with other guards every couple of feet. It was standard that the king was constantly guarded, so Arla had long forgotten to even take note of them, but today, because the room was so vacant, her eyes wandered to the only people in the room.

"Good morning, Father," she said as she bowed before him.

He grunted at her greeting. "I want you to stay with me today for my meeting. I believe it will be interesting to you. Maybe if you are good, I may ask for your input."

Arla choked back tears of happiness. "Of course, Your Highness."

He was truly changing towards her. Wanting her here in the first place was a sure sign that maybe he was finally seeing her as his daughter again.

A huddle of boots echoed down the long hallway as someone entered through the doors. She turned to the sound of clinking armor and saw Leo, Uro, and Rose approaching them. Instantly, she was nervous. *What are they doing here?*

"Ah! Soldiers, you have arrived early." Mathus spoke, a hint of amusement in his voice.

"Apologies, Your Highness," Leo replied, his tone as placid as ever. "It took less time than I thought to make our way here." His eyes flicked to Arla and then back to the king, not betraying anything that had happened the night before.

"No matter," the king replied. "We can start our meeting now."

The hair on Arla's neck stood up. Something seemed wrong. Why did her father bring them here? Did he know about their friendship? What did he want with them? Leo did not make any movement to look or acknowledge Arla, and the others followed suit. It was the best course of action; they needed to act like they didn't know each other.

Mathus rested his hands behind his back and asked, "Do you know why I summoned you three here?"

Uro glanced at Arla and quickly looked away. If Mathus noticed the exchange, he did not show it.

"I have summoned you here," the king continued, "because I want you three to lead another tour out into The Forest."

Arla's stomach plummeted.

He couldn't be serious.

Leo stood in silence for a moment before responding. "May I ask what the intention of this journey is for?"

Her father rooted into the ground, a power stance through and through. "There is great magic in The Forest, and it will make Ulsana stronger."

Arla couldn't breathe; he was sending them back into that nightmare?

She knew she wasn't supposed to speak, but she couldn't just stand there.

"Father," Arla pleaded, "there is nothing in that place. I took the last plant and there is nothing left to retrieve." This wasn't true. Arla was sure there were plenty left protected in that horrifying mist, but if she could convince her father there weren't, then maybe it would deter him.

Mathus shot her a glare to warn her to shut her mouth. "I don't want the plant, dear daughter," he answered. "You went into The Forest and gained magic we are only beginning to understand. I want them to retrieve it for me."

"How can they retrieve magic? It's not possible," she said, ignoring the king's warning looks.

"If you, of all people, can gain magic in there, then there must be a source," Mathus snapped. "Something that can be found and taken."

Was her father delusional? How could he be so sure? She opened her mouth to protest again, "But—"

"I will go," Leo stepped up, a hand resting on the pommel of his sword. "Uro and Rose do not know the way, but I remember. I will go."

No.

Her father was not going to accept any type of refusal, he was going to send them or they would die, that was the choice. His mind was made up of whatever he believed The Forest had. Leo must have realized this and once again, he volunteered to go.

Uro grabbed Leo's shoulder, clearly understanding the same thing, but he was shrugged off by his captain. Leo was yet again trying to protect them.

Mathus waved a lazy hand. "So be it. You may go in their stead and if you do not return in two weeks, I will send *them* in the next attempt."

A desperate panic overtook her. "Please, Father, you can't send him back," she begged. "We barely survived the first time!"

"Silence!" Scarlet traveled up his neck to this face, flaring his nostrils in rage. Mathus's eyes bulged like one of The Forest creatures, ready to strike. Her throat closed up, shuttering into submission. "I told you not to speak unless spoken to and yet you continue to blabber!"

She watched Leo stare at her father, with a chilling indifference, ready to accept his fate. His mask of ice hid the true feelings Arla knew he must be feeling. Leo had almost died the last time they were there, and surely, he knew he would not make it the second time, but worse than that, he would have to once again lead a group of men and women and watch them die with him, which for him, was a worse hell.

From behind Leo's sturdy shoulders, Arla saw Uro, triggering a memory of a promise she had made to him. When he was afraid Leo would get punished, he asked her to help him, and she promised she would do all she could. She intended to keep that promise. And so, she reached deep within herself and opened up her throat, willing her voice to be heard no matter the consequence.

"I owe them my life." Her voice came out strong, determined. "I would not be alive if it weren't for them. If they go, I will go too."

She looked at her father, not dropping her gaze, openly defiant for the first time in her life.

Arla was sure the king would not risk losing her now that she had magic, with so much to still discover and use. She was sure he was going to—

Her father's callused hands struck her across the face, the blow nearly knocking her off her feet.

A high-pitched shriek pierced her skull.

Arla shut her eyes tight from the sound.

Blood sprayed onto the floor.

Whose blood? Her blood?

A flash of a familiar king, his hand reeled back crossed her mind's eye, and then the image was gone, replaced by a pulsing throb in her skull a moment later, delayed from the shock.

Looking at the ground, the blood wasn't there anymore.

"Leo, don't!" Uro's cried out.

A blur.

A resounding crack.

When Arla's vision finally cleared, guards had drawn their weapons. The pointed tips of their swords surrounded Leo, who now was on his knees. The cloth on his shoulder was torn away, revealing a weeping wound that was still smoking from the burn.

Mathus was heaving, blood gushing from his hideously twisted nose.

A gasp escaped her lips when she realized what had happened.

Leo had hit her father.

"You dare touch me, Low-Born!" Mathus screamed, the heat radiating from his body threatening to boil everyone in the room.

The young captain clutched his wound as it continued to bleed, panting in pain, but his eyes were blazing and directed at her father. The guards closed in, ready to strike.

Before Arla could shout, her father raised a hand.

"No," Mathus commanded the guards, his free hand gently holding the side of his nose. "Take him to the dungeons instead." He approached Leo, his nose still bleeding. "You will be punished in a different way and when it is done, you will beg for the edge of a sword." He waved his hand, ordering his guards to grab Leo and drag him away.

"No!" Arla, Uro, and Rose shouted in unison, all running to Leo. A wall of flame erupted around the captain, stopping them all in their tracks, dividing them from him.

As she watched the guards through the fire, she met eyes with her father. And in that moment, she saw the ugly thing he truly was.

Arla opened her mouth, willing the Whispers to return. "*Mo'tek en rela'io!*"

The stone from beneath them shifted and turned into mud as the spines of her mud lizard slowly lifted from the sludge. A hand shot out, hitting her across the head, sending splotches of light across her vision.

The lizard returned to the ground without fully emerging. A cloth looped around her and gagged her mouth, stopping her next words. Arla tried to move, but the guards already had her in their grip.

Uro and Rose managed to toss a few attackers away from them before being overcome by the sheer number of guardsmen. Mathus looked at her with utter disappointment and for the first time in her life, she didn't care.

"Take them all to the dungeons," he ordered.

Arla kicked and screamed as she was dragged out of the room. The last thing she saw from the room was Leo, still bent over, gasping for air as Rose and Uro were subdued and forced through a door on the opposite side.

CHAPTER 31

The dungeon was disgustingly moist. It smelled of piss and salt from the sweat and tears of the past prisoners who crouched in the same corner where Arla was sitting now. There was a thick grime of fungus growing on the wall that pressed against her back, the only thing that could possibly have lived in this sun-deprived hole in the wall. The steel bars crisscrossed in squares in the door opposite the fungus wall that separated Arla from an empty passageway that only seemed to lead to more darkness.

It had been a full day since she was dumped in here by the royal guards. Or at least, she guessed it was since there was no window to the outside world here. She had tried shaking the bars, screaming out through the leather cylinder between her teeth to anyone who could hear her, but when that all failed to free her, she slumped to where she sat now, deciding it was better to save her energy.

So far, she had not heard Rose or Uro in any of the adjacent cells, so the guards must have thrown them somewhere else. She hoped that at least they weren't injured and were trying to find a way to escape like she was.

She pulled at the metal cylinder lodged in her mouth, trying to loosen it again somehow. The iron scrapped against her teeth, shooting a small sharp pain up behind her nostrils. She flinched and withdrew her hands. It was impossible to remove this type of muzzle. It was created to be a cage for your mouth that was bound around your head by various leather straps typically used on High-Born criminals to prevent them from speaking, so they couldn't use their magic. She gave the muzzle another strong tug before shouting in exasperation when it did not budge.

Leo's wound would have gotten worse by now and she doubted anyone was tending to it. Something like that could get infected. Worry started to overtake her as she yanked at the muzzle again. They would at least keep him alive until his execution day, right? Dread continued to fill her as those thoughts passed across her mind. Leo was going to be killed. No. He was going to be tortured first. She knew her father. He would not give Leo a quick death. He would make sure to humiliate Leo and have him beg for death before he did it.

Her eyes started to sting with the threat of tears again.

Why did Leo do it? Uro tried to stop him, but Leo did it anyway. He must have known the consequences. Leo was not a rash man, he was a captain, for Whispers sake. *What was he thinking?*

Footsteps echoed down the hall, the sound of a cloak sweeping behind the person approaching her cell. Arla stiffened. Her father's square jaw and swollen nose broke through the light first as the rest of his daunting stature followed. Someone had reset Mathus's broken nose, but they could do nothing for the lumps and bruises.

This was the face she had so desperately wanted to smile at her for years and now it was the same face she wanted to lunge at with sharpened claws.

"Arla…" he tsked through the bars. "Even with magic, you are a sore disappointment."

Before she would have tumbled into a deep abyss from those words, but now there was something else that bubbled instead, a rage itching to lash out.

Are you going to kill me too? she wanted to ask, but the metal cylinder would not let her speak.

He lingered there, just out of arm's reach from the bars, studying her face, like he was looking for certain features. "When you were born, your mother didn't last the night."

Arla flinched. She had never heard her father speak of her mother. Ever. She had asked so many times when she was young, and he had refused to say anything. Refused to let anyone say anything. The sudden mention of her seemed… suspicious.

"I thought it was such a waste to die over bringing another girl into this world, but still, I was glad to have any heir at all," he said in a lulling voice of nostalgia, before shifting to a sharp tinge of resentment. "You were supposed to be like me. Strong. But instead, you ended up just like your mother. And with no magic! Even your weak mother had magic, but you couldn't even manage that. You shamed me in front of my people. In front of everyone." He sighed.

"But now you have your own Whispers. Magic that is different from the rest of us. Something that cannot be wasted. And I thought that perhaps you weren't a complete disappointment. That you could be saved." His voice darkened. "But then you defended that boy... and I realized you sympathize with them, don't you? You pity those ground-dwelling vermin.

"You disobeyed me. You spoke when I told you not to. You dared to draw your magic against me. After everything I've done for you... why did you do this to me?"

Arla couldn't believe what her father was asking her. Like she had been the aggressor. That she was the villain who hurt him.

In a regret-ridden voice, he said, "Maybe it's my fault. I should have hardened that soft heart of yours. Maybe then..." he trailed off and then shook his head. "There is still time to learn. You can still prove you are worthy of being a Seojin." He leaned close to the bars. "Today, I will draw that weakness out of you, and you will thank me for it one day."

And then he was gone.

Worthy of being a Seojin. A week ago, there was nothing Arla had wanted more, but now, she could toss it into the sewers for all she cared. If being a Seojin meant being like her father, she did not want it. She had been living in a fog all her life, and now her vision was clear. She was so blind by her desire to prove herself she didn't think to see how truly terrible her father was.

What was it from him that she wanted so badly?

Her father only started paying attention to her when she had gained magic and like a fool, desperate for love, she wilted into his palm, wanting to do anything to stay in his graces.

She had cried and begged for years to gain her father's love. Why did she even want it? He had never treated her kindly, never paid attention to her, and... she touched the tender spots on her arms.

He. Hurt. Her.

But worse than anything else was that for years, he made her feel like she was worthless. She believed she didn't deserve kindness from anyone unless she proved it.

But Leo, silent, grumpy, reserved Leo, had told her over and over again that she didn't need to prove herself, she didn't need to try so hard to get people to like her.

We are told we are not worthy of a good life because we can't wield magic. That's bullshit. We are just as worthy as anyone else.

And that includes you, Princess.

Her heart constricted. He was the first person to ever say that to her. The first person who ever protected her instead of hurting her. She twisted her hands into fists. It was time *she* protected *him*. And to do that, she needed her magic. She yanked at the cylinder again, but it did not budge. There had to be a way to get out of this thing. Pulling was useless. She looked at the prison bars. Maybe if she slammed the cylinder hard enough into the bars it would bend enough for her to get out a Whisper. It would also probably dislodge some teeth.

She sprung up to her feet, determined. She had to try.

A scream pierced her skull, scattering Whispers into her head. Arla clutched her ears and doubled over. It was The Woman, she was sure of it. Gritting her teeth against the iron muzzle, she screamed—not from pain, but frustration. She yelled back at the howling in her head.

Enough of this!

She screamed, louder than *her*. As loud as she could. Loud enough that her throat strained and her tonsils became sore.

If you are trying to tell me something, she shouted in her head, *say it!*

The screaming in her head intensified so much that Arla thought her eardrums might burst. White light sliced through her vision.

The agony almost made her turn away, just to get some relief, but she forced herself to stay. To trudge through the misery. Arla was sick of seeing bits and pieces, it was time to see what The Woman was trying to tell her.

I am ready, she told The Woman, *show me.*

Shards of glass ripped through her as she was thrown into a pool of a thousand voices. Her very essence stretched across lands as her mind struggled to hang on. She willed herself to stay together even though she was sure she would rip to shreds any moment and then—everything snapped into place—but she wasn't in her own body anymore. She could feel the weight of it on her soul, the different height, the different skin, the different posture. She was The Woman.

A young man, older than Arla, with jet-black hair was holding her hand, but there was something so cold in his eyes it made her inwardly shudder. The crown above his head glittered in the candlelight.

Arla knew this High-Born. She had seen his painting all around the castle.

The First King of Ulsana, Namkil Seojin.

Arla was his betrothed, no, *she* was The Woman. This wasn't a vision of the future; it was a memory of the past. The scenery changed and Arla was in a barn, hands caressing another, a man with blond hair and deep cobalt eyes. A farmer. He was a farmer. He handed her a bouquet of red flowers. The same ones that fell from the trees in The Forest. The ones that burned and poisoned.

Stop! She wanted to shout as her own hands took them and pulled them to her chest. Like she was cherishing them. Against her will, Arla's hand—The Woman's hand—touched the soft petals.

Why weren't they burning her?

A hand slapped her across the face.

Blood splattered onto the floor.

She knew this place, it was the throne room, but there was only one portrait on the wall and the furniture was different, from an older time.

A violent threat hissed in her ear. "If you think you can run away with that Low-Born trash, you are delusional!"

And then suddenly Arla was floating, high above the treetops of the bright and luscious green Forest, and then settled like a ghost, seeing everything.

"Run!" The Woman grabbed the farmer's hand and raced past the trees. Horses whined as they chased them. Arla could feel her fear. They weren't running fast enough.

The horses circled them. A soldier grabbed the farmer by the hair as King Namkil Seojin got off his horse. The Woman was crying, begging him, but it did not stop the dagger as it pierced through the farmer's heart. Wailing, The Woman fell to her knees as the king wiped the blood from his weapon.

"I told you not to be stupid," Namkil said. There was no remorse in his voice, just disappointment, like someone reprimanding a child.

The Woman continued to cry as she watched the blood flow from her dead lover's chest and into the ground beneath him.

"Come," Namkil ordered. "We shall dine together and forget about this mess."

The Woman shrieked and lunged at a nearby soldier, who pushed her away, but it was too late. Her hand had stolen the dagger from his side.

Arla couldn't move, she could only watch, like a prisoner in someone else's memory.

The king dove to stop her, "No!"

She drove the sharp blade straight into her chest. Her body hit the forest floor before anyone could catch her.

A sudden and violent gust of wind blew through all of them, snapping branches off of trees. The ground shook, knocking several soldiers off their steeds. The farmer's blood-soaked The Forest floor, like a never-ending stream, turning into black ooze, poisoning the ground beneath it. The trees shriveled and blackened as they drank his blood and groaned as they slowly came to life.

And then true horror ensued.

The trees shot out their sharpened limbs and skewered men and horses alike. Their blood splashed to the ground, feeding the rage of The Forest and bringing to life more trees.

Arla watched in terror as the ground fractured like gaping wounds and creatures of smoke and ash crawled out, shredding the soldiers apart, splashing their hot, sticky blood everywhere.

"Retreat!" King Namkil Seojin shouted. He rode away, barely making it out of the tree line before darkness swallowed everything up behind him.

Arla's head whipped around as she careened down into nothingness and then crashed right back into her body in the dungeon. She let out a struggling gasp as she tried to get her breathing back.

It was a nightmare. Something she wished had never happened, but it did, didn't it?

And then she understood the real story. The first king was The Woman's fiancé, but she fell in love with a Low-Born, and they both died because of it.

A faint voice echoed in her head. Arla looked up, but no one was there. The Woman was struggling to say something, tugging at her.

I am here, she called out to her.

Silence.

I saw it, she said to the echo in her head. *I'm sorry for what happened to you.*

It felt like fragments; there were still missing pieces. Their deaths had turned The Forest into the cursed place it had become. But there were still so many unanswered questions. There had been many deaths in The Forest across all of time, so why did it care about The

Woman's in particular? And why was The Woman's spirit still there? But of all the questions, the one she wanted to know the most still lingered.

What do you want with me? she asked.

Still no answer.

Regardless, if The Woman had loved a Low-Born, then at least she would be on Arla's side with what would come next.

I have to save Leo, she said. *Will you help me?*

An invisible hand pressed on her chest, right over her heart.

And with that, Arla nodded. They were to work together.

CHAPTER 32

Arla was hauled from the dungeon by the same guardsmen who put her in there. Her feet dragged behind her, making a line in the dirt as she kept both her hands in fists. She didn't try to hold up her body weight; if they were going to take her, she was going to make sure it was going to be difficult and wear them out. The muzzle was still fastened around her head, and her wrists were tied behind her as she was brought outside of the castle grounds and to an arena she had never seen before.

It was enormous. Enough to fit hundreds, if not thousands, of people.

Her father sat in a large wooden chair with a sleek columned back placed in the center of the only balcony above the arena. Ametha and Jun were thankfully not there.

A bright red cloth covered the awning over their heads, creating shade from the beating afternoon sun. Guards stationed themselves against the back wall while a few advisors in her father's council stood on either side of Mathus. Surprisingly, Norendra was not present either. Did she know that Arla was being held against her will? Did she even care?

A few turned to her as she was dragged onto the balcony. From the corner of her eye, she caught Wilkins's father, Gerald, staring at her with judging eyes. All the others' attention was fixed on the center of the arena below.

To her horror, a shirtless Leo was already chained up in the middle of the flat, circular arena. Each of his arms was pulled up above his head to a metal post above him. Heavy iron shackles held his feet down to the ground, forcing him to kneel.

The wound on his shoulder had festered. She was right, no one had bothered to try and dress it. That was probably why he was sweating profusely, his eyes drooping in exhaustion; a fever had already caught him. Her heart broke seeing him like this, uncared for and hurting, but as broken as she felt, another feeling quickly took over.

Blood-boiling rage.

She struggled against the guards who yanked her down to a chair in the corner, a few feet from the king. Her muffled screams were ignored as they tied her wrists to the armrests and her ankles to the sturdy legs of the chair, tight enough that she couldn't wriggle free, but she made sure to keep her fists closed.

Hundreds of spectators sat behind a wall that surrounded the arena. High-Borns waited in their designated sections with curious or bored faces. They looked like they were coming to see a show, rather than the long death of a good man. Even a winding line had formed outside through the entrance where more people were waiting to join the crowd, even though there weren't enough seats. It was sickening.

The only ones who seemed to understand this was an execution were the Low-Borns, who fidgeted uncomfortably in the standing area, trying to get a better look at Leo. Worry crossed most of their faces.

"If you are quiet and good," her father's voice slithered to her, "then I might find mercy with the other two."

He means Uro and Rose.

Arla stilled.

The edge of his lips curved up into a slight approval as he turned back to the entertainment below.

Good. Let him think I am obeying.

Ever so slowly, Arla slipped a jagged rock out from the inside of her fist. All night, she had chipped away at the wall, until a piece fell off. She had inspected it and concluded that it was sharp enough for the job. She was first going to use it to cut away the straps in the dungeon, but she didn't have enough time before the guards came for her.

Little by little, she cut away at the rope around her wrist, without drawing attention to herself. Those guards had underestimated her. They thought she was too distraught to think of escape.

Her father's messenger, a tall, lanky man, got up and walked to the edge of the balcony. He looked out into the crowd as he announced, "People of Ulsana, we are here today to witness the hand of justice against a terrible crime." Turning to Leo, he continued, "Captain Leo Treterra. You have been found guilty of attempting physical assault and displaying treacherous behavior against our most noble and gracious king, Mathus Seojin."

Attempt? Leo had broken her father's nose. Arla looked to Mathus now, whose nose was straight once more with a thin line of cloth glued across it which would have been obvious to see if there weren't layers of caked-up makeup on his face to hide it and his bruises. The people in the arena would not be able to see his injuries.

She glared at her father, wishing her magic could seep out of her and strangle him.

"Such acts are grave offenses against the Crown and shall not be tolerated. Let the guilty and all in attendance take heed of this proclamation." The messenger paused for dramatic effect as the High-Borns booed and grumbled against Leo. "For these crimes, you have been stripped of your title and will be sentenced to death by a thousand lashings."

Arla wanted to throw up.

A thousand lashings. He would bleed out long before then.

"Let this all be a lesson for all Low-Borns," the messenger continued. "This will be the same punishment you receive if any dares to make the same offense to any High Born. Never forget your place here."

The nobles cheered, clapping in glee as they leaned forward, waiting for the main event.

The messenger returned to his place in the back of the balcony and a man in black entered the arena, carrying with him a thick leather whip that split into three ends, each fitted with sharpened silver.

The crowd roared in anticipation.

Arla struggled against her ropes, her heart racing. The rock wasn't sharp enough; she wouldn't be able to cut through it in time. The man in black raised his arm, the long whips lifting in the air in obedience.

No. No. No. No.

The silver-pointed leather cut into Leo's muscled back with a sickening snap, tearing open the skin, and splattering blood in all directions. Leo let out a shout through gritted teeth, biting back the worst of his screams.

Arla cried out, tears running down her cheeks. The Whispers raged in her head, demanding to be freed, but her mouth could not move.

She thrashed in her chair like a wild animal. They couldn't do this. She wouldn't let them; even if she had to rub her wrist raw until the rope gave out, she would do it.

A hand gripped her shoulder, tightly.

"Do not struggle so much, Princess." Gerald Dermarcu stood above her, his face grim. "It will all be over soon."

She wanted to spit in his face. *Coward!*

After his son's death, he remained at Mathus's side, doing his duties as diligently as Norendra did. Not once did he ask about his son or what happened in The Forest.

Arla glared at him, wishing she could kick this wretched man down. He slammed his hand over hers, sending a sharp cry from her mouth as she dropped the rock to the ground. Her heart dropped seeing it tumble away from her.

"I said, do not struggle," he hissed. "This is what he deserves."

Wilkins's father was as bad as his son was. Entitled and self-absorbed, willing to forget his son died just so he could climb the political ladder with her father. Gerald did not meet her glare, instead looking out into the crowd. She hated all of them. They deserved to suffer for what they were complying with now.

Gerald pressed harder into her hand. A sharp object cut into her fingers. She paused and realized what it was.

A blade.

Small and broken from something else, but a blade, nonetheless. Without looking down, Gerald left her, taking his position back by Mathus's side.

She blinked in disbelief for a second.

Gerald had given her a blade.

She didn't question whether it was a trap. It didn't matter. All that mattered was that she freed herself. Without hesitating, she chiseled away at the rope in her hand, keeping most of the blade hidden within her palm.

The whip cracked again, opening another gaping wound across Leo's back. The crowd gasped at the amount of blood the second spilled. Arla desperately cut into her ropes faster.

I'll be there soon. Don't die, don't die.

Tears blurred her vision as she heard the third crack of the whip, and then a fourth and fifth. Leo was unable to contain his screams now. She choked back tears as the binds would not unravel faster. Blood started to drip from her palm, and her grip tensed around the blade.

Please. Please.

A chorus of aggravated whining vibrated outside the arena. Everyone turned to the entrance as a bundle of hooves stampeded against the ground. Someone was yelling, pointing at something outside, but Arla could not see. And then the wooden entrance door splintered open, giving way to a herd of horses tumbling into the arena. The crowd erupted in chaos as the horses separated, running in all directions, kicking up dirt and dust into the air.

Her father shot up from his seat, shouting at the guards to contain the horses. The guards by Arla's side moved toward Mathus, more concerned for his safety than making sure she stayed put.

"They're taking him!" the messenger shouted, pointing.

Down the arena, amongst the chaos, Arla saw Rose in the middle, subduing the man in black, taking the whip from his hand and headbutting him between the eyes. Across from the executioner, Uro was there, untying a barely conscious Leo.

Arla's heart almost burst from relief. But then she saw the guards closing in and her father making his way to the balcony, his hand outreached. "Hal—"

No!

She threw herself backward, tipping the chair and sending herself crashing backward. Her back screamed from the impact as the wood split beneath her. The chair shook with enough force that she used it to thrust her blade one final time through the last thread of the rope and it unraveled.

Mathus turned to her, eyes wide.

Pulling her hand free, she cut at the leather straps around her head holding her gag, slicing parts of her face at the same time until finally, she was free.

The iron cylinder clattered to the floor.

She grabbed the first Whisper within her reach.

"Uthred 'el thur-nabu qil-i buthra-dana!"

"Hal'en!" Mathus shouted at the same time.

Her father's fire erupted from the ground, racing towards Uro and Leo. But then lightning crackled from the earth, blocking its path, and from nothing came a cloud of sparks that formed into a half-solid fox-like creature as tall as the walls of the arena. Its long ears sparked with shots of light and its long tail wrapped around Uro and Leo, creating a wall of defense. It roared at the guards closing in, daring them to come near.

Mathus pivoted and stormed toward her, his face glowing red. Arla desperately cut the rope around her other hand, finding it was just as stubborn as the first. Mathus was over her in an instant and grabbed her by the throat, lifting her and the chair above the ground. She gasped, dropping the blade.

The lightning beast flickered in and out, before completely disappearing, but to her great relief, Leo and Uro were gone along with Rose.

They had escaped.

His finger pressed into the soft parts of her throat, cutting off her air. Pressure built in her head as the breath left her.

The Whispers furiously shot back.

In one great push, she rasped out, *"I'et lamel al'para-tet."*

Vines smashed through stone and wrapped around her father's arm, yanking him backward. He shouted, burning them with fire, but another thorned vine swung and smacked him in the face, forcing him to drop her to the ground.

The back of the wooden chair splintered against the stone floor.

Everyone was running now, away from them and out of the balcony entirely. The guards tried to get to them, but her vines snapped back.

The vine curled around her hand and ankles and ripped the ropes off of her, leaving burn marks on her joints. The pain was sharp, but there was no time for a reaction. Rolling to her side, she grabbed the blade again and crashed through the distracted guards, and tumbled down the stairs, tripping over her vines and landing on her knees. The vines thrashed wildly out of control, hitting the wall and floor and people everywhere they swung.

Back on her feet, her knees bruised, her ankles throbbing, she ran.

CHAPTER 33

She skidded into a tunnel as she heard shouting behind her, stuffing the small blade into her pocket. She needed to find them, to make sure they were okay. Whipping around the corner, she crashed into a trio of people. She reeled back as the tip of a sword pressed against her chest.

Arla shook her head to regain focus and looked up to meet Rose's eyes. Uro was standing next to her, holding up Leo, who was half-conscious, fighting to stay awake.

Tears streamed down her face, unable to contain her relief. "I'm so glad you're alive!" she cried out, opening her arms towards them. Rose's sword remained on her chest, pressing deeper.

Arla hesitated, baffled. "Rose?"

Rose was glaring at her with such hatred, she thought she might melt right there.

"Over here!"

The four turned to see Gerald waving them down to his side of the tunnel. Rose whipped back around to Arla and for a moment, Arla feared Rose would drive the sword through her, but instead, the great warrior reluctantly sheathed it and raced toward Gerald.

Dermarcu led the way down a deeper tunnel, winding back and forth. These passageways were different from the ones Arla knew in the castle; they were wider and filled with more rats, but Gerald navigated them with ease.

"How did you escape?" Arla shouted at Uro as she tucked her blade into her pocket.

"Gerald freed us," Uro said, huffing at Leo's weight.

They ran until they no longer heard the clatter of pursuit behind them, and only then did they slow to a fast walk. Arla wanted to make use of this time to look at Leo's wounds as they continued to travel, seeing if she could do anything. He seemed like a limp doll, only barely aware of what was going on. His lips were cracked, dried from lack of water and the blood from his wounds was still pouring out of him too fast.

As she reached for him, Rose slapped her hand away. "Don't touch him," she hissed.

Arla retreated, giving her a hurt look.

"If we follow these tunnels far enough, we can get to the outer limits of the city where you can find escape," Gerald said, his uneven breathing echoing against the rounded stone walls. He was definitely not used to running this much. Arla used to be like that too until she went into The Forest, where walking and running for their lives were the usual states of being.

Turning to Gerald, Arla asked, "Why are you helping us?" "I thought you were loyal to my father."

"I could never be loyal to a man who sent my only son to his death," Gerald said, his voice edged with scorn. *So that's what this was, revenge.* He led them down a steeper tunnel. "I should have run away with Wilkins like this when I had the chance." His voice shook. "I should have saved him." Gerald kept his eyes ahead of him, but Arla could see his throat bob heavily, like he was holding back tears.

Arla couldn't help but feel bad for this man. She couldn't imagine what it was like to knowingly send your child to death.

Gerald stopped suddenly. "Princess. Tell me. Did my boy die a brave death at least? He was always so courageous."

Arla remembered how Wilkins panicked and pushed soldiers into the path of the creature that ultimately killed him. The way he demanded their water and made fun of her journal. Gerald looked at her with hope in his eyes.

"Yes," she lied. "He did."

Gerald looked relieved, letting out a sigh as he smiled slightly.

They had reached the end of this tunnel, with a choice to go left or right. Gerald stepped forward, looking in both directions and then remembering. Pointing to the right, he said, "We must go this way."

His step dug into the loose gravel of the dirt.

An orange glow warmed the darkness ahead. A roaring filled their ears and suddenly a burst of molten fire filled the entire horizontal tunnel ahead of them. Arla leapt back and stumbled into the trio behind her. Gerald still stood in the passageway, caught in the flames.

He screamed in agony as the flames enveloped him. Arla reached out trying to grab him, but the fire was too hot.

And when the inferno finally fizzled out, there was nothing left of him but a wisp of ash.

Slow, methodical footsteps came down the tunnel.

"I know you are there," her father's voice echoed down to them.

Her heart raced, pounding blood into her ears.

How did he find them so fast?

Arla turned on her heels to her friends. She wanted to scream at them to run, but she knew her father could throw flames down the entire tunnel and kill them just as he did Gerald. Running was not going to work. For as long as they lived, her father would hunt them, no matter where they went. No place would be safe.

There was no other choice.

"You have to go," she told them, trying to hide the quiver in her voice. "I will try to slow him down enough for you to find another way out."

"No."

Rose and Uro turned to Leo, who was wide awake now, panting from the agony of his still-bleeding wounds.

"Please," Arla begged, her heart aching. "You have to go. He'll kill all of you if you don't."

"No," Leo rasped, every breath sounded like he was being strangled. "I'm not leaving you."

Arla smiled, tears brimming her eyes. Her kind, stubborn, grumpy snail. Before Rose could push her away, Arla cupped Leo's face and kissed him. His lips were cracked and caked with dirt and sweat, but they felt warm and perfect to her.

She pulled away, looking directly into his beautiful brown eyes. "You were the only person who ever made me feel like I was enough. You never wanted anything from me, except to be safe. Thank you."

Arla stepped back, looking at Uro and Rose.

"Please, run." She lifted her hand. *"I'et lamel al'para-tet."*

Vines burst through the ceiling, cracking the stone and dirt above, raining rocks down between them. She heard Leo's scream of protest, but it was quickly muffled out by the crumbled wall that now separated them.

And then she was alone again.

CHAPTER 34

She looked back at the dark tunnel. Her father's footsteps were getting louder.

"I have lost my patience with you," Mathus growled as he stalked the darkness. "I gave you so many chances and as always, you ruined it for yourself."

"I disagree, Father." Arla backed away from his approach. "I think for the first time in my life, I did something right for myself." The tunnel was too narrow; he would send another blast of fire and she would be dead. She needed to reach a wider area. "You should have left my friends alone."

"You dare command your king?!" he shouted through the dark.

"Yes." Arla felt a draft as another tunnel path opened up to her right. "I do."

She sprinted down the hollow corridor, the gravel kicking up under her feet. Another blast of fire roared from the rear. The cloth on her back seared as she rounded the corner to another tunnel leading further down. Panting heavily, she kept turning and turning, until the passage finally opened up to an undercroft with rows of stone arches across a flat ground.

"All your life you've been a stain on my reputation." Mathus, in his great stature, almost filled up the entire tunnel as he appeared from its depths. Shaking his head, he said, "I should have gotten rid of you a long time ago."

A stream of fire burst into life in front of Mathus's feet and raced towards Arla, who managed to dodge it in time. Just as she caught her footing, a second line of flames galloped toward her face. She barely lunged out of its path.

Sweat beaded her forehead. The scars on her arms inflamed, triggering a throbbing ache around them. They remembered the heat that created them and went into a panic.

"*I'et lamel al'para-tet!*" she shouted.

Vines stretched to grab Mathus's legs, but they instantly shriveled to crisps from the heat emanating from his body.

"*J'en-ath gurth-u dal!*" The earth split beneath, opening a large hole.

The first creature she had ever summoned had returned with its large, fanned skull and scaled black lizard body. It climbed out from the ground and snapped at her father with its razor-sharp teeth. The beast's tail swung and hit her in the side, knocking her off her feet. She gripped the ground in frustration; she still had so little control over these monsters.

As she scrambled back to her feet, Arla felt the fatigue creeping in. She had to hang on, just long enough for the creature to stop him, but her red-eyed beast only made it past a couple of steps before it was incinerated by her father's white-hot fire.

Hope drained from her. The creatures were no match for him. He would just burn them all to death. She wasn't going to beat him this way. At this point, she didn't know how much more magic she had left. Her movements were getting sluggish. Magic really did take a toll.

But it took a toll on everyone, didn't it?

Maybe she could tire her father out by forcing him to use up his magic too. And that's when she felt the blade in her pocket, tucked away from earlier.

Mathus sent another flame down to the ground toward her. She dove to her right, but not fast enough. The edge of her shoe melted, leaving her skin underneath to bubble and sear. Crying out, she pulled it to her chest. She needed to keep moving. She waited for her father to go after her, barely dodging the next attack.

The game of cat and mouse continued as Arla tried to lure her father to keep using his magic against her. Over and over again, she would move forward and dodge at the last moment.

"Enough!" He sent a wave of sizzling hot air across the entire undercroft.

It went through her body like a hot summer wave, making her feel dizzy. She could barely breathe properly from all the running as the torrid air filled her lungs.

"If you are trying to outlast me, it won't work," he spat. "I have held my magic for longer than this."

Then I'll have to weaken you myself. Arla grabbed the blade from her pocket. She called upon more vines that wrapped into themselves to create the clumpy monsters like before, but he burned through them all. She was draining herself too quickly.

She willed the vines to push her father, but they only made him move a couple of steps back or a couple to the left, but never enough to do any real damage. She ran forward, taunting him to shoot his flames, and then reeled back just in time to dodge them.

Arla scrambled to her feet, pulling the small blade from her pocket. She shouted the words that brought forth another creature to attack him and just as his attention was on the creature, she lunged and cut her father in the arm with the small blade.

Finally! Her heart swelled in hope.

His eyes grew wide in anger. "Enough of the games!" He drew in a long breath. "*Xio-numa-the!*"

She had never heard him say those words before.

Fire raged around them and clamored to meet each other in the center where it became a towering inferno creature with the body of a giant horned man. Its rippling muscles were lined with veins of lava as it stood on two hooved legs. Everything it touched melted. The cracked earth beneath it glowed red underneath his feet.

The suffocating heat brought Arla to her knees. She fought to remain conscious as her head hit the floor. Her eyesight struggled to stabilize the swirling ground. It was too hot everywhere. The last of her energy drained from her like the horned giant was sucking it from her body.

She felt her father hover over her.

He spread his arms open as the monstrosity of eternal fire came to him. "I *am* power, Arla," he said smugly. "Ulsana stands today because of my strength! You have no idea what it is like to be a ruler. A true king must be unbending, or else the kingdom will fall."

She gripped the ground, scratching her nails into the solid stone beneath her. *Get up. Get up. Get up.*

With a heaving sigh, Mathus said, "What a disappointment you've been."

A sputter of laughter broke from her lips. And then more laughter and more, until it became an uncontrollable cackle, the sounds of a mad woman.

"Your strength?" she laughed as she pushed herself up to her knees. "You think you're strong because you belittle people?" Arla thought about all those times she reached out for her father's mercy. How much he enjoyed crushing her. Calling her weak, stupid, useless. "If you were truly as powerful as you claim you are, you would have gone into The Forest yourself to save your son," she spat. "But you didn't, because you're a coward. Covering your fear in shows of flame."

His fist slammed into her face, spraying blood from her mouth as his blazing knuckles sizzled against her skin. Her teeth shook from the impact, threatening to fall out.

She laughed even harder, almost tearing up from the hilarity. Sixteen years she had cried and begged and prayed for this man to love her. To accept her. *What a waste of time.*

"Admit it, you're weak without your magic," she croaked out. Her legs were shaking so violently, she thought she might collapse back onto the ground. She didn't know how long she could stay up, even in this kneeling position.

The fire creature that roared above him returned to his body, leaving only him. "I don't need to waste all this power on you. You are nothing!" he grimaced, spitting hatred into her face.

"I am *not* nothing," she seethed, glaring up at him. "I survived nightmares in The Forest you could never imagine. *You*. A king who has never gone to battle in his life. You have never faced monsters whose blood eats away everything it touches. You have never looked into darkness so endless you can't remember what light is anymore. You have never done those things. But I have. And if you had gone into that Forest, you would have learned a valuable lesson."

Mathus looked down at her, a flame hovering in his hand, ready to burn her until she screamed for mercy. "And what is that?"

She smirked. "Always be aware of your surroundings."

Arla swiped her legs under her father, stumbling him backward and into the crack in the ground where her first creature had dug itself out of. He screamed as he fell, a deafening thud at the bottom.

Slowly, she crawled her aching body forward and leaned over the gaping hole.

Mathus was wailing, holding his broken leg, the ivory bone jutting out of his shin. He shouted words for his fire, but they could not reach the surface above. The hole was too deep. She knew it wouldn't kill him to fall in, but she also knew neither he nor his fire could get out. Everyone had a limit, and Mathus's was that his fire could only go so far.

Arla slumped her shoulders, relieved.

It was over.

She had led, pulled, and pushed him to that very spot where he would finally fall, and now she had won.

"You think this will stop me?!" he screamed as he shot more fire up the walls of the hole, but they still did not reach the top. His words seemed empty now that he could not reach her. "I will kill you and your Low-Born filths when I get out of here. You will never escape me!"

Something yanked violently in her chest.

Rage boiled inside her, but it wasn't her fury. The wind caught and the Whispers flooded her mind. In a flash, The Woman's face appeared before her.

Without any control, Arla opened her mouth, speaking words she had never heard, even amongst the Whispers of her own mind.

The wind raged and lifted her father from the hole.

What are you doing? she shouted at The Woman.

Flashes of a dead Forest and a child emerging from the dirt blanketed her vision.

Arla's body was not her own as she reached out and grabbed both of her father's wrists.

He screamed out his Whispers of flame and death, but they were swallowed up by the wind.

Stop, Arla screamed at The Woman. *Let go!*

Biting her tongue, she tried to barricade the words from coming out. Swallowing each and every one of them, letting them fill her to the brim. But The Woman was too strong, and the words tumbled out. Letting every feeling of agony, pain, and sorrow go through her and into the language of The Forest. But it wasn't just her pain, it was The Woman's, and it was fury beyond this world.

Mathus cried out in agony as wind and fire engulfed them both. While it beat against his body, it left Arla unaffected.

Wild fear overtook his eyes.

No! Arla shouted from a distant place deep somewhere The Woman hid her away.

Her mouth moved and the inferno raged again, taking her father. His screams filled the air as his skin melted off his bones and his hair turned to ash until there was nothing left of him.

In a flash, the heat snuffed out and Arla crashed backward. She gasped, gaining full control of her body again. Whatever energy she just had was stripped from her, leaving her empty.

Slowly, she looked to the empty space in front of her where Mathus had once been.

Dead.

Her father was dead.

The King of Ulsana was gone.

Her hands shook at the overwhelming truth of it. She cried out in horror as the arched ceilings carried her voice across the hollowed undercroft.

What had she done?

CHAPTER 35

The skies had grayed, blocking out the sun as light rain sprinkled against the large window, a sure sign that fall was ending and spring would come within the weeks ahead. Linuth was curling Arla's hair with a heated iron, placing it high on the top of her head. Norendra stood behind her, telling her all the steps she would have to take.

"You only get one chance," she said. "They will judge you forever for every mistake you make today."

Being judged was something Arla was used to by now and it had bothered her less and less as the days after The Forest had gone by. At this point, she was numb to it. She was numb to most everything, still in shock from what she had done.

"You are ready, Your Highness," the elderly woman said, revealing the mirror to her.

Arla looked like a goddess.

Her golden dress was the most exquisite thing she had ever seen and everything about her glowed, except for her eyes, which were deadened and hollow. Linuth worked a different type of magic with the powdered makeup to conceal any bruises and burns on her face, which still throbbed. They did not ask many questions about it.

Maybe they assumed she had gotten them when she was taken to the dungeons and whatever happened on the balcony of the arena.

A handful of guards and her ladies-in-waiting escorted her out of her bed chambers and down the hallways with Norendra following close behind her, muttering more directions.

"Take slow, long strides so you do not trip over your dress," she muttered just as the Throne Room came into sight. Its great double doors were thrown open and a great pure white velvet carpet was rolled out from the door to the glittering throne, which looked cold and empty. Every inch of the room that was not the carpet was filled with standing High-Borns from every corner of Ulsana and the edges of the room were lined with so many guards, it looked like they themselves were the wall.

Every eye in the room turned to her as they did on the night of Jun's party, but the looks were different this time. They no longer looked at Arla with disdain and pity; instead, their faces expressed concern and doubt, the same feelings that she, herself, was feeling right now.

"Stand straighter," Norendra dictated.

Arla lifted her chest, trying to keep her chin high.

As Arla waited by the edge of the door, just as her teacher instructed, there was an awkward silence as the spectators watched Arla and she watched them back. It was surreal, what was happening now.

A royal herald approached her and turned to the crowd. "Presenting Arla Seojin!" The trumpets played and Arla slowly walked down the carpet. The throne chair got bigger and bigger, larger than it should have ever been or ever was.

"Walk slower," Norendra commanded behind her. Arla held her breath as she kept going, pushing herself to move as slowly as she could, hating every minute of this. She was only a few feet away with only a set of three elevated steps separating her from the end of her journey. She lifted a heeled foot, putting weight on her bandaged one that still stung from her father's fire. Wincing, she wobbled slightly before quickly putting her heel down on the first step.

Finally, she settled into the cold chair, which creaked from her weight. Did the chair know that she was a fraud? That she had killed its former master?

Norendra approached her with a book. "Arla Seojin, firstborn of Mathus Seojin, you are here today to be appointed as the new Queen Regent of all of Ulsana. As Queen Regent, you are sworn to protect all the lands of every corner of our great kingdom and see to it that we prosper with strength and longevity so long as we are under your rule. Do you swear on your life and blood to uphold these duties that every great ruler has done before you?"

I don't know.

"Yes," she breathed.

A flash of her father disintegrating into ash lingered in her mind, sending chills down her spine.

"And do you swear to uphold the laws and traditions of Ulsana as long as you hold this title?"

Arla stayed silent, her jaw tight.

Her hesitation earned a slight downward tug of the advisor's mouth.

"Say yes," Norendra hissed lowly at her.

"Yes," she replied.

"And do you, as acting Queen Regent, promise to relinquish your title and claim to power peacefully when your brother, Jun Seojin, comes of age to take his rightful place as heir?"

"Yes." This one she said quickly. The only thing she was truly sure of.

"Then as decreed by Ulsana, I anoint you, Arla Seojin,"—Norendra placed the golden crown of rubies and diamonds, the same one her father had worn only a few days ago, on her head—"Queen Regent of Ulsana. May you be blessed by The Forest and its Whispers."

"May you be blessed by The Forest and its Whispers," the crowd chanted solemnly in unison. And then they erupted in obligatory cheers and clapping. Looking out into the crowd, Arla didn't know which cheers were truly real and which weren't. Surely, none of them were happy to see her as their new leader, a sixteen-year-old girl with no experience.

Queen Regent.

A temporary title of power given to the eldest heir if the true heir was too young to take their crown. Arla naturally obtained the role and would keep it until Jun turned sixteen. Until then, she would have all the power a queen normally would.

Her gaze fell on Ametha, who held an ecstatic Jun in her arms. He was clapping his hands, mimicking those around him, but the former queen did not share his joy; Ametha was glaring up at her. As the widower of a former king, she had no power, instantly subverted by the eldest child. Arla wondered if Ametha hated her for it and what that would mean for them.

Looking deeper, Arla saw that within Ametha's look of contempt, there was a tinge of fear. The oath ordered Arla to relinquish her crown to Jun when he turned sixteen, but there had been known royal regents of other kingdoms who kept their power when the true heirs had mysteriously taken ill or disappeared. With no proof or anyone to go against those regents, they became the true and only ruler of the kingdom.

As Arla scanned the room, she noticed there were other looks of suspicion or rejection. She knew they did not see her as their leader. The people knew she had magic and helped the Low-Borns escape and her father mysteriously disappeared just after that, his body was never found, but proclaimed dead only a day later. It was suspicious for sure.

But tradition was tradition, and the advisors knew that a throne could not be left empty for too long, lest they dared expose themselves to chaos, so they crowned her.

It felt like Arla was sitting there forever, blankly looking out into the crowd, trying to seem like a controlled, calm leader, when inside she was drowning in waves of guilt and sorrow. The ceremony had mercifully been short and at its end, when Norendra wasn't looking, Arla slipped out and escaped to the garden where her statue would be waiting for her.

Alone at last, Arla sat on the garden bench, next to her affectionately grotesque statue. It was only at this moment that she let herself relax a little bit. She needed space and time to process everything that had just happened. All the events that led her to this seemingly impossible moment.

"Well, I see some things never change, my queen." Simion slinked out from around a nearby corner.

She inwardly groaned; his face was the last one she wanted to see today. What was he doing here anyway? Had he been waiting there for her?

"What do you want, Simion?" she asked curtly.

Simion bent on one knee, bowing his head. "I have come to swear allegiance to you and offer you my services of knowledge to become an advisor to your council."

"I don't have room in my council," Arla reminded him. She planned to have the same advisors her father did.

Simion nodded, still kneeling. "Of course, but I implore you to consider my application. I have eyes and ears everywhere. I am knowledge itself in Ulsana, which means I know a great many things, Your Highness." Simion slowly got up, a grin plastered on his face. It twisted of deception. "Things such as, what really happened to your father in that undercroft."

Arla froze.

The royal scholar casually looked at his fingers. "It would be a great shame if anyone were to find out how the king truly perished." He circled her. "A child who kills their own father for a throne... a most treacherous thing. Enough to get them executed. A baseless rumor, of course. But if enough people believe a rumor, it does not matter if it is true or not." He flashed a snake-like grin. "You will find me very useful, Queen Regent."

Arla wanted to threaten him back. To call her creatures to corner Simion against the garden walls and tell him to leave Ulsana and never come back. But that would never stop his mouth from leaking rumors. Whether it was here in Ulsana, another kingdom, or even from the edges of Terren, the exile land of no kings, Arla would not be able to stop gossip from moving from person to person.

The only way to truly stop him from blackmailing her was to kill him, but she would not do that, because she wasn't a murderer.

Liar.

She cringed.

You are a murderer.

She curled her lips up into an untrue, strained smile and said, "I do believe I will find you very useful, Simion. I accept your application and look forward to your services as an advisor to my council."

"As do I, my queen." He bowed and slinked away from her, leaving her colder than she had ever been.

* * *

The infirmary was thankfully mostly empty. Arla dressed in her stolen kitchen maid's dress and wore a hood to conceal her face as she made her way through the rows of cots. It took asking a dozen people to find where they were keeping the injured. She walked the hallways endlessly until she finally found the room she was looking for.

It was mostly empty except for the cot at the end of the row.

Leo was already sitting, trying not to lean on the wall, with bandages looped around his chest and back. Seeing him so hurt made her heart ache.

"Leo..." she murmured as she stood before him.

Leo's eyes widened and then looked around to check no one else was around before he let himself relax.

"Are you feeling okay?" she asked as she sat beside the cot.

"My back is itchy, but I think I will survive. Good thing I am a side sleeper, or this would have been a true disaster," he joked.

It had been a few days since they had seen each other. She wanted to come sooner, but she was constantly watched and could not escape long enough to visit. Leo's eyes grew serious as he lightly touched her bandaged cheek. Yes, the cut she made herself to get out of the muzzle. She knew what question he was asking.

"I'm fine," she assured him.

He frowned. "You shouldn't have left us. What if you were killed?"

"I wasn't."

She knew what choice she made, and she still did not regret it. She reached out and put her hand over his, which made him flinch. Even after all that passed between them, he still seemed surprised by her touch. Under the guise of a kitchen maid, no one would suspect that she was the new ruler of Ulsana. Hopefully.

"How did you escape him?" he asked in a hushed voice.

Arla hesitated. "The ceiling collapsed, and I just ran faster than he did."

Leo turned his hand over, placing his palm against hers, and squeezed, trying to comfort her. It felt horrible to lie to him, but she wasn't ready to tell the truth, not only because she, herself, was still trying to come to terms with it, but she was afraid of what Leo would think of her if he knew. What if he pulled away from her and told her she was evil? That he couldn't stand to be near a killer? What if he never wanted to see her again because of it? Her heart wouldn't have been able to take it.

She mentally traced the bends and curves of his scratched-up knuckles and tried to memorize the feel of his calloused palms against hers, wishing they could stay like this forever.

"I hear you have become queen regent," he said.

She nodded grimly. "They made a mistake. I'm not a queen. I don't know how to lead a kingdom. I've barely even lived a real life."

"You will figure it out."

"How do you know that?"

"Because I know you're strong and capable. You always have been."

He seemed too sure of her, but he didn't know what she knew. Of her true fears. Of how The Woman could take over her body and how scared she was that she might lose control of herself again. Or how she couldn't sleep now because her father's death haunted her dreams. In these nightmares, she heard his screams as she burned him alive.

No, it was too much for an injured captain to take on, and too much for Arla to confess right now. So she sat there in silence instead, just trying to stay in the moment and be grateful that Leo was alive and healing.

"I'm sorry I pulled you into that mess," she said softly.

"You didn't do anything wrong," Leo replied, his tone serious. "I chose to hit him."

"Why?"

She searched his face for answers. Of why he would risk so much for her. Why he lost control. His gaze was soft and open and a little defeated. "I think you know why."

Her heart swelled.

She leaned forward, her other hand pressed into the cotton blanket at the edge of his bed. She wanted to be near him, to close the gap between their lips.

"Arla..." Leo said in a low sotto voice. His hazel irises swirled with waves of sorrow. "I am a soldier."

For a moment, she didn't understand what he was trying to say. It didn't matter that he was a soldier. It wasn't a bad thing, so why mention it? *Because I am not a soldier*, she thought to herself. And then Arla understood what Leo's words truly meant.

"And I am a queen," she responded, her voice empty.

Low-Borns and High-Borns could barely be friends, let alone... whatever they were. There was no future here.

She slipped away from him, creating distance the world put between them.

"I'll come to visit again," she promised as she got up.

He nodded, his face solemn. As she walked away, she heard him say, "Next time, bring food."

She turned and smiled, meeting his playful look. "I will and I'll make sure it's not cooked by me."

CHAPTER 36

Arla stood alone in the darkness looking out her new window. She was in a much larger bed chamber now in the central tower. It wasn't as big as the royal rooms where a queen regent would have typically slept, but Arla had decided to let Ametha and Jun stay where they were. It was too much, she thought, to ask them to give up their only place of solace when Ametha had just lost a husband.

Besides, she didn't want to stay anywhere near where her father once slept. Not after what she had done.

She knew rest would not come for her tonight, just like it had not come the night before. The screams of her father would echo in her head until she woke in a cold sweat. So instead, she took to staring out at the city through the glass, watching candlelight illuminating the windows of various homes and shops.

Alone with her thoughts, her sorrow morphed into anger. How could The Woman just kill her father? She had used Arla's body as her own weapon.

Is this what you wanted? she said to the void of her mind. *You wanted revenge for what happened to you? Was that your plan all along? To kill a Seojin king?*

I was just your plaything this entire time.

Of course, she was.

She had thought The Woman was on her side, but now she knew better, and this Woman was not going to be another person that controlled her. Arla was done with allowing other people to make her feel weak. She would never again beg for someone's approval or mercy.

So, what next? she asked. *What do you want?*

Silence.

Answer me, she demanded.

A faint sound encircled her mind as a mysterious wind picked up inside her bedroom even though no window was open.

She was here.

Clenching her fists, Arla readied herself for a fight.

Are you going to kill me too? She asked.

The breeze curled around her.

No, The Woman said in a hushed tone.

Arla quivered. "Then what is the point of all this?"

The air lifted and settled above her, thick and heavy.

An icy chill trickled down her head, through her chest, and into her heart. Arla's body froze as fear overtook her. But it wasn't the still air or The Woman's voice that left her blood cold.

It was the next words she heard.

Like a hiss of smoke, The Woman's voice seeped into Arla's ears.

You must save them.

He is coming.

And then, The Woman was gone.

BONUS CHAPTER

Want to know what Leo was thinking?

Sign up for my newsletter to read Leo's POV
in this exclusive bonus chapter here:

https://pages.jynamaengbooks.com/kowbonuschapter

LEAVE A REVIEW!

Have thoughts on what just happened?

Reviews are the life blood of my work, and the more I get, the more incentive I have to write another book. So please take some time to write a review! I will greatly appreciate it!

And be sure to reach out to me via email or social media to let me know you left a review! I would love to see what you wrote!

A QUEEN OF WHISPERS

Arla and Leo will return in A Queen of Whispers.

Join my newsletter or follow me on Amazon or
social media to know when it releases!

www.jynamaengbooks.com

ACKNOWLEDGEMENTS

It is true what they say, no great endeavor is ever taken on alone. And this book is no different. I would not have been able to create A Kingdom of Whispers (KOW) without all those kind-hearted, enthusiastic people who chose to help me along the way. This page is dedicated to you all.

Thank you to my beta-readers, who shaped KOW into what it is today. To M.A. Frick for her thorough in-line notes that forced me to fill in plot holes. To Victoria Louie, for reading the earliest draft that needed the most work. To Kayla for her extensive chapter-by-chapter notes that gave me the guidance I needed to ensure the book flowed evenly. And to Brittan Scott who helped me see how I could better my voice and tone. This story would not be what it is today without you all, so a thousand thank yous forever and forever!

Eternal gratitude to my editors Hina Baber and Ashley Olivier. Hina was the one who told me this story would be a trilogy and gave me the resources I needed to structure it the right way. I definitely needed her phone calls which always taught me more than I hoped and gave me a sense of sureness in my next steps. And a big thank you to Ashley, the editor that got me through the finish line with her quick turnaround and editing.

A great big thanks to my writing group on Discord for giving me notes and being so enthusiastic about my journey.

A personal thank you to my boo, Chris, who allowed me the time and space to write this book.

And a thank you to my friends who always gave me encouraging words and supported me through this entire journey of trying to get something I love out there into the world.

And a big appreciative hug to the 20BooksTo50K collective, whose advice and strong community helped me learn everything I needed to get this book published the right way. As Craig Martelle always says, a rising tide lifts all boats, and you all have lifted mine.

About the Author

Jyna maeng

(pronounced Gina Mang ← rhymes with Bang)
Jyna considers herself a multi-potentialite with many careers as a retail worker, swim instructor, actor, software engineer, and now author. She has an overactive imagination and a worrying addiction to chocolate and often wonders what it would be like to taste feelings. Her greatest dream is to wake up one day with a superhuman power that lets her eat whatever she wants at any quantity without consequences.

Join her in these places:
Newsletter: www.jynamaengbooks.com/backmatternewsletter
Tiktok: @jynamaengbooks
Instagram: @jynamaengbooks